The critics review *Marty Pants*

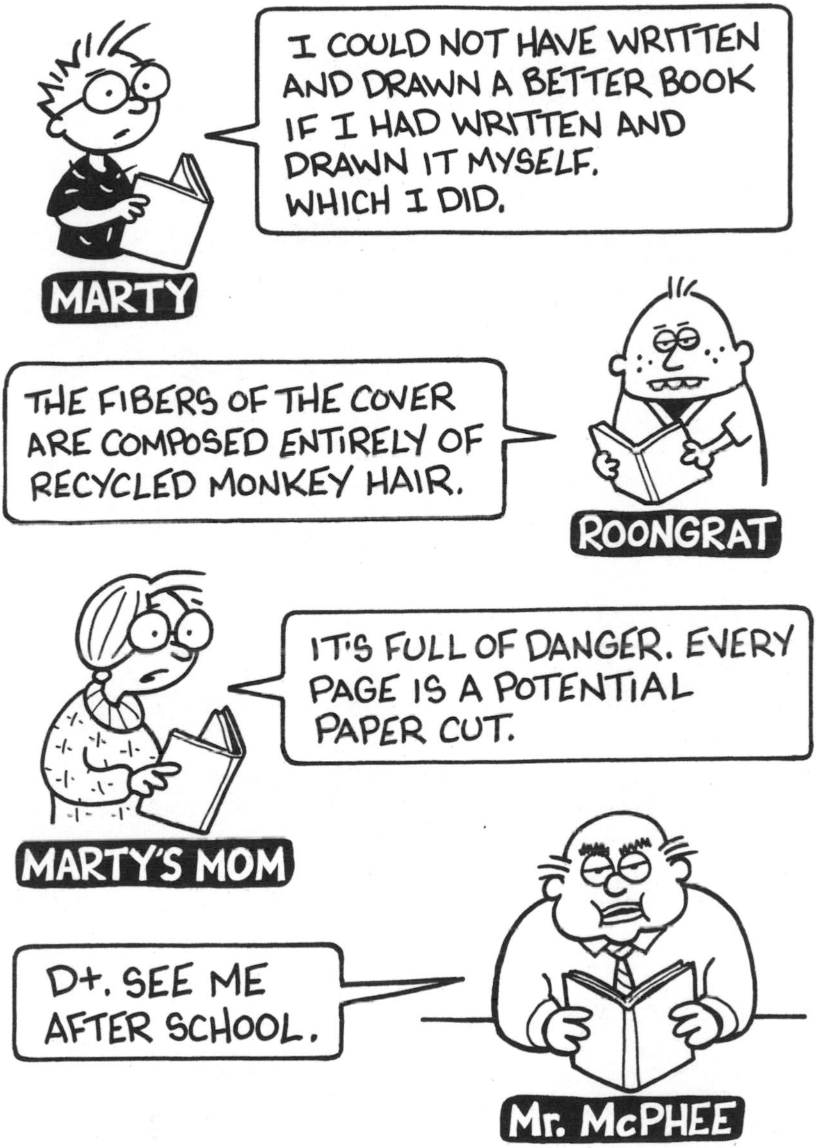
I COULD NOT HAVE WRITTEN AND DRAWN A BETTER BOOK IF I HAD WRITTEN AND DRAWN IT MYSELF. WHICH I DID.
MARTY
THE FIBERS OF THE COVER ARE COMPOSED ENTIRELY OF RECYCLED MONKEY HAIR.
ROONGRAT
IT'S FULL OF DANGER. EVERY PAGE IS A POTENTIAL PAPER CUT.
MARTY'S MOM
D+. SEE ME AFTER SCHOOL.
Mr. McPHEE

Marty Pants

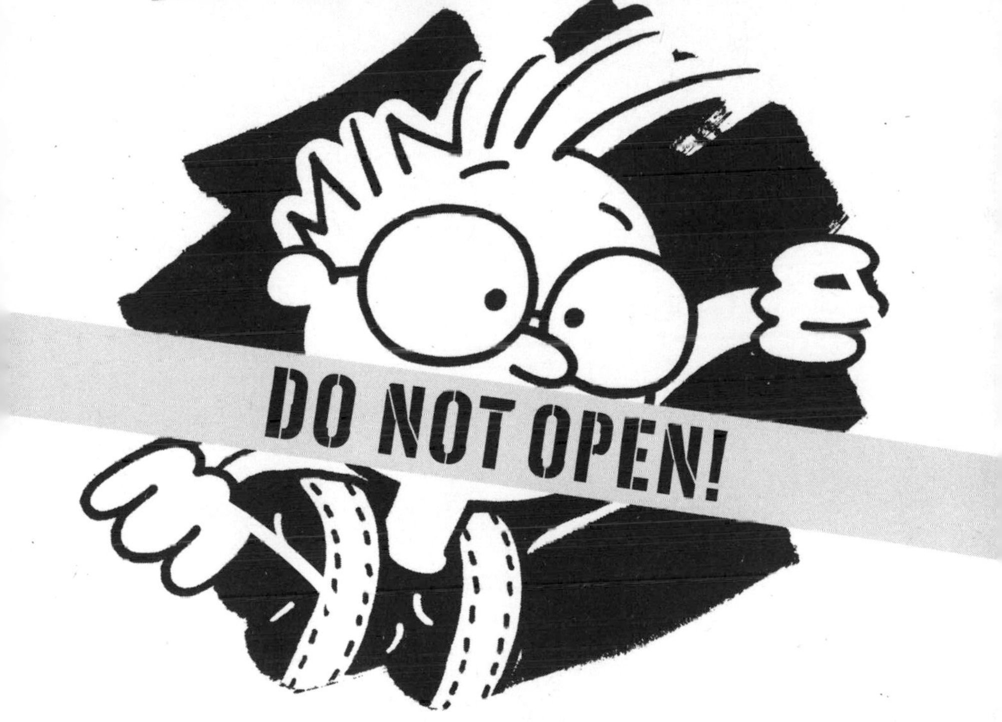
DO NOT OPEN!

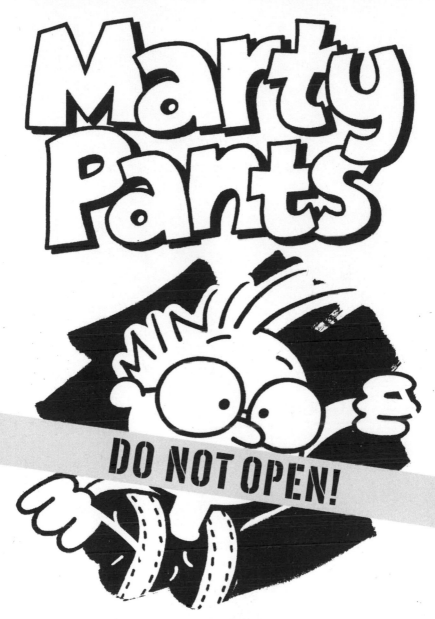

Mark Parisi

HARPER
An Imprint of HarperCollins*Publishers*

To Mom and Dad—
Thanks for always supporting me.

Marty Pants #1: Do Not Open!

www.harpercollinschildrens.com
ISBN 978-0-06-242776-2
Typography by Joe Merkel
    19 20 21   CG/LSCH   10 9 8 7 6 5
❖
First Edition

IF YOU'RE ALIVE TO
READ THIS BOOK, YOU
HAVE ME TO THANK.

YOU'RE WELCOME.

CHAPTER 0

sneak preview

I burst through the front doors of the school with a vicious animal in my arms and a stolen document in my mouth. The contents of this document are earth shattering. Literally! I'm being chased by a large, angry . . .

You wouldn't believe me if I told you, but I'm going to tell you anyway.

Where should I begin? I suppose the beginning is as good a place as any.

let's talk about me

I'll start with the basics. My name is Marty Pants and I wear black. I heard somewhere that artists wear black.

I didn't choose to be an artist. I was born that way.

ARTISTIC VERSION OF ME

I don't really have four arms and legs.

I created my first work when I was just a baby, and my dad captured the moment on video. I was eating strained carrots and sneezed on the wall.

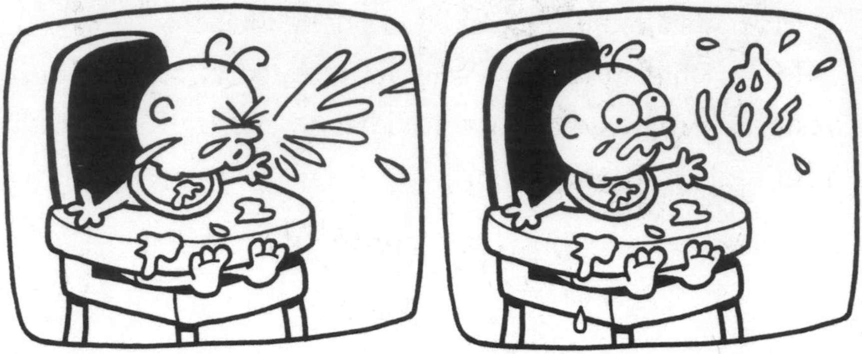

I know that doesn't sound like much, but the splatter looked like a famous painting called *The Scream*. My dad posted the video online, and it got millions of views. People ate it up!

I tried to recapture my glory in kindergarten by chewing up crayons and sneezing on construction paper, but I got sick of that pretty quickly. All over the teacher.

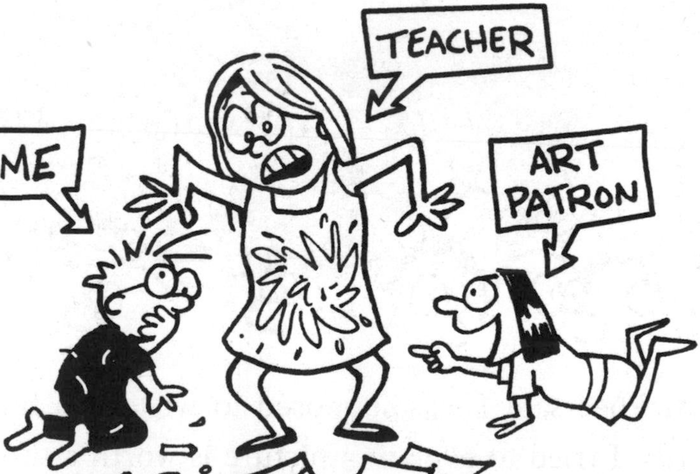
TEACHER
ME
ART PATRON

My dad called it my Jackson Pollock phase.

My art has always been unappreciated at school. But yesterday, my teacher, Mr. McPhee, came right out and admitted I'm a true artist!

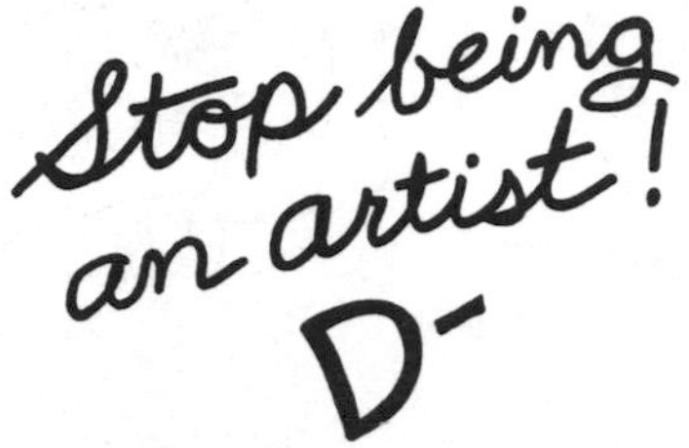
Stop being an artist!
D-

He wrote that on my homework.

The assignment was to comment on overpopulation and the effects it could have on our planet.

This was my paper.

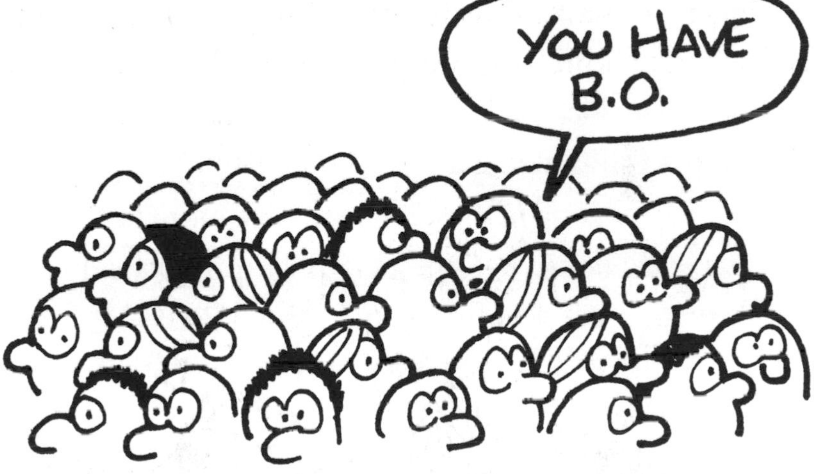
YOU HAVE B.O.

McPhee said I was supposed to write two hundred words. I tried to explain a picture is worth a thousand words so I deserve extra credit, but he's obviously not very good at math. And he certainly doesn't understand art. Maybe I was lucky I didn't hand in my first draft.

I'M GOING TO THE BATHROOM RIGHT NOW.

My dad told me someone who doesn't understand art is a *rube*. *Rube* is now my favorite word. McPhee is a rube. He's supreme king, lord, emperor, and prime minister of the rubes. He doesn't understand anything creative, especially not a brilliant artist like me.

And like all good artists, I have an eye for detail. Make that an *exceptional* eye for detail. I'm always noticing things no one else seems to notice.

For instance, right now I notice something that I consider strange.

My cat is devouring my face.

CHAPTER 2

scratching the surface

Jerome and I are pals. So why did he suddenly decide to eat my face?

1.) He's rabid

2.) I'm dead and he's devouring the carcass

3.) I'm delicious

4.) All of the above

There's another option. He thinks I'm cat food. I had a tuna sandwich earlier so I smell like his food. Also, I'm not moving, which is something else his food does.

I shift my body so Jerome will realize his error, but he's obviously too embarrassed to admit when he's wrong so he keeps on licking me. And cat tongues feel like sandpaper.

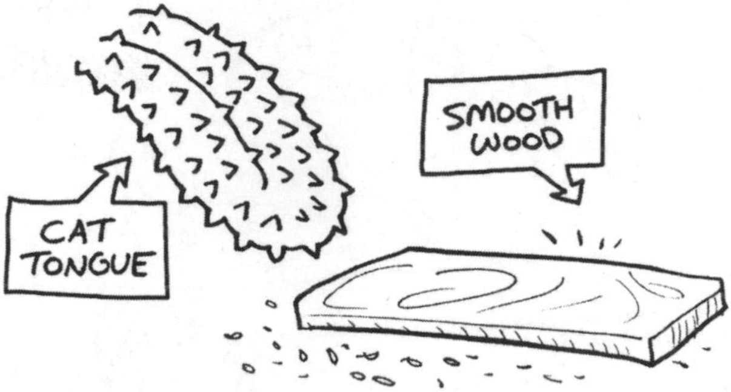
SMOOTH WOOD
CAT TONGUE

I don't think Jerome has actually eaten an entire human before, but I wouldn't put it past him. He's tough and I'm the only person in the world he gets along with.

I can pick him up no problem, but if anyone else tries it, things don't go well.

Just ask my dad.

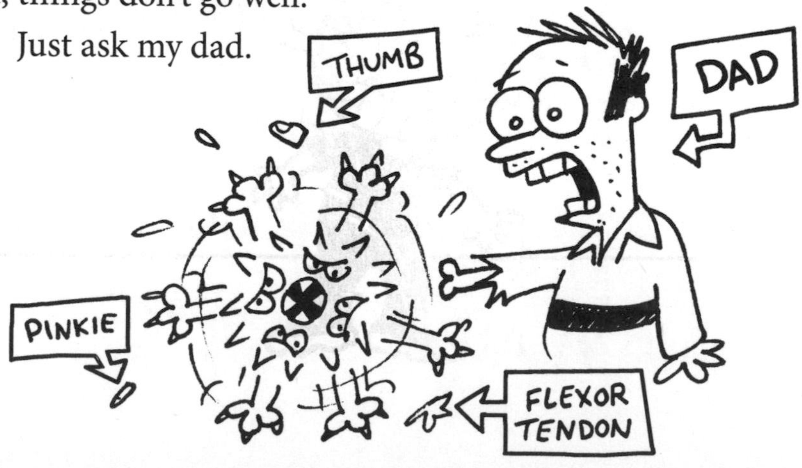
THUMB
DAD
PINKIE
FLEXOR TENDON

The damage really wasn't that bad, but that's how my mom describes it. She overreacts to scratches.

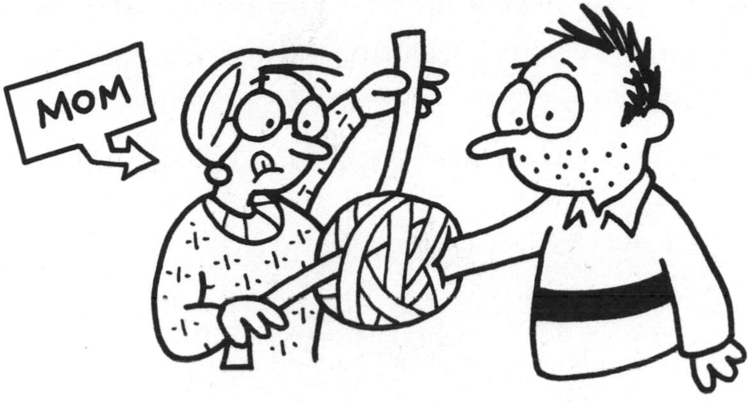
MOM

She also went overboard when my sister stubbed her toe.

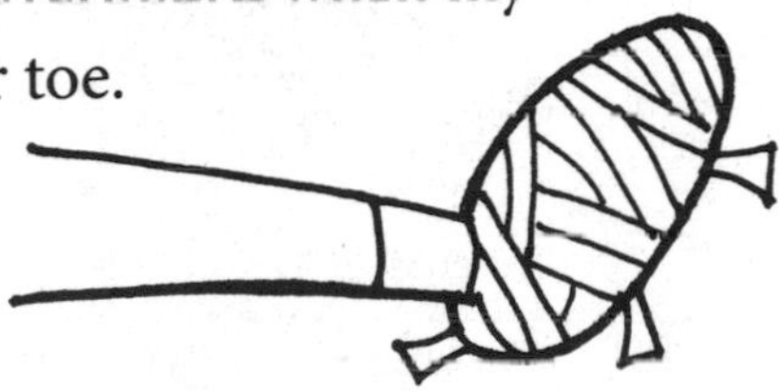

And the time I had a headache.

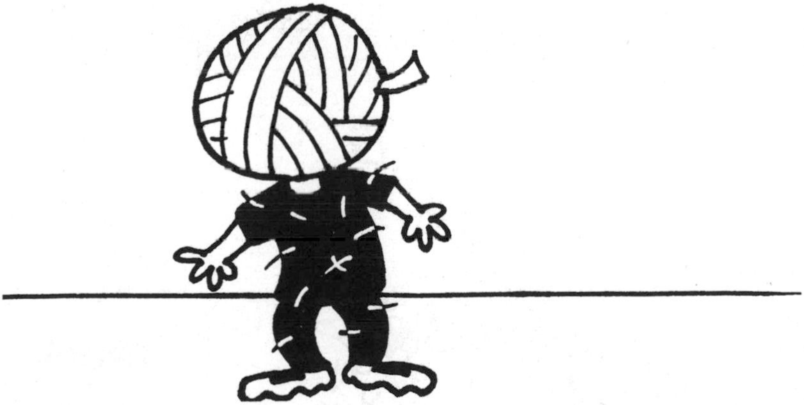

My dad, on the other hand, is pretty mellow about stuff. He's not a big talker unless you mention old music.*

Somehow, he talked my mom into letting me keep Jerome. And that was a big deal because my mom's over-protective.

In fact, if it were up to her, I'd still have training wheels on my bike.

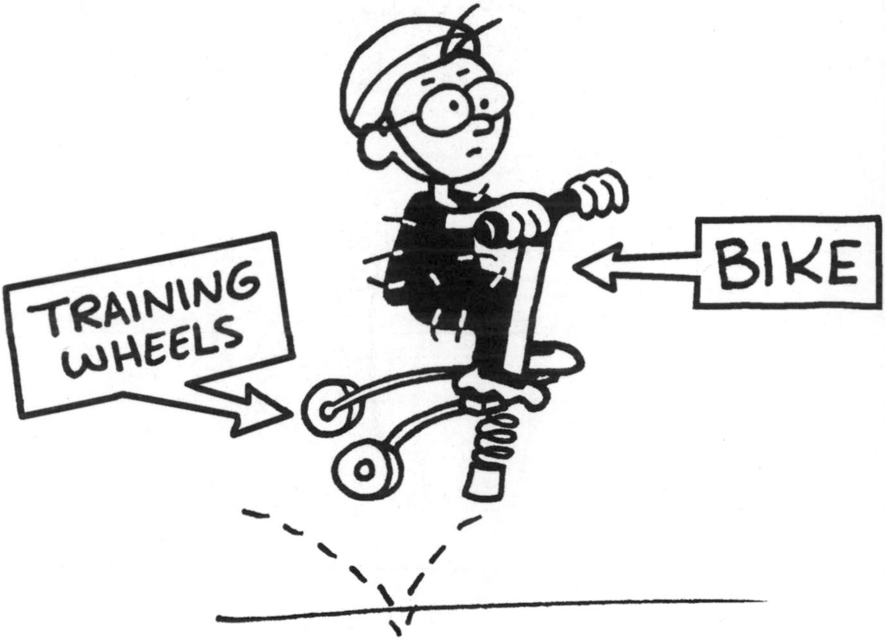
TRAINING WHEELS
BIKE

Yes, I know that's a pogo stick, but I'm no good at drawing bikes. They're difficult, so I draw pogo sticks instead.

Speaking of difficult, here comes my sister.

* Then he won't shut up.

CHAPTER 3
give me space

My sister's name is Erica. Except when it's

Erika

or Ericka

or Ericca

or Eriquahh.

She changes the spelling almost as often as she changes her mood. I usually just guess.

As soon as Erickka storms into the room, I can tell she's gearing up to annoy me. But I won't let her get to me. Not this time. No matter what she says.

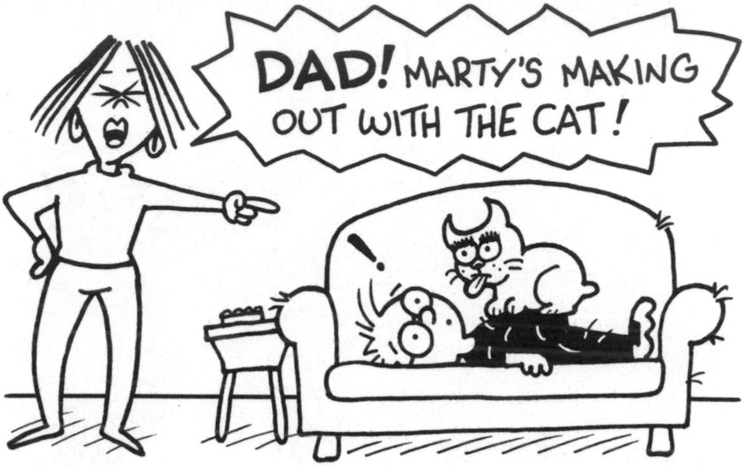
DAD! MARTY'S MAKING OUT WITH THE CAT!

"Marty," my dad calls from the kitchen, "stop making out with that cat."

"WHAT?!" I yell. "I'm not . . ."

"Kissing the cat is weird," my sister says. "Is that how you practice for your girlfriend?"

"Analie is NOT my girlfriend!"

Errikah smiles. "Interesting. I never mentioned Analie."

Gurk! She tricked me!

"I hope Analie likes guys who are covered in cat hair," she adds.

I hope so, too, I think to myself.

"It's my turn to watch TV," Eriicca declares. "DAD! MARTY'S HOGGING THE TV!"

"Stop hogging the TV, Marty," my dad says. "Why don't you come here and we'll talk about music?"

"But I'm watching alien movies!"

"Not anymore, space cadet," Errrica says as she sits down and flicks through the channels.

Okay, that does it.

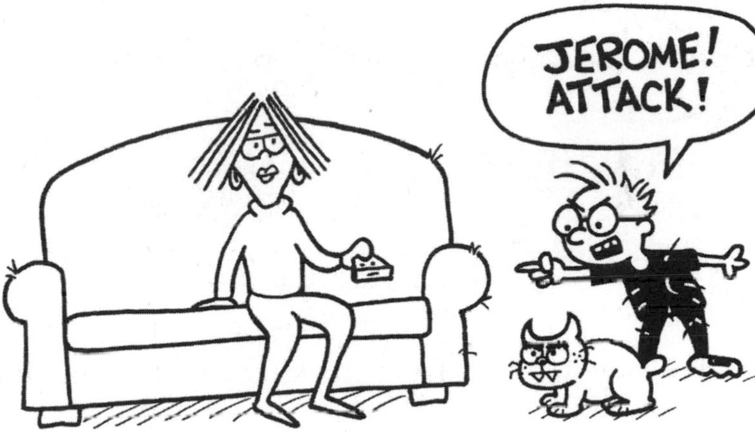
JEROME! ATTACK!

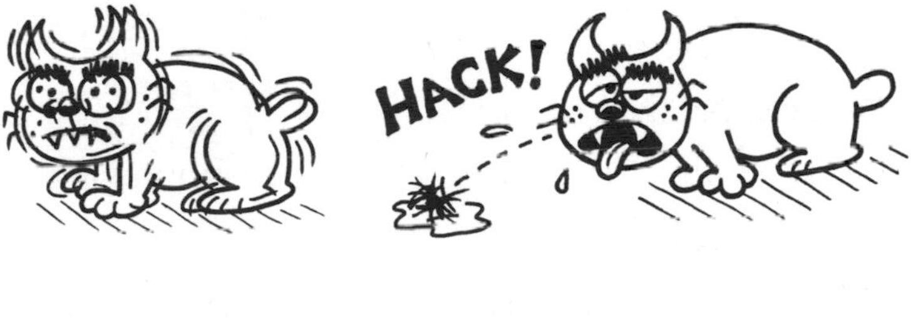
HACK!

"EW!" screams Ericcah. "DAD! MARTY'S GROSSING ME OUT!"

"Stop grossing out your sister, Marty."

I race into the kitchen to plead my case.

"DAD! Eriickaa just . . ."

"Marty, is that lipstick on your face?"

"What?"

"It's red around your mouth."

"That's because Jerome was kissing, I mean, licking me!"

"If you want to wear lipstick, it's fine with me, but maybe you shouldn't be kissing the cat."

Before I can respond, my mom walks in, fresh from her business trip.

"WHAT'S THIS? MARTY'S PUTTING LIPSTICK ON RATS?"

I take a deep breath.

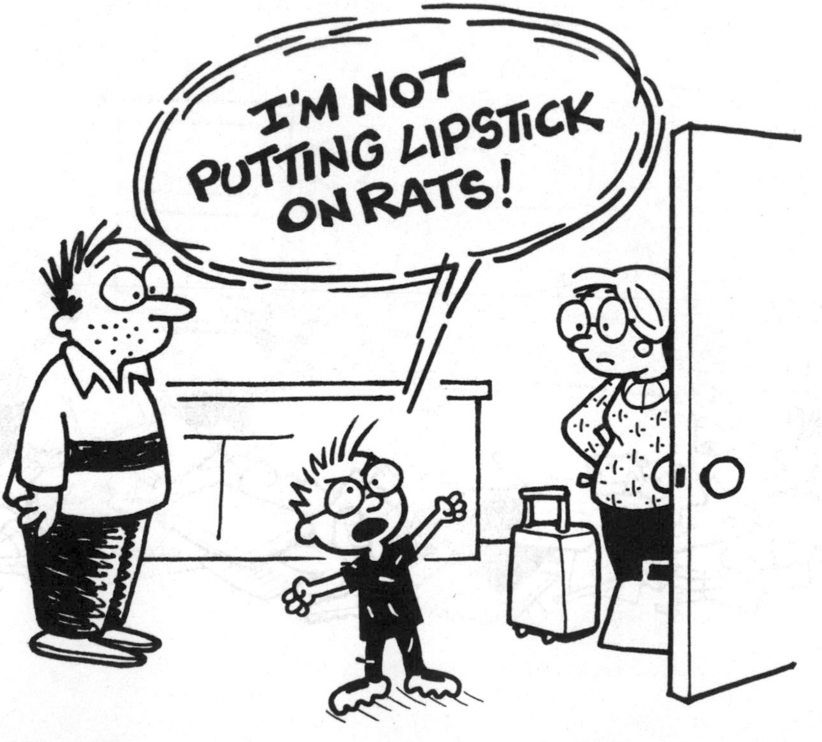
I'M NOT PUTTING LIPSTICK ON RATS!

Of all the sentences I never thought I'd say, that one's pretty high on the list.

Here are more from that list:

- I **AM** putting lipstick on rats.
- Let's all smell monkey butts.
- My sister is a ray of sunshine.

"Use your inside voice, Marty," my mom says. "Have you cleaned your room yet?"

"It's SPOTLESS!" I assure her as I bolt upstairs to my room, which is exactly what I said it was: Spotless.*

* There's not a dog named Spot anywhere.

Now I'm all wound up, so I plop into my quiet place, my beanbag. The beanbag of solitude. I come here to relax.

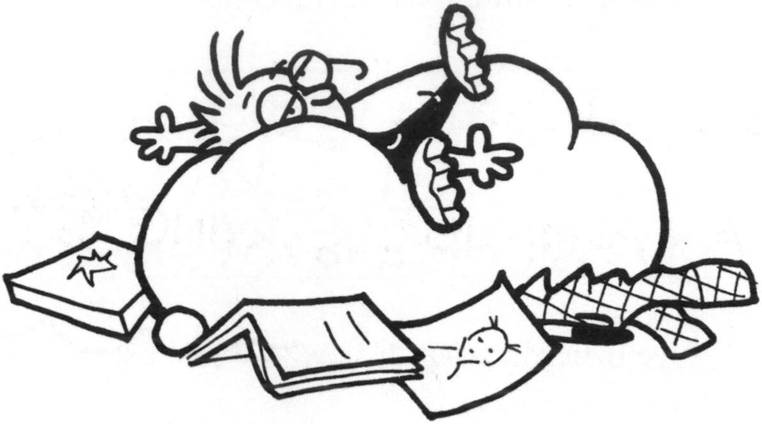

Ah, peace.

It's not easy being misunderstood.

But my Zen is soon broken by a crinkling noise. I look around and see Jerome pulling a purple piece of paper out of my backpack.

I rescue it from his feline jaws and discover it's a note.

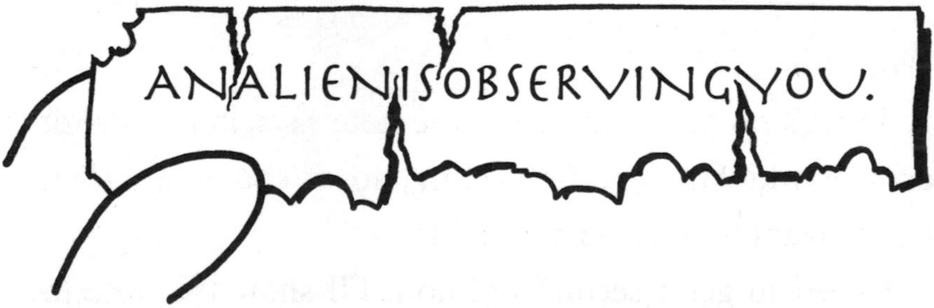
AN ALIEN IS OBSERVING YOU.

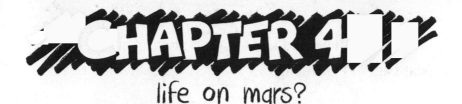

CHAPTER 4

life on mars?

AN ALIEN IS OBSERVING ME?

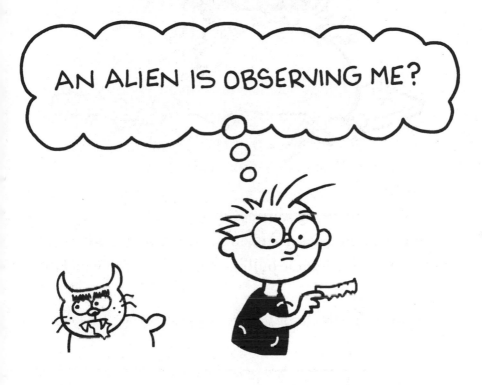

Wow.

There's no mistaking what the note says, but is it legit or a prank? I'm very interesting, so of course an alien would want to observe me, right?

I need to get a second opinion. I'll show the note to someone else. Someone I trust. Someone with a level head.

Not that kind of level head. I mean someone who's smart and rational. And I know just the person. Parker.

Parker's a buddy I can count on to give me serious advice in serious situations. Believe it or not, not everyone takes me seriously.

"Where are you off to, Marty?" my mom asks.

"Parker's house because of *mumble mumble mumble*," I mumble as I snap the door shut behind me.

It's a warm Sunday afternoon, and I look up into the sky. Not an alien in sight. But when I look straight ahead, there's danger!

I make a quick detour.

CHAPTER 5

get fuzzy

Peach Fuzz!

His real name is Salvador Ack, but he has a light, fuzzy mustache so I call him Peach Fuzz. Not to his face, of course. He's a high school kid who pushes me around like it's his hobby.

His other hobby is spitting.

It's always bad news when I run into him, but due to what happened on my bike ride yesterday, I fear for my life!

I try not to move as I hide in the bushes. Partly because I don't want Peach Fuzz to find and kill me, and partly because I now have something new to worry about.

Gurk! They say spiders are more afraid of us than we are of them. I have a complicated opinion on that. (Opinion: That's a dirty, filthy lie!)

I can't decide what to do. I guess it comes down to who's going to kill me first, Peach Fuzz or the spider.

I try to calm myself down by imagining that the spider's name is Shermy.

Shermy is a friendly name.

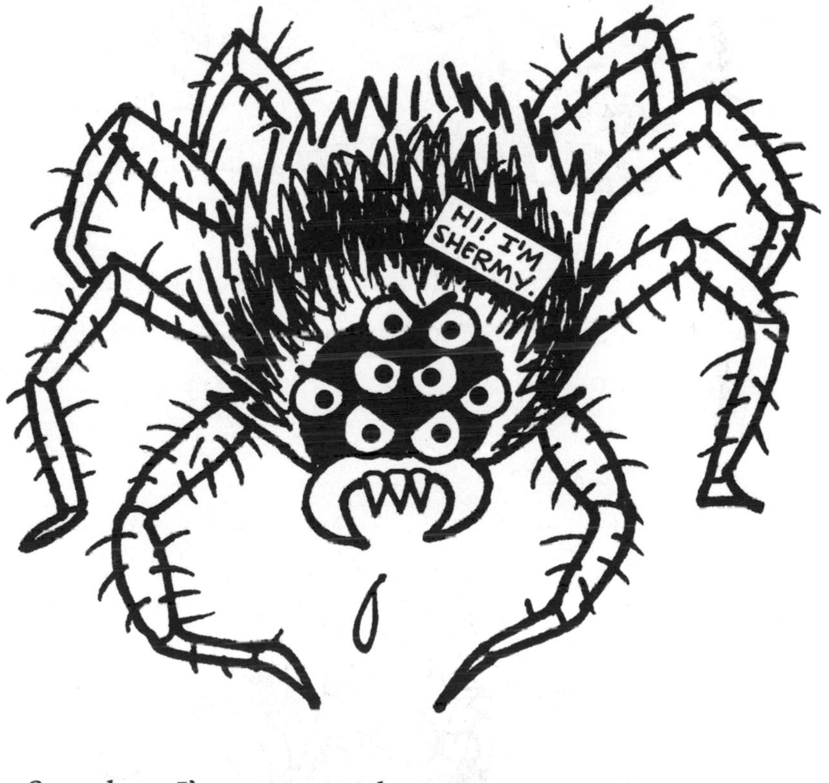
HI! I'M SHERMY.

Somehow I'm not any calmer.

They say before you die, your life flashes before your eyes.

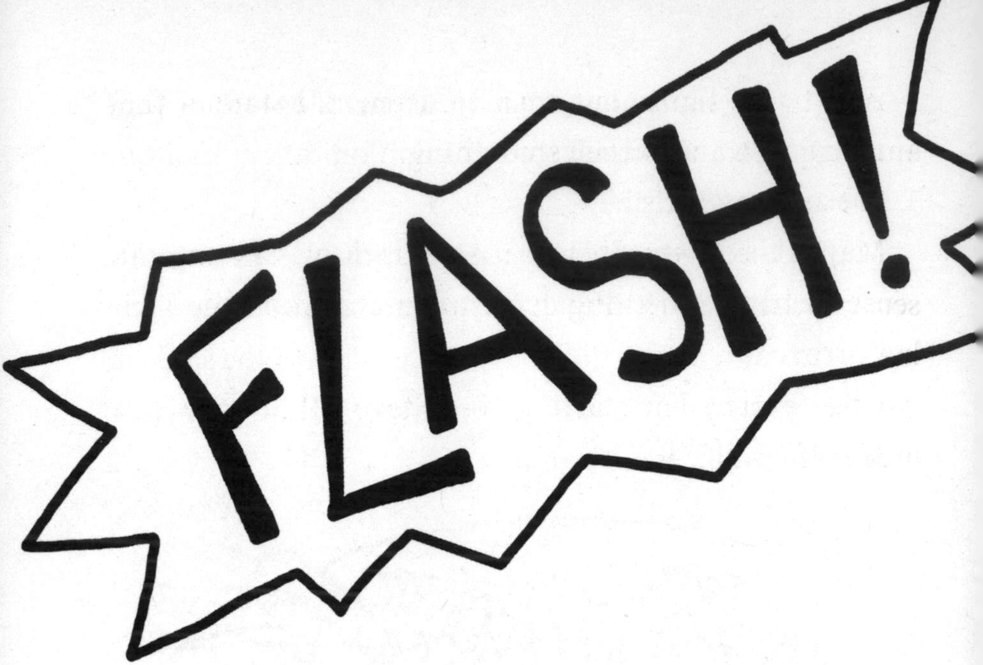
FLASH!

Nothing. I'll take that as a good sign.

As I try to figure out what to do next, I stare at that amazing web and realize something.

Shermy's an artist.

Maybe that's why Shermy's not attacking. Shermy can sense we have something in common and won't bite a fellow artist.

I feel better. I'm starting to believe I'll survive this ordeal after all.

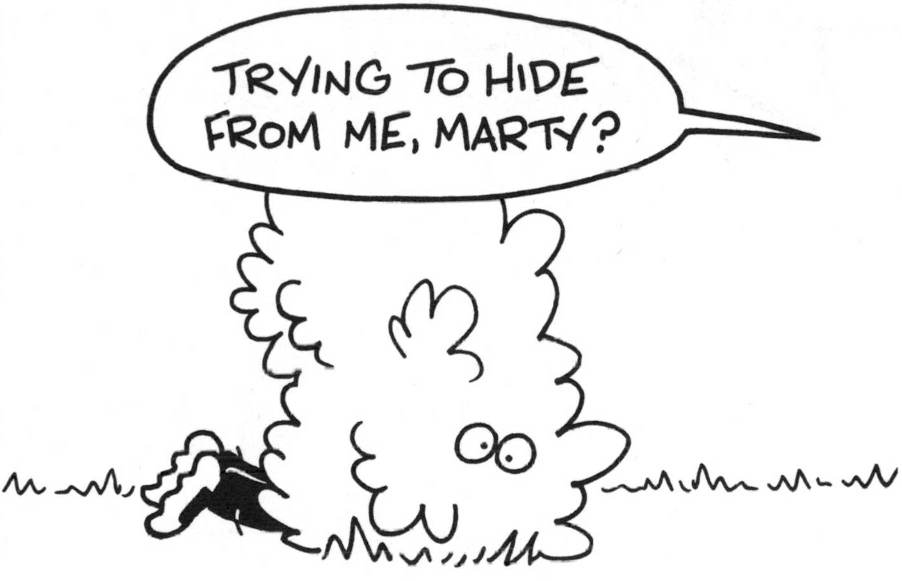
TRYING TO HIDE FROM ME, MARTY?

Gurk! Peach Fuzz found me!

I'm dead.

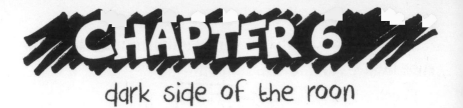

CHAPTER 6

dark side of the roon

Wait, I know that whiny voice. It belongs to Roongrat Mitten. That means the coast is clear. I totally outsmarted Peach Fuzz!

Now I have to ditch Roongrat. He's harmless but a little annoying. Roongrat's a major know-it-all, and he also happens to be one of my closest friends. Why am I friends with someone who annoys me? I ask myself that question every day.

ROONGRAT
KNOW-IT-ALL
DOESN'T REALLY KNOW IT ALL

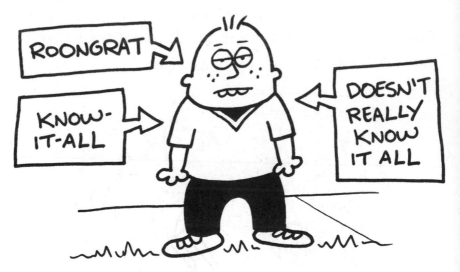

"Hiding? I'm not hiding," I lie. "I'm just looking at this awesome spider web." I point to it.

Roongrat puts his foot through it.

I stand up and give him my why-did-you-do-that-you-rube look.

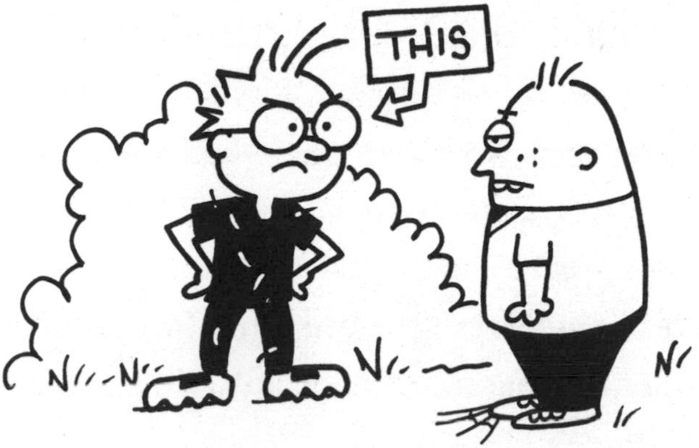
THIS

Roongrat doesn't seem to pick up on it, so I come right out and say, "Why did you do that, you rube?"

"Spiders need to keep making new webs," Roongrat insists. "Or it all builds up inside them until their butts explode. It's a fact. I did that bug a favor."

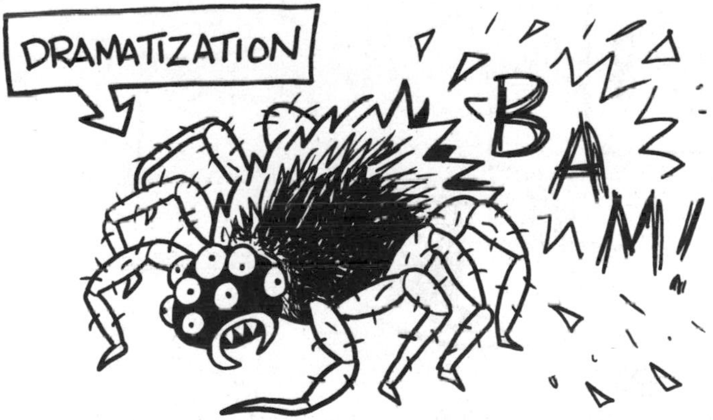
DRAMATIZATION
BAM!

He says things with such authority you almost believe him. Almost.

"My mom told me your birthday's coming up," he says, changing the subject. "What kind of cake are you getting?"

"I don't know." I DO know. Chocolate. I just don't feel like telling him.

"Get chocolate. I like chocolate."

Now I don't want chocolate.

"Chocolate improves your brain motions," he says. "It's a fact. All the geniuses eat chocolate cake . . . Einstein, Sherlock Holmes, Oprah . . ."

Roongrat freezes in midsentence.

Maybe his "brain motions" didn't get enough chocolate cake.

Then I notice he's staring at something on his leg.

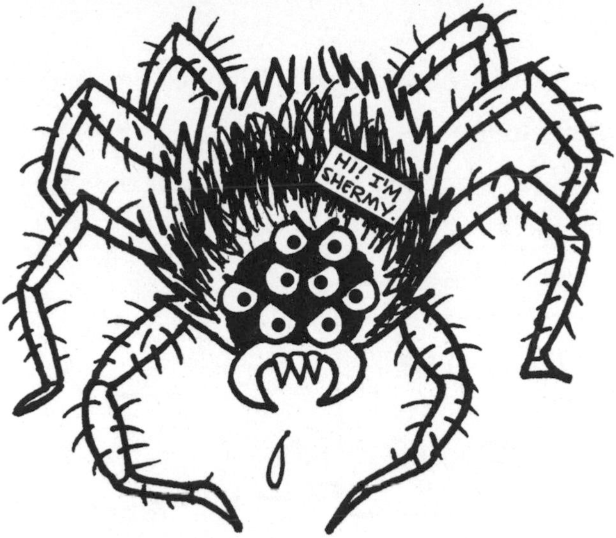
HI! I'M SHERMY.

Roongrat goes from standing still to the opposite of standing still.

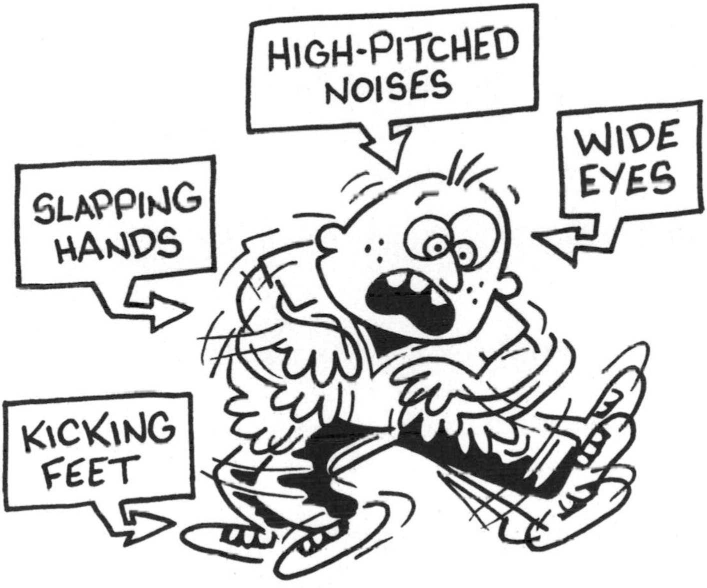
HIGH-PITCHED NOISES
WIDE EYES
SLAPPING HANDS
KICKING FEET

HOW TO DO "THE ROONGRAT"

It's entertaining, but I can't help feeling sorry for him. The spider, I mean.

Roongrat falls backward, wriggles out of his pants, and runs off!

IRONICALLY, SPIDER-MAN UNDERPANTS!

Someday they'll invent a technology that allows you to unsee things. Until then, that image will remain burned into my retinas. I may even need therapy.

Good thing I'm heading to Parker's.

CHAPTER 1

psych

Parker Fedora opens the door before I even knock.

"Hi, Marty!"

Incidentally, Parker is *not* my girlfriend. She's just a friend I've known since preschool who happens to be a girl. I trust her instincts. She's always giving me a fresh perspective on things.

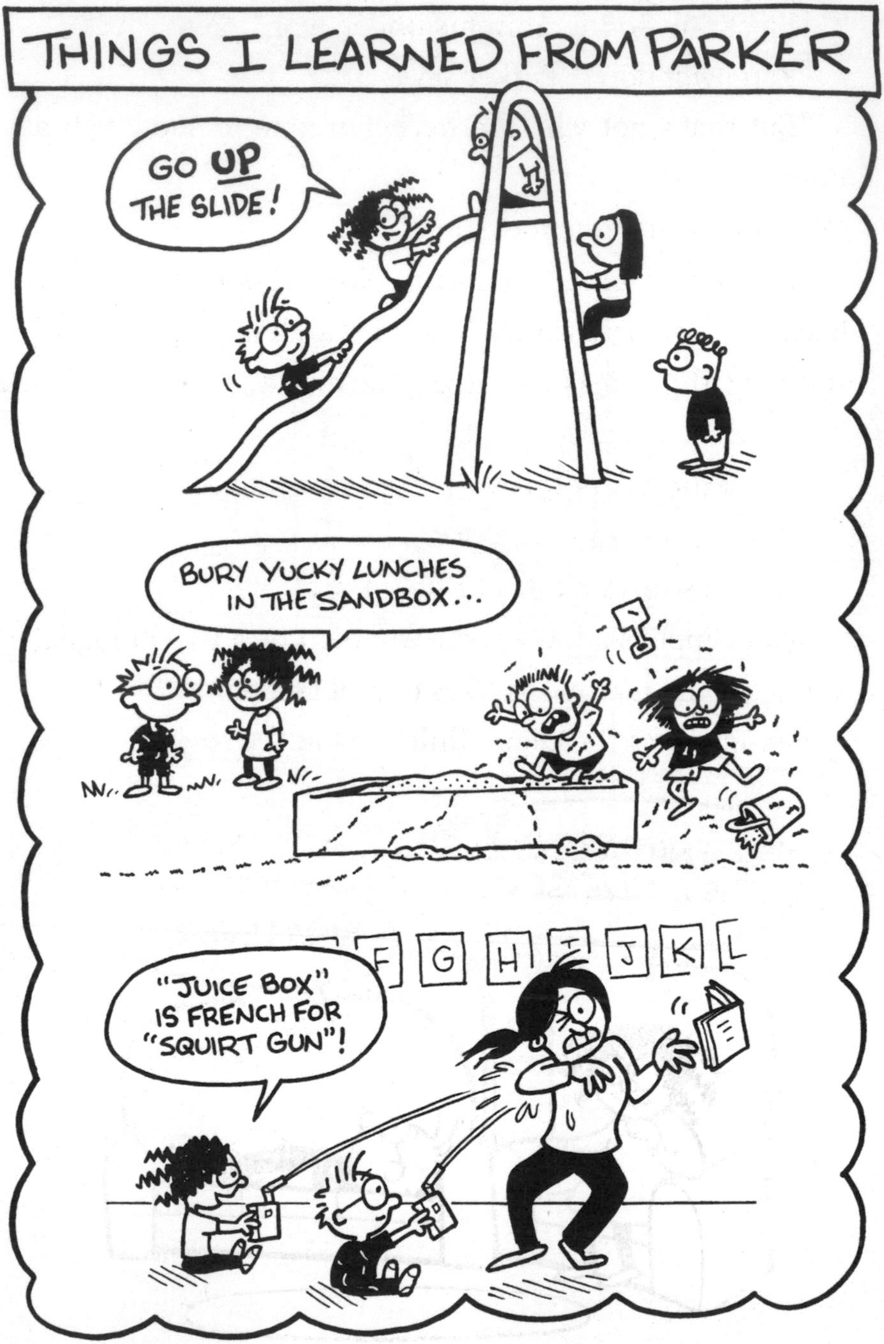
THINGS I LEARNED FROM PARKER
GO UP THE SLIDE!
BURY YUCKY LUNCHES IN THE SANDBOX...
"JUICE BOX" IS FRENCH FOR "SQUIRT GUN"!

"I just saw Roongrat in his underwear."

"You *what* now?" Parker says.

"But that's not why I'm here. I'm here to show you a note."

"Oooh, you wrote me a note?"

"I didn't write it," I explain. "My cat found it in my backpack. It's here somewhere." I search my pockets, but suddenly the note is nowhere to be found.

"Maybe I lost it."

"What did the note say?"

"It said an alien is . . ."

"Marty, why don't you lie down first?"

This happens a lot. Parker wants to be a psychologist, and for some reason she likes to practice on me.

Parker sits in the chair while I lie on the couch.

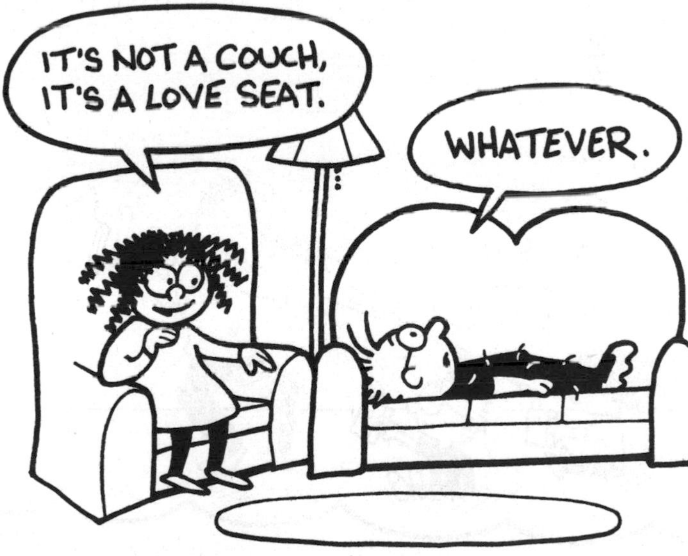
IT'S NOT A COUCH, IT'S A LOVE SEAT.
WHATEVER.

She tells me I'm the best patient a psychologist could ever hope for.

"Thank you for the compliment," I say.

"We'll have to be quick, though, because my dad made a new rule: no boys over when he's not home. Or else."

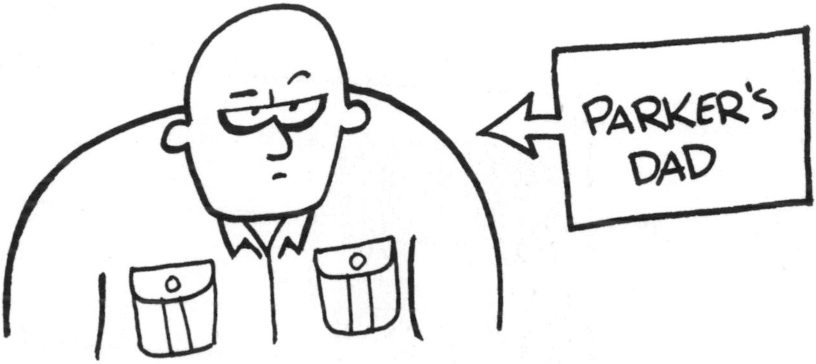
PARKER'S DAD

"Or else what?"

"Or else he'll use their skin and bones to make furniture."

"Oh. He was speaking metaphorically, right?"

"I'm not sure. Anyway, let's start."

"But . . ."

"The clock is ticking, Marty. Tell me about the note."

"It says an alien is observing me."

"How exotic!" Parker says. "And this note totally exists, right?"

"Totally."

"By any chance, have you been watching movies about aliens lately?"

"Yes, but I don't see what that has to do—"

"Remember when you watched all those zombie movies and thought the pigeons outside your house were zombies?"

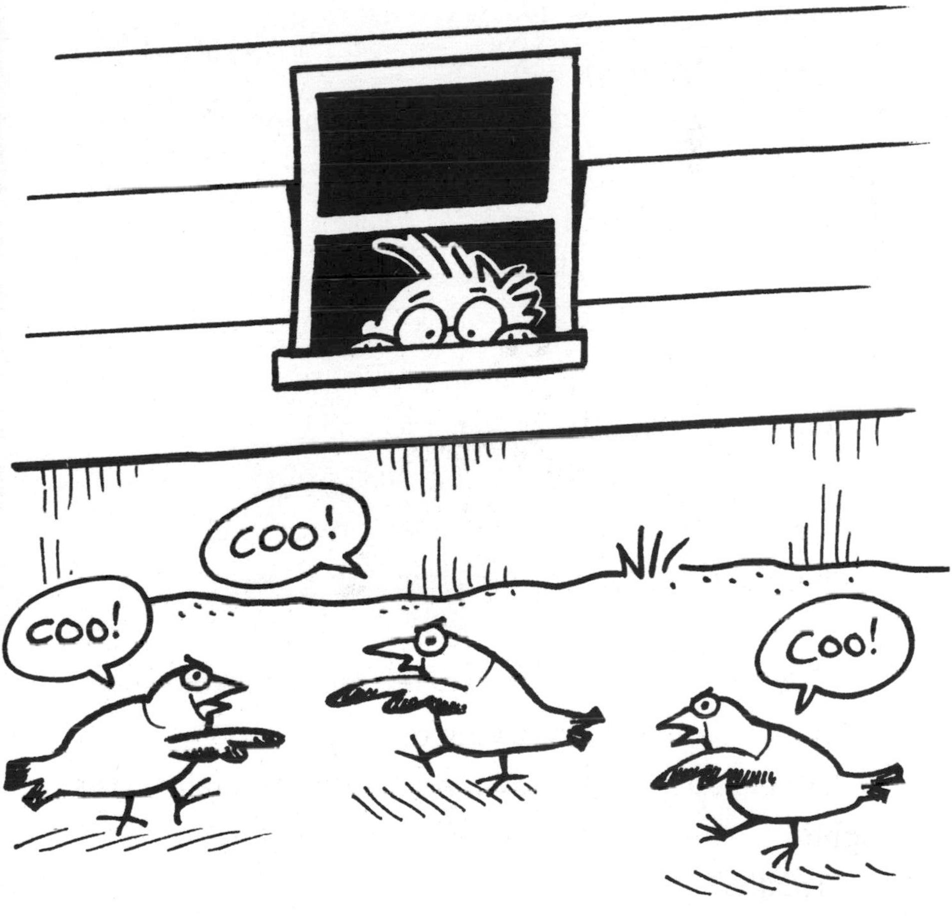
COO!
COO!
COO!

"Your point being?"

"You went door-to-door with a bullhorn trying to evacuate the neighborhood."

"Of course I did! No one listened to me, but the noise scared away the pigeons. And, in case you haven't noticed, there are now exactly *zero* zombies in my neighborhood."

"Point taken," Parker admits. "Your parents were concerned about you, though."

"You know parents. They worry about the wrong things."

"True enough. And some kids teased you."

"Most kids don't notice the things I do."

"That's for sure. Have you told anyone else about this, um, note?"

"I came to you first, Parker."

"Good thinking. My advice is have your fun, but don't say anything to anyone else."

"Why? It's the most important thing that's happened to me all week!"

"Think about it and I'm sure you'll figure it out."

I guess this is what psychologists do. Let you figure things out on your own.

Parker winks and says, "That will be five hundred dollars, please."

"Put it on my tab," I tell her as I get up to leave.

"One more thing," Parker says as she walks me to the door. "Who supposedly wrote this note?"

"No idea," I say.

Parker's face goes white. "OH NO! My dad's in the driveway! He'll turn you into FURNITURE!"

"I don't want to be a human credenza!"

DRAMATI-ZATION →

I run to the front door, but Parker pulls me back. "He'll see you! Climb out the window!"

"Good plan!" I dart to a back window and struggle to open it as the footsteps get closer and closer.

"It won't budge!" I say in a panic.

Parker reaches over to unlock the latch and the window flies open. I don't have time to escape gracefully, so I just dive out headfirst.

At least it's a soft landing.

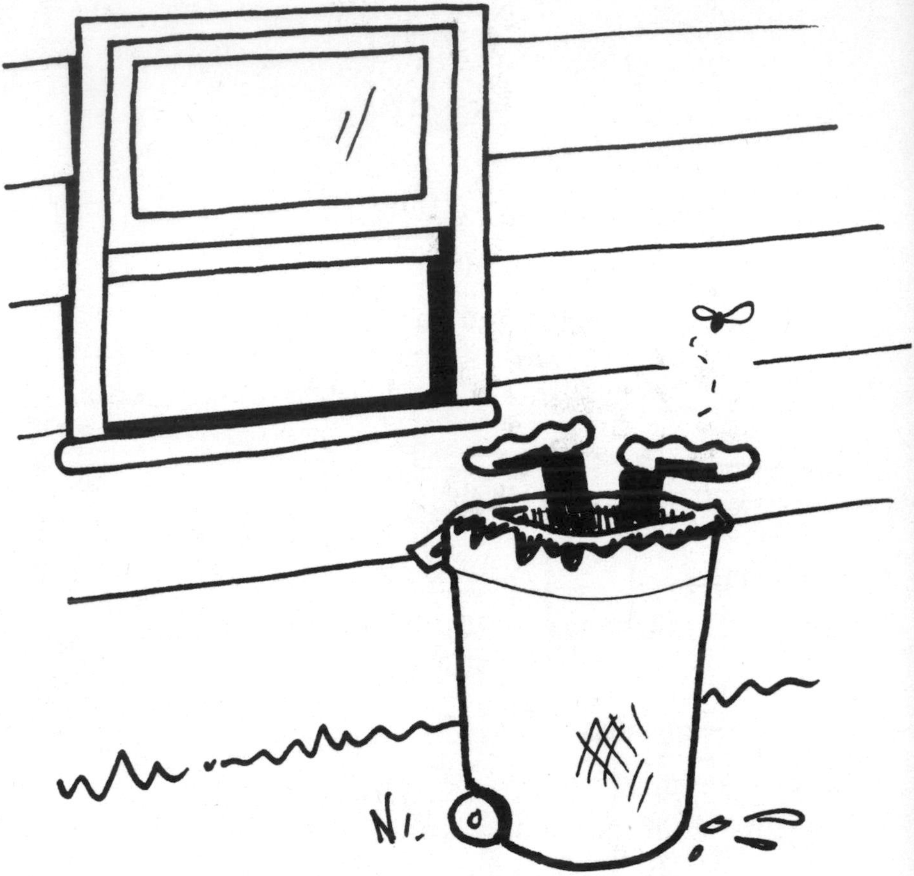

Turns out it wasn't her dad after all. It was the mailman.

I stay put until he leaves, just to be safe. In the meantime, I notice a perfectly good Twinkie that someone threw out. The next thing I notice is someone staring at me from across the lawn.

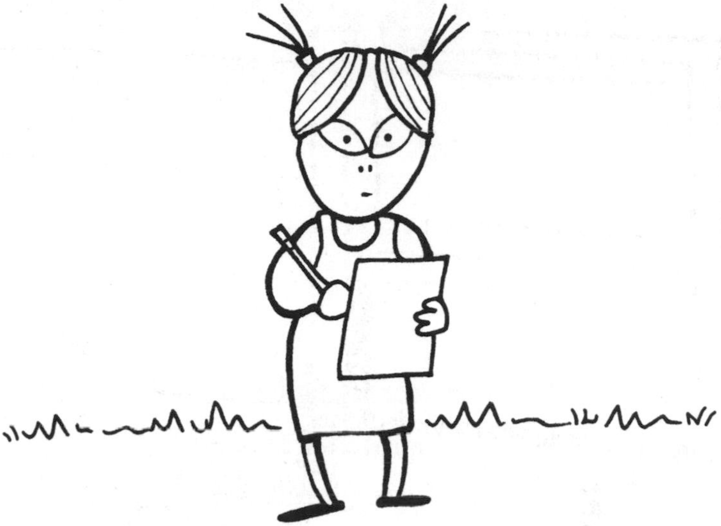

It's Analie, the girl my sister thinks I'm in love with! I try to act cool, but am not sure I'm pulling it off.

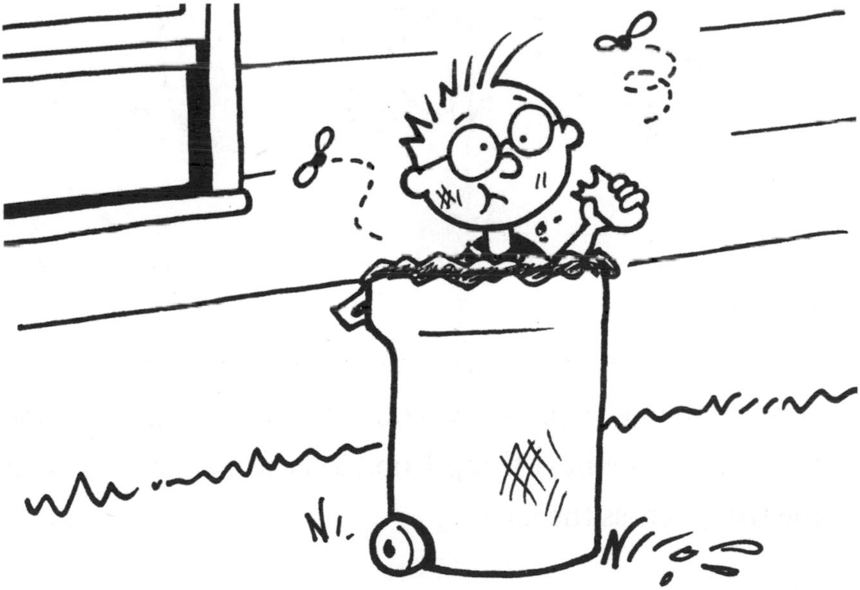

CHAPTER 8

a lot to digest

Analie's the new kid in class. She wears purple and sits in back, where no one pays much attention to her.

Whenever I do anything embarrassing, she always seems to be there to witness it.

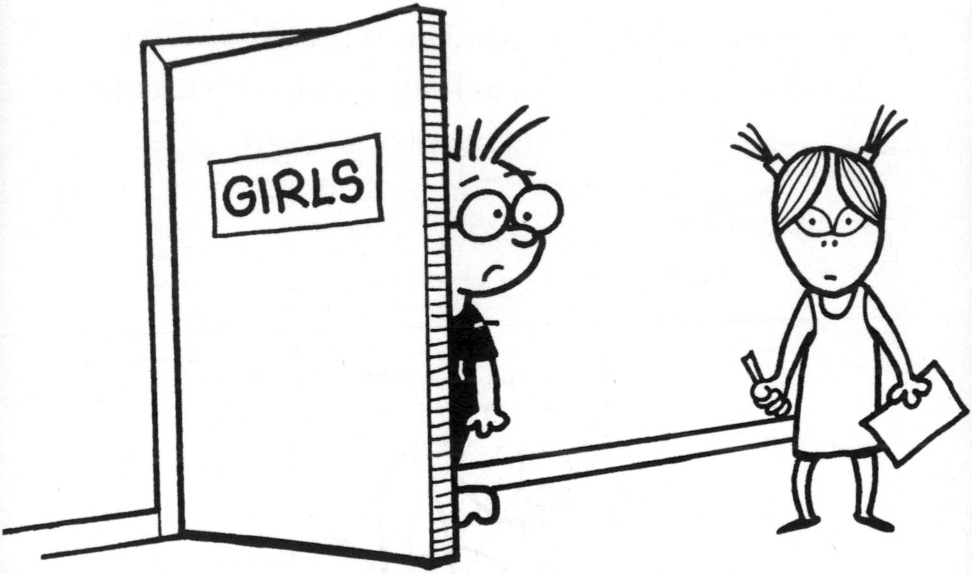
GIRLS

My sister thinks I'm crazy about Analie because she found an innocent drawing I did.

ME   ANALIE

Ericaaa thought those were hearts around my head, but that's what a rube would think. I'm obviously being attacked by a swarm of bloodthirsty moths.

"What's that stink?" my dad asks when I walk in the door.

"Probably Erriccka," I say as I run upstairs. Then I take a long shower to wash off the smell of garbage.

Unfortunately, shame doesn't wash off.

I sink into my beanbag of solitude and unwind.

As the stress leaves my body, I see something sticking out of one of the beanbag creases.

AN ALIEN IS OBSERVING YOU.

I found the note! Parker advised me not to talk to any-one about it, though. Does she think I'm making it all up? Nah.

I reach over to grab the note, but it's gone! It vanished into thin air!

No, wait. There it is.

Jerome! I shouldn't be surprised. Jerome has strange ideas of what counts as food.

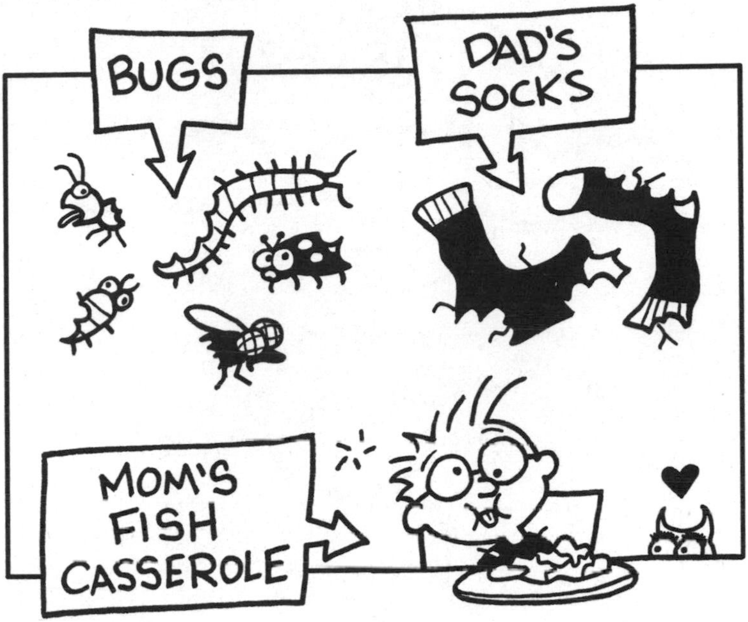
BUGS
DAD'S SOCKS
MOM'S FISH CASSEROLE

The note is gone, but that's okay. I have it memorized.

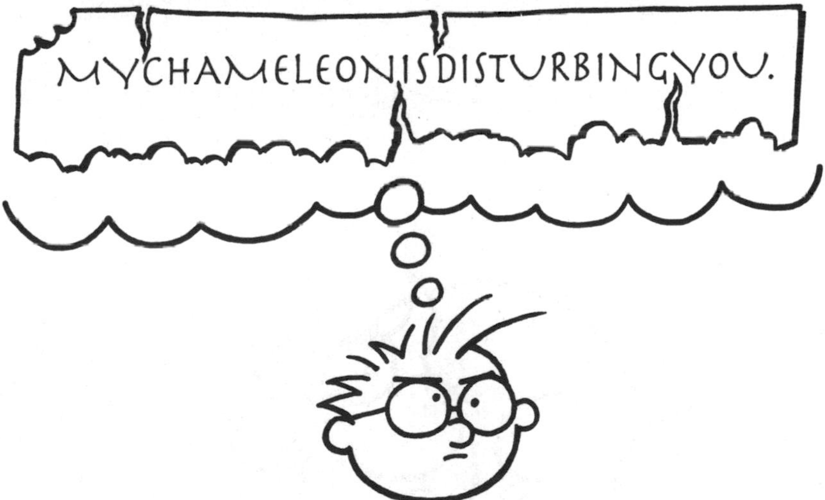
MYCHAMELEONISDISTURBINGYOU.

That's not right. Focus, Marty!

ANALIENISOBSERVINGYOU.

That's it!

But before I try to figure out who the alien is, I need to answer one question.

Do aliens really exist?

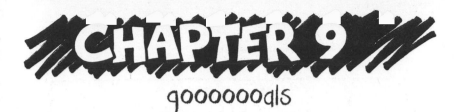

CHAPTER 9

gooooooals

I'm having trouble concentrating because I have too much mind clutter.

Will anyone come to my birthday party?
Can I burp the alphabet?
People eat mushrooms.?
I don't want to be furniture.
Why is paper money worth anything?
monkey butts
Will Peach Fuzz kill me quickly or slooowly?
Clean rooms are overrated.
Where are the zombie pigeons right now?
When will I be famous?
exploding spiders
Can I fart the alphabet?

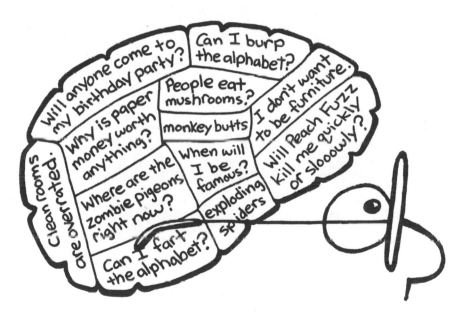

If I hope to get anything done, I need to organize myself. My mom gets organized by writing lists. She's obsessive about them.

Here's one she wrote:

My Lists

- Groceries
- Bills to Pay
- Party Supplies to Buy
- Kids to Invite
- Things to Pack for Business Trip

That's right. It's a list of her lists.

I hate to admit it, but my mom is right. Making lists has really helped me become organized.

Tonight I'm making a list of my goals.

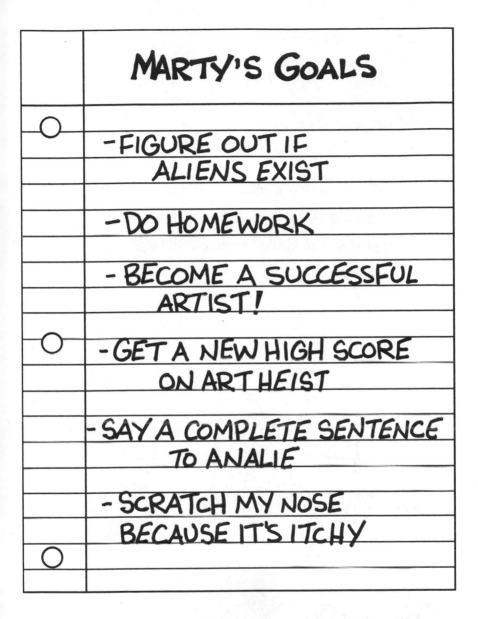

	MARTY'S GOALS
○	-FIGURE OUT IF ALIENS EXIST
	-DO HOMEWORK
	- BECOME A SUCCESSFUL ARTIST!
○	-GET A NEW HIGH SCORE ON ART HEIST
	-SAY A COMPLETE SENTENCE TO ANALIE
	- SCRATCH MY NOSE BECAUSE IT'S ITCHY
○	

My mom says you should put one easy thing on your list so you can cross it off right away and feel productive.

So, I start with the easy thing.

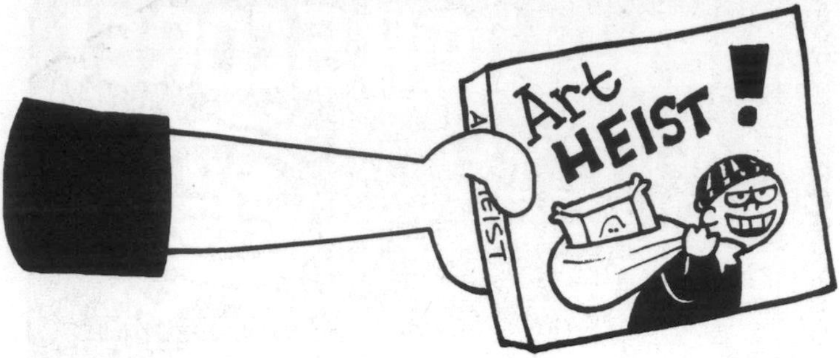
Art
HEIST!
ART HEIST

Art Heist is my favorite video game. You break into museums, steal paintings off the walls, and replace them with forgeries. You draw the forgeries yourself with the controller. Like this:

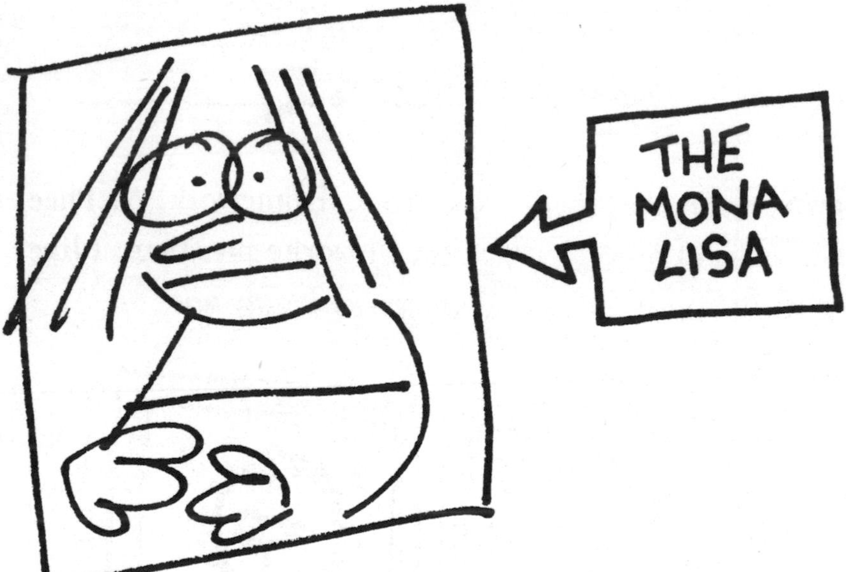
THE
MONA
LISA

Okay, not my best work, but on level one you only have to fool the security guards, and that's not hard. They're rubes.

NEW HIGH SCORE!
MARTYP
YOU ARE
THE
#1 ARTIST!

I rule at this game! I grab my marker.

~~- GET A NEW HIGH SCORE ON ART HEIST~~

Now, on to something harder. Homework. McPhee wants us to do a report on our favorite president. I like Washington and Lincoln but can pick only one.

n.

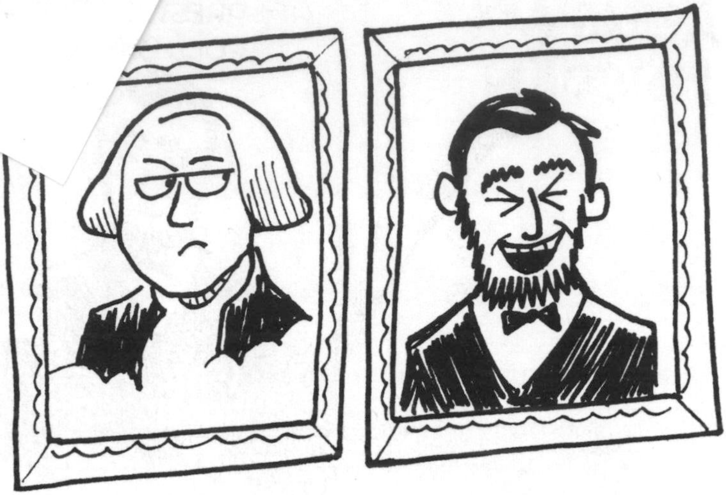

I spend all evening on my paper, and when I'm done, it's a masterpiece. Even a rube like McPhee will love it.

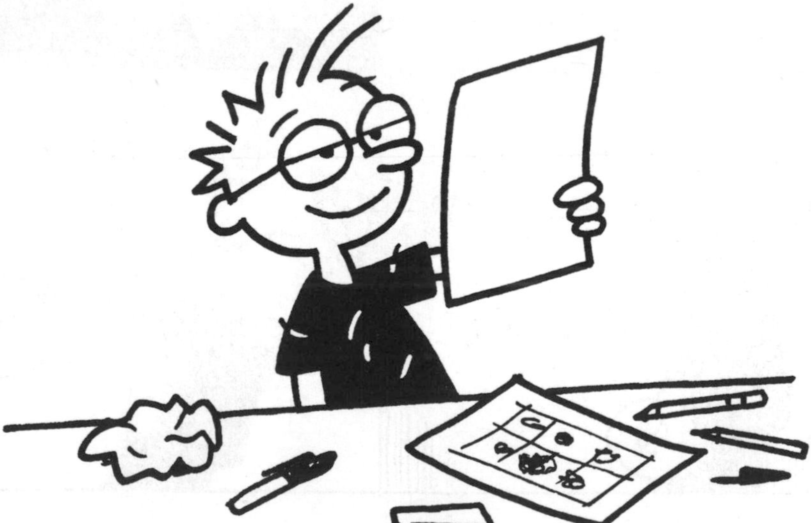

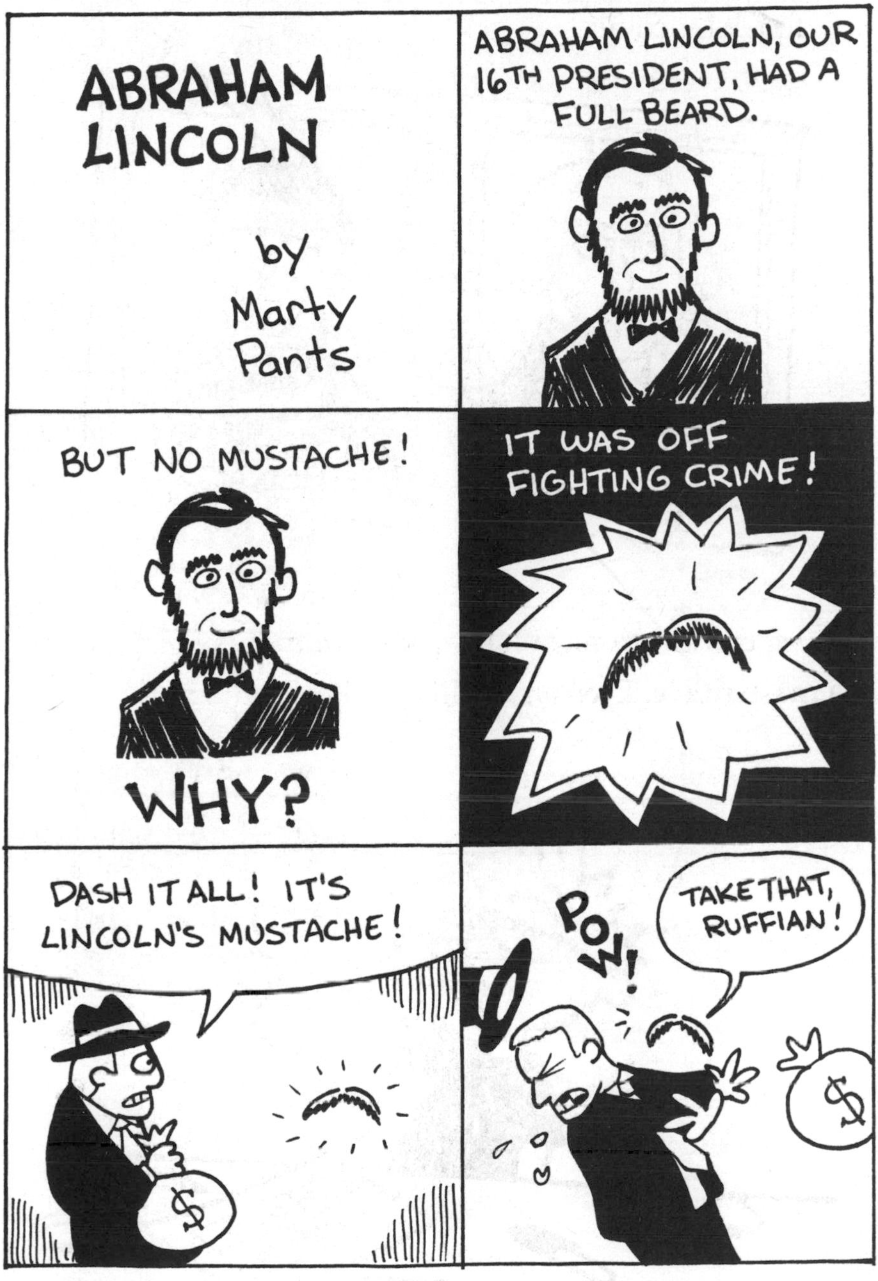
ABRAHAM LINCOLN
by Marty Pants
ABRAHAM LINCOLN, OUR 16TH PRESIDENT, HAD A FULL BEARD.
BUT NO MUSTACHE!
WHY?
IT WAS OFF FIGHTING CRIME!
DASH IT ALL! IT'S LINCOLN'S MUSTACHE!
POW!
TAKE THAT, RUFFIAN!

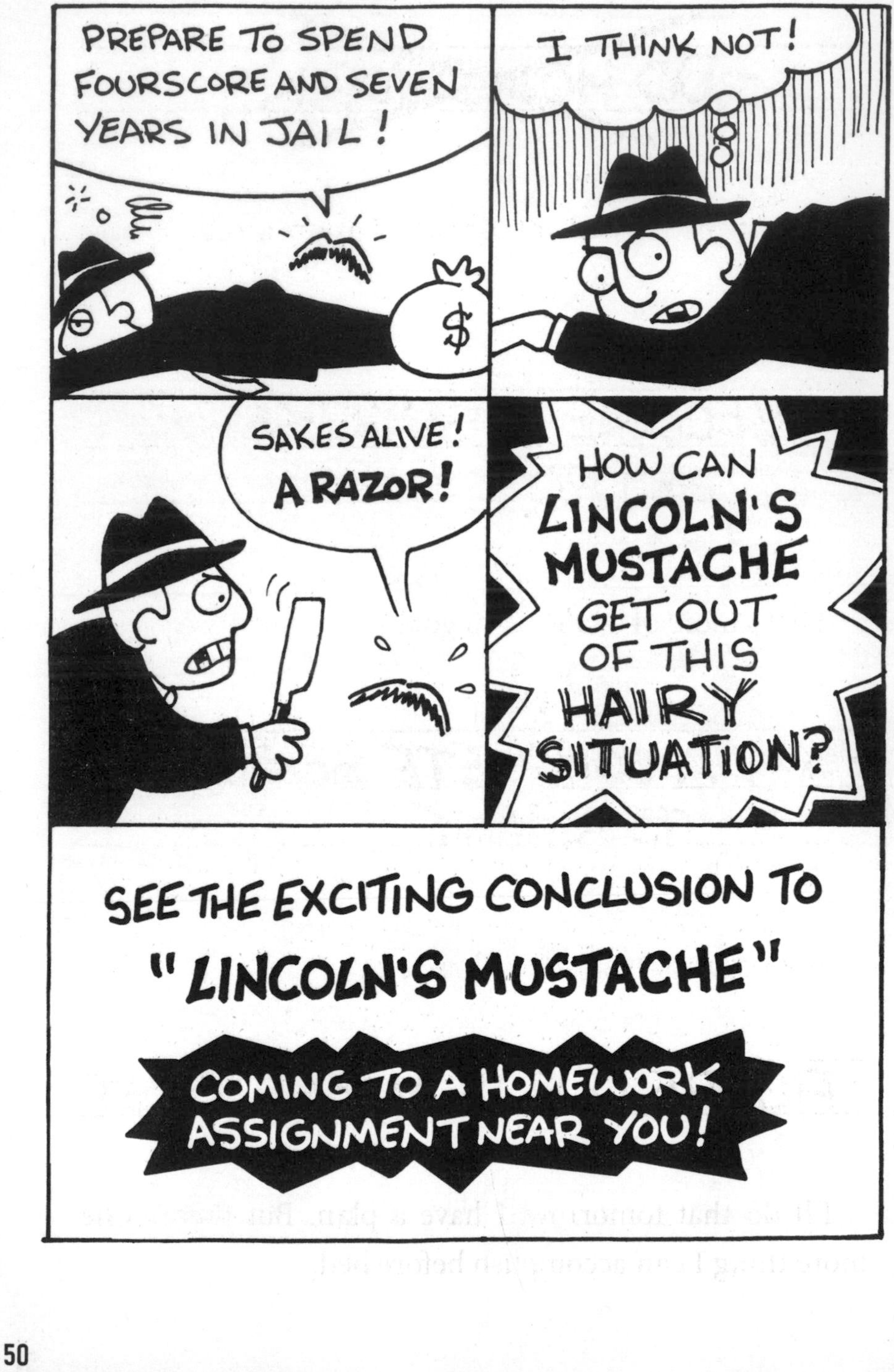
PREPARE TO SPEND FOURSCORE AND SEVEN YEARS IN JAIL!
I THINK NOT!
SAKES ALIVE! A RAZOR!
HOW CAN LINCOLN'S MUSTACHE GET OUT OF THIS HAIRY SITUATION?
SEE THE EXCITING CONCLUSION TO
"LINCOLN'S MUSTACHE"
COMING TO A HOMEWORK ASSIGNMENT NEAR YOU!

- DO HOMEWORK

Two items crossed off already. I'm on a roll! What's next?

- BECOME A SUCCESSFUL ARTIST!

That's more of a long-term goal.

- SAY A COMPLETE SENTENCE TO ANALIE

Honestly, that may never happen.

- FIGURE OUT IF ALIENS EXIST

I'll do that tomorrow. I have a plan. But there's one more thing I can accomplish before bed.

- ~~SCRATCH MY NOSE BECAUSE IT'S ITCHY~~

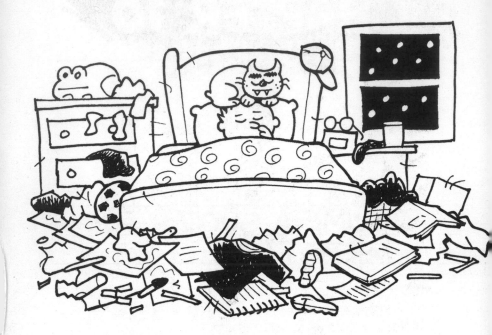

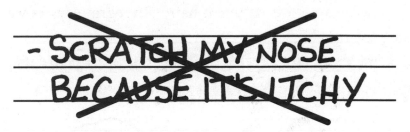

CHAPTER 10

manic monday

"You're always covered in cat hair," Roongrat says as we walk to school.

"That's my look," I say, making the decision at that moment. Every great artist has their own unique look.

PABLO PICASSO

STRIPED SHIRT

(Tried it. The neighbors thought I was an escaped convict.)

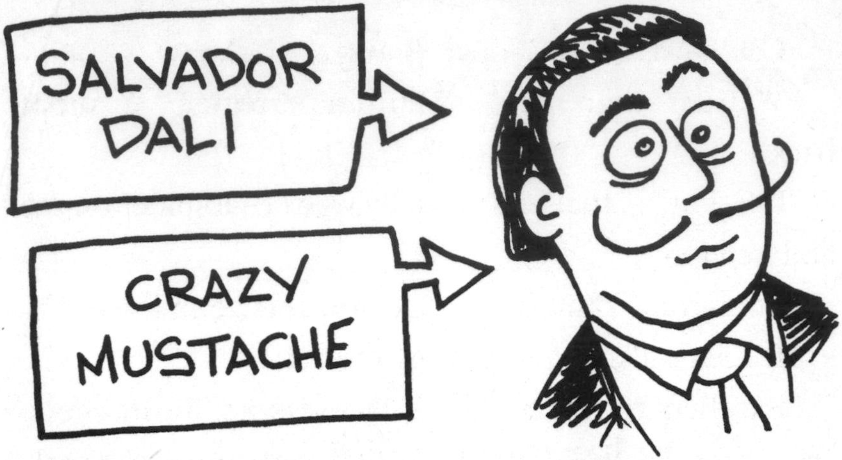
SALVADOR DALI
CRAZY MUSTACHE

(Tried it. Took my mom all day to get the marker off my face.)

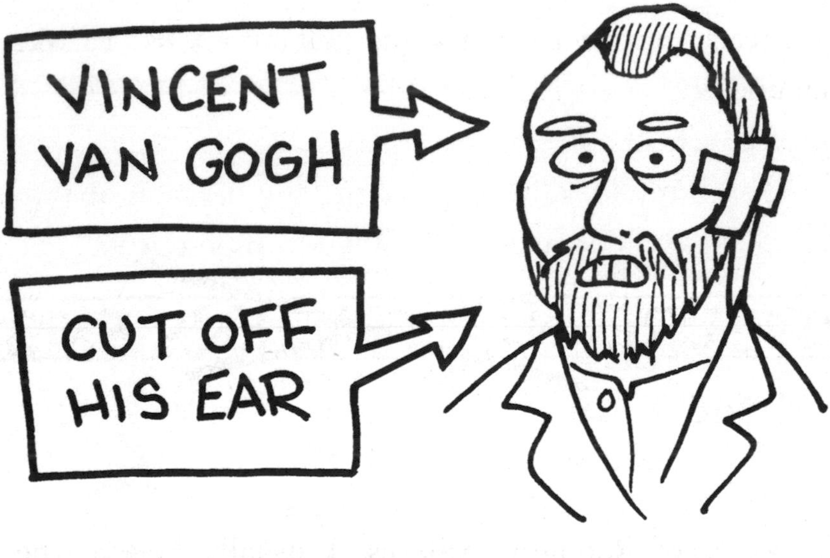
VINCENT VAN GOGH
CUT OFF HIS EAR

(Tried it. Just kidding. I don't even like cutting my nails.)

"Cat hair is a weird look," Roongrat declares.

"Weirder than Spider-Man underpants?" I shoot back.

"I . . . but . . . that was a deadly wolverine spider on me and I had to . . ."

"Roongrat," I interrupt. "Do you believe in aliens?"

He seems glad I changed the subject.

"Excellent question. Aliens do not exist," he answers. "It's a fact. Earth is the only planet in the universal galaxy that supports the functionality of respiratory life based on the carbon sciences. Why?"

"No reason."

I reach into my backpack and pull out my list. I make an update.

~~-FIGURE OUT IF ALIENS EXIST~~

Whatever Roongrat believes, I usually believe the opposite.

So, I believe in aliens now.

We walk to school with our thoughts.

CHAPTER 11

i'm a believer

Roongrat sits at his desk, but I pause a moment. I wonder if someone in this room is the alien.

The bell rings, so I rush to my seat. As I sit down, the pencil in my pocket breaks and stabs me in the thigh. I twitch and make a weird noise.

OOCHIE GAZOONGA!

Luckily, the bell was still ringing so no one noticed. Well, almost no one.

Sitting up front is my teacher, Mr. McPhee.

McPhee reminds me of a sleepy tortoise, only less exciting.

But this is his lucky day. My Lincoln report will add a thrill to his sad, misguided, rube existence.

I hand him my homework, but I'm not sure what to make of his expression when he looks at it. It was probably something he ate.

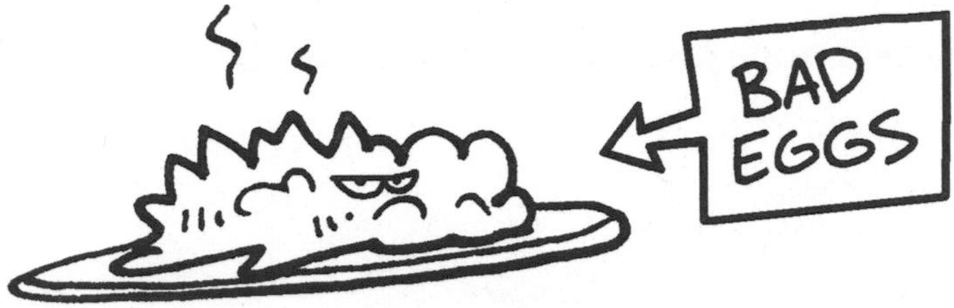
BAD
EGGS

"Marty, can I see you after school?"

Why would McPhee want to see me after school? I bet he wants to buy the rights to my Lincoln report and claim he wrote it himself and sell it for billions of dollars to a Hollywood producer and get rich and famous off my hard work!

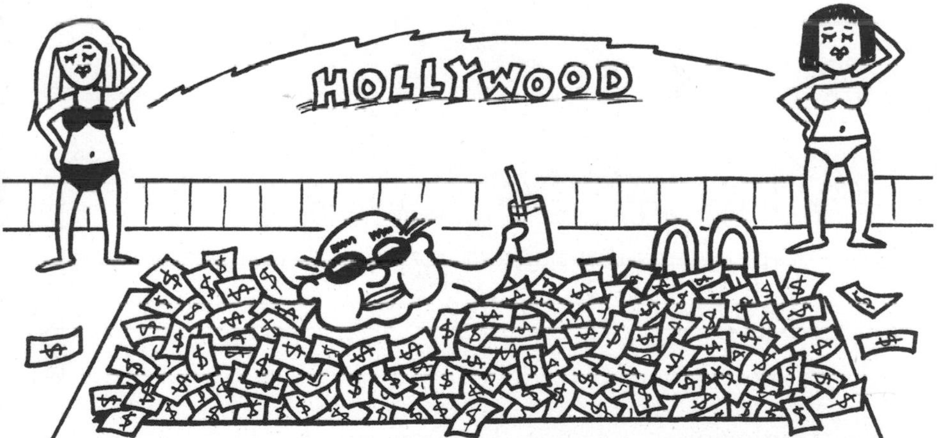
HOLLYWOOD

Uncool, McPhee! Uncool!

It turns out McPhee wants to play hardball.

"You have to redo this report," he tells me after school. "It's not factual."

"It's called creative writing," I explain.

"This is not a creative writing class," he says. "Hand in a proper paper by the end of today or you're getting a D."

I can't believe this!

"And Marty," he adds, "stick to the facts."

I did stick to the facts! I just stuck in some artistic license.*

* Artistic license = made the rest up

CHAPTER 12

do not open

I don't like being in school after school hours.* It feels wrong. Besides, I have better things to do.

LOOK FOR THE ALIEN
PLAY ART HEIST
WATCH PAINT DRY

"Hey, Mr. McRube, how can I redo my report when the class computer isn't working?" is exactly what I would say to McPhee if he hadn't just left the room. But he did.

So now it's up to me to problem solve.

* Or during school hours.

I look around and notice McPhee's personal computer is unattended on his desk.

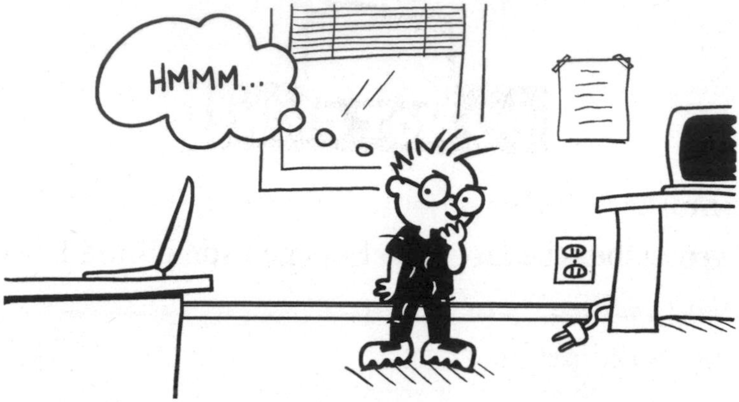
HMMM...

Perhaps he knew the class computer was on the fritz so he left his laptop there for me. He probably wants me to take the initiative. Yeah, that's it.

I accept the challenge and sit at his desk. The chair is still warm.

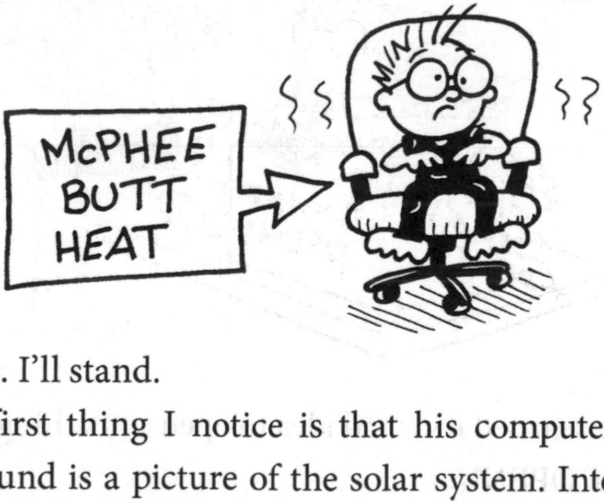
McPHEE
BUTT
HEAT

Gross. I'll stand.

The first thing I notice is that his computer screen background is a picture of the solar system. Interesting. That's where aliens come from, I'm pretty sure.

Then, as I poke around a little more on his computer, I come across a file that catches my eye.

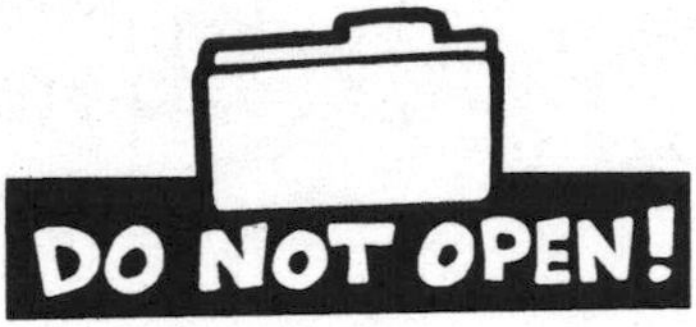
DO NOT OPEN!

Hmm.

I remember the last time I opened something labeled DO NOT OPEN!

Things did not go well.

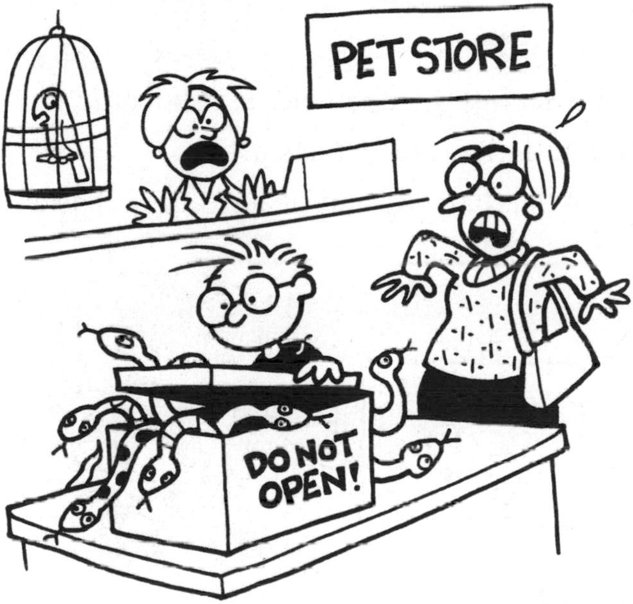
PET STORE
DO NOT OPEN!

So, I've learned it's a bad idea to open something marked DO NOT OPEN!

I open it.

MARTY! WHAT DO YOU THINK YOU'RE DOING?!

Yikes! McPhee snuck up on me! He's quick for a sleepy tortoise!

"Yuba . . . hoba . . . whaba . . ." He sounds like me when I try to talk to Analie.

"WHAT DID YOU SEE, MARTY?!"

"Nothing!" I lie.

"Why were you snooping on my computer?! Go home! You're getting a D, and I'm calling your parents!"

I've never seen him this way before. The sleepy tortoise turned into a snapping turtle!

As I pack up to leave, one thing's crystal clear. McPhee has something to hide.

I told him I saw nothing, but I did see one word.

Annihilate

It sticks in my head. When I get home, I ask my dad for his opinion.

"Dad, what does the word *annihilate* remind you of?"

"A great name for a rock band," he says. "When I was growing up, rock bands had the best names. For instance . . ."

"Time out, Dad! I'm looking for a one-word answer!"

"One word. Can you make it multiple choice?"

"Fine," I sigh. "What does the word *annihilate* remind you of? Aliens, bongos, or celery."

"I'll go with aliens," he answers.

Aliens! That's exactly what I was thinking!

what's the buzz

I meet Parker at the common. We used to play here when we were younger, but these days we just hang out on the swings and talk.

"I think I know who the alien is," I tell her.

"Alien?"

"The alien from the note," I remind her.

"Of course." She nods. "Assume the position, Marty."

"So, Marty, tell me. Who do you think . . ."

"McPhee."

"Our boring teacher is an alien?"

"I'm sixty-eight percent sure."

"How so?"

"It makes sense. The note said the alien is observing me. McPhee observes me."

"Did the note ever turn up again?"

"Yeah, but then my cat ate it."

"I see."

"I also snuck onto McPhee's computer," I tell her.

"No way!" Parker seems impressed.

"I saw the word *annihilate*. Aliens love that word."

"Your mind is an exciting place, Mr. Marty."

"Thanks."

"Have you mentioned your suspicions to anyone else?"

"Not yet, but . . ."

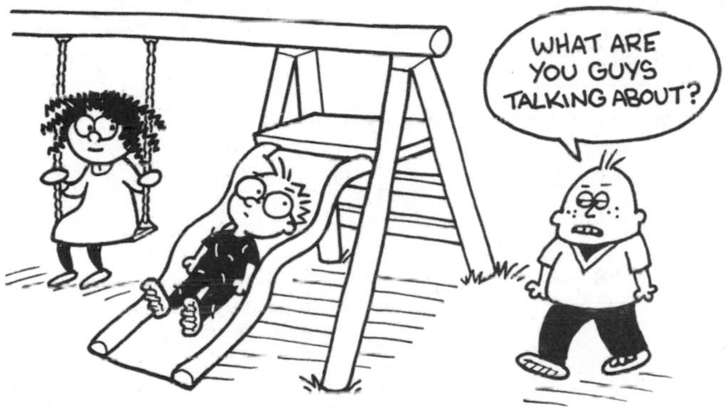
WHAT ARE YOU GUYS TALKING ABOUT?

Roongrat shows up so I switch topics. I mention that McPhee *hated* my Lincoln report and he's going to call my parents.

"Next time you should have Simon show you how to draw," Roongrat says.

"Next time you should have Simon show you how to *wash a monkey*!"

I wish I'd had time to think of a better comeback.

Roongrat considers Simon Cardigan to be the school artist. Everyone seems to, but Simon's a complete rube. He doesn't have a creative bone in his body.

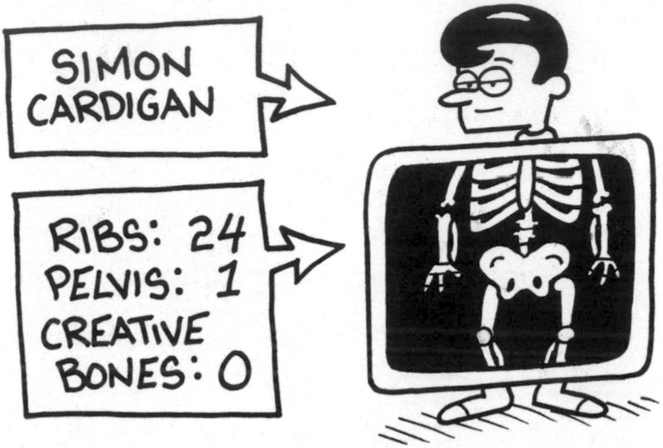
SIMON CARDIGAN
RIBS: 24
PELVIS: 1
CREATIVE BONES: 0

He only draws *one* character. It's a famous cartoon character that, for legal reasons, we'll call AnemoneBob TrapezoidShorts.*

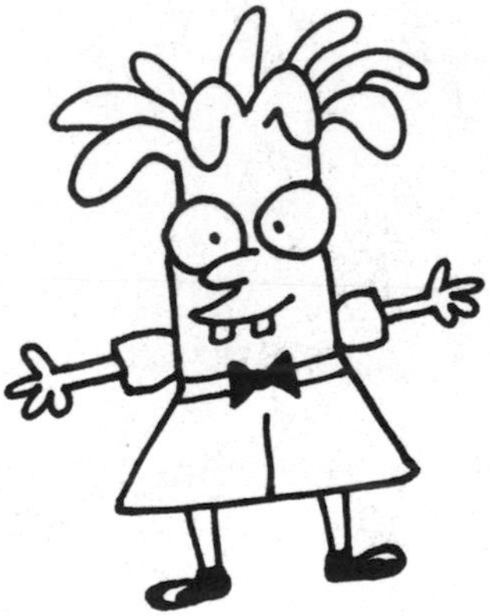

He shamelessly draws it all the time, especially on girls' notebooks. Parker has an AnemoneBob on her notebook.

* Not the real name of the character. You know the real name.

Roongrat has about twenty. I suspect Roongrat's trying to move up the popularity ladder by cozying up to Simon.

Talking about Simon makes me angry, so I start swinging.*

Parker turns it into a competition and starts swinging higher. She knocks Roongrat on his butt.

From the ground Roongrat says, "Swinging was invented by ancient Egyptians. It moves stomach food into the intestines to make room for dessert. It's a fact."

"Beat this!" says Parker, as she swings dangerously high.

"BLAAARGH!" I say.

And that's because a fly went up my nose!

I don't know if you've ever had a buzzing insect in your

---

* Not punching, swinging on the swing.

nostril before, but it immediately takes precedence over whatever else you're doing.

I jump off the swing and run around in circles trying to blow it out. Parker thinks it's hilarious.

Roongrat just makes things worse. "It's a fact certain bugs tunnel up your nose and lay eggs in your brain matter."

Thanks, Roongrat!

When blowing it out doesn't work, I try something else. Digging in.

"IT'S A BIG ONE!" I say. "I ALMOST GOT IT!"

At that moment, I lock eyes with someone across the street.

I sneeze and the fly shoots out. The traumatized bug takes a moment to recover, and then buzzes off home.

The traumatized Marty does the same.

CHAPTER 14

bushwhacked

I step in the front door just as the phone rings. I run over and look at the name.

MCPHEE

I think fast and answer it in my English accent. "Hallo, guv'nah! Wrong numbah!" Then I hang up. That will buy me some time.

The phone rings again, and my mom grabs it before the ring is even finished.

"Oh, hi, Mr. McPhee . . ."

Gurk! My only hope is it's a completely different Mr. McPhee. I mean, what are the odds it's the same Mr. McPhee I'm thinking of? There must be dozens! Hundreds! Gazillions!

The expression on my mom's face says it all. Of all the Mr. McPhees in the world, it's the only one I didn't want it to be.

Either that or it's something she ate.

BAD EGGS

I step outside so I won't be around to hear this conversation.

Over by the bushes, where Roongrat had his pants scared off, I notice Shermy the Spider already made a brand-new web. And trapped a fly!

I begin to wonder if it's the same fly I met earlier.

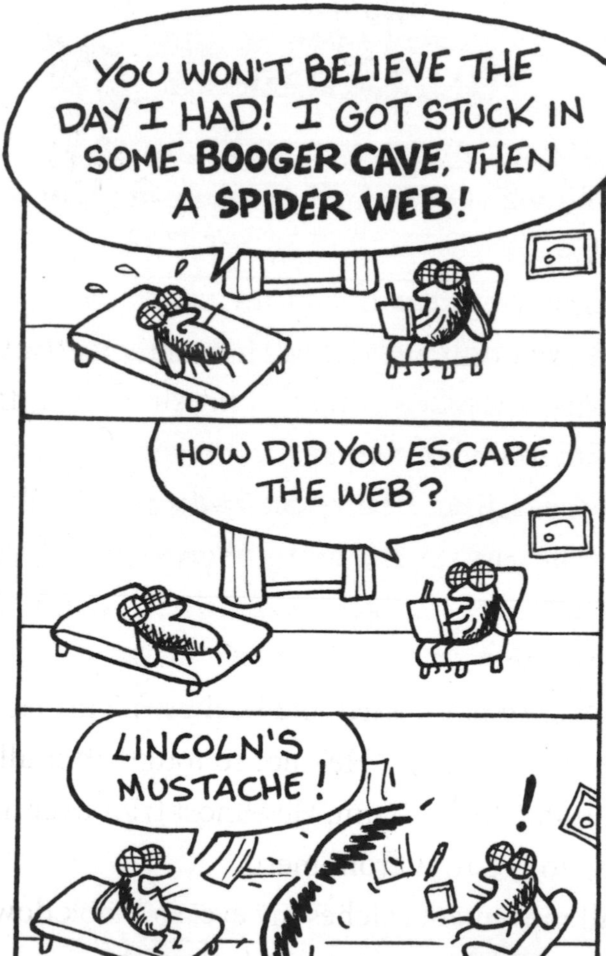
YOU WON'T BELIEVE THE DAY I HAD! I GOT STUCK IN SOME **BOOGER CAVE**, THEN A **SPIDER WEB**!
HOW DID YOU ESCAPE THE WEB?
LINCOLN'S MUSTACHE!

Suddenly, I'm pushed face-first into the bushes. Without looking, I know who it is.

"Yer clumzy, Weddy!"

Peach Fuzz calls me *Weddy*. He means *Wetty*. Get it? Wetty Pants? Ha ha. I get up and brush myself off. And try hard not to weddy my pants.

"I owe ya sumthing," Peach Fuzz says as he holds up his fist. I hope he's about to open it and give me back years of lunch money, but I doubt it. I defensively put up my fists and brace myself.

Peach Fuzz looks scared and backs off. Ha! He didn't expect me to fight back! He's not so tough after all. I feel braver and step toward him. He almost trips over his own feet trying to get away from me!

A small movement catches my eye, so I look down and everything suddenly starts to makes sense.

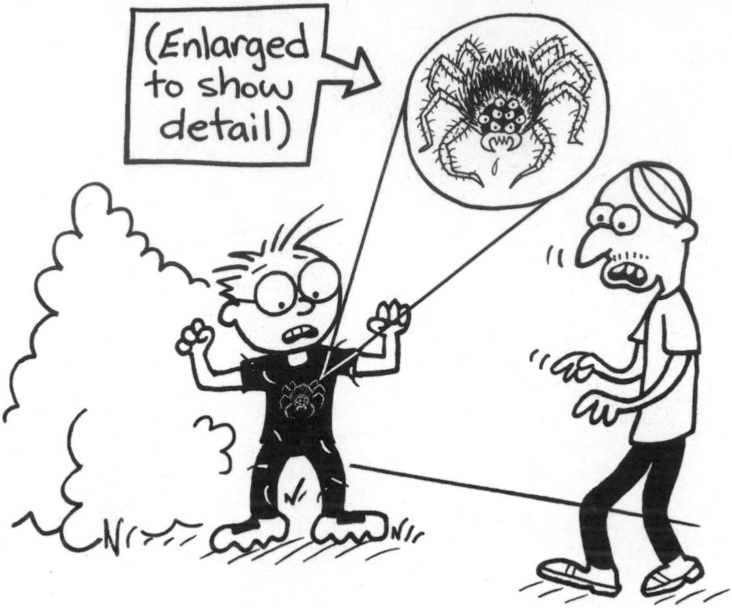
(Enlarged to show detail)

I feel a rush of terror. I can see Peach Fuzz is scared, too. If I can keep my head, I can use this to my advantage.

"Th-This is my new poisonous wolverine spider," I say in a voice higher than usual. "His name is Shermy. He can jump six feet. Wanna see?"

Peach Fuzz takes two steps back. "Get away frum me wid dat."

"C-Come on, pet him," I say.

"I'll katch ya later, Weddy," Peach Fuzz growls. He turns away and spits on the ground. "And I WILL katch ya later."

Whew. Another close call.

With Peach Fuzz gone, I can now act like I normally would in this situation.

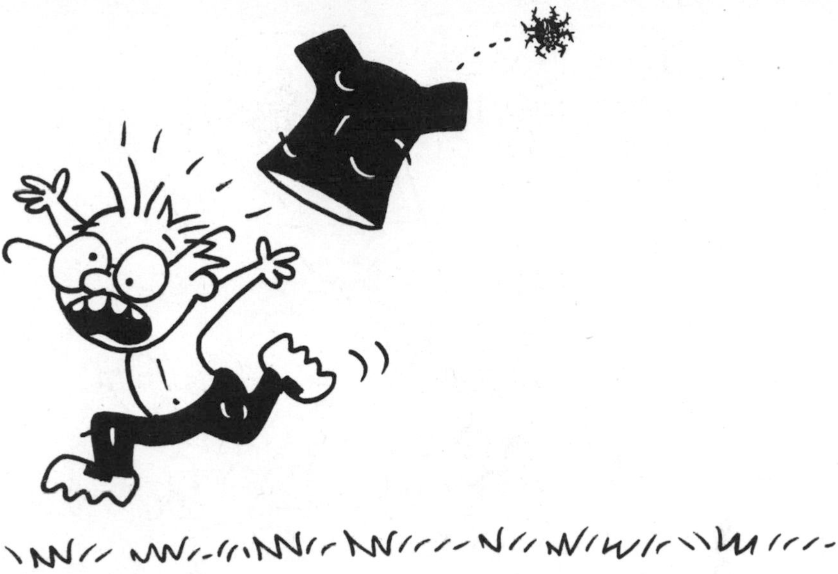

My heart is beating a million times a minute!

I played that perfectly, though. Things could not have gone better!

Before I head inside for dinner, I spot a familiar face on the corner.

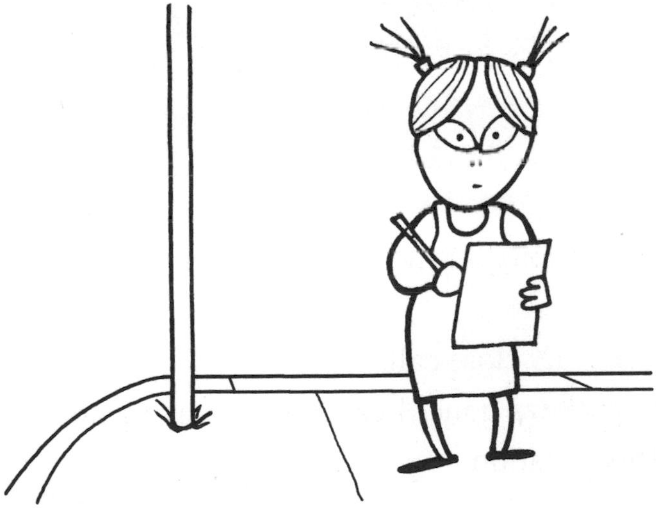

So I wave.
Then I realize this is what Analie is seeing.

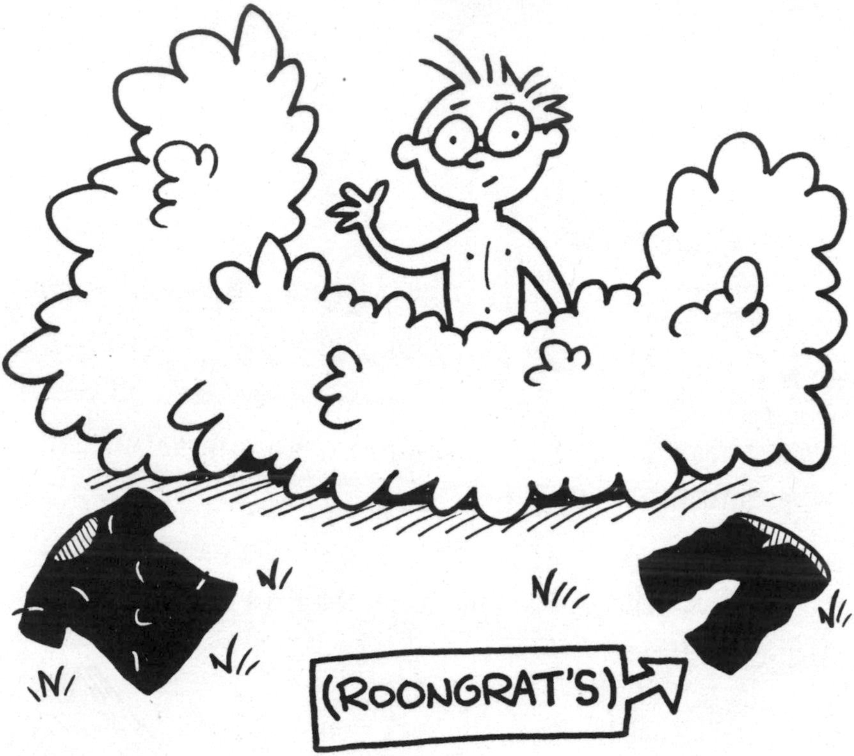
(ROONGRAT'S)

I'll be able to retrieve my shirt, but not my dignity.

CHAPTER 15

letter man

I go inside and it's almost dinnertime. My mom is telling Eriqa how proud she is of her. Apparently, Ericcca got an A+ on her test, scored two goals in soccer, and cured every disease known to mankind. Not really, but that's what it feels like.

...AND YOU STRAIGHTENED THE LEANING TOWER OF PISA?

IT WAS NOTHING.

When my mom runs out of awesome things to say to Errika, she shifts her attention to me. In her lecturing voice, she tells me I need to do my assignments "correctly." She says I'm "underachieving" and I'm really "smart."

This makes Errickaa snort food out her nose.

A lot of things seem to be going in and out of noses lately.

"Are you listening to me, Marty?"

Oh yeah, my mom's still talking.

"Avidly," I say. As I listen, there's one thing I don't hear. There's no talk of me snooping on McPhee's computer and opening that file named DO NOT OPEN! Apparently, McPhee didn't bring up any of that when he called the house.

He's definitely hiding something.

My dad says he liked my report and Mr. McPhee's a rube.

Then my mom and dad get into a discussion. My mom seems to be winning this discussion.

I leave the table unnoticed and take a handful of crack-ers to my room. Time to skim the words for tomorrow's vocabulary test.

Annihilate
Protagonist
Imminent
Absurd
Feeble
Assumption
Deprive
Terminate
Exasperate
Industrious
Wisdom

As I go over the definitions, I notice something. These words may seem innocent to the average mind, but I notice things others don't. I'm a noticer. It can be a curse to be a noticer. It would be easier to be blissfully ignorant like everyone else and not notice things, but there it is, plain to my noticer eyes.

These are the words a dangerous alien would use! Just look how they flow together.

"We will *annihilate* Earth, and any *protagonist* who senses the *imminent* danger will instead decide the idea is *absurd* and that *feeble assumption* will allow us to *deprive* humans of their world as we *terminate* the planet and no one will *exasperate* us, not even an *industrious* student with *wisdom*."

Coincidence? I think not. That's probably the alien motto.

The alien manifesto.

It may even be the lullaby they sing to their alien babies.

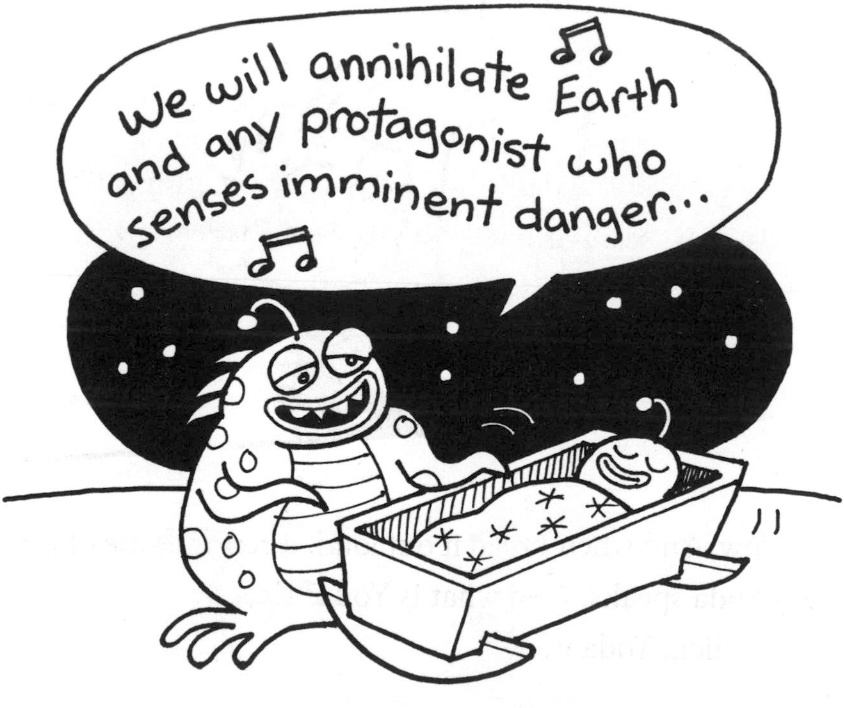
We will annihilate Earth and any protagonist who senses imminent danger...

I try something else. I take the first letter of each vocabulary word: *A, P, I, A, F, A, D, T, E, I, W,* and this happens.

A- nother
P- lanet
I-
A- m
F- rom
A- nd
D- estroy
T- he
E- arth
I-
W- ill

Wow. And when I read it out loud, it reminds me of the way Yoda speaks. And what is Yoda? Exactly.

An alien, Yoda is.

CHAPTER 16

eyes wide open

I have trouble sleeping.

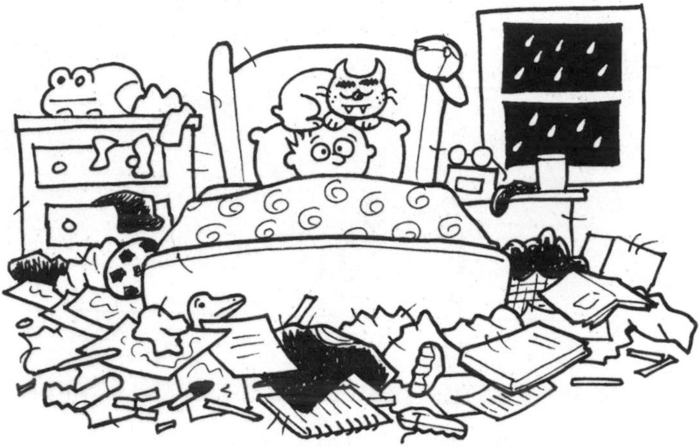

It's not because Jerome is on my head. He always does that.

It's not because of the rainstorm outside.

It's not because of the cracker crumbs in my bed, although that doesn't help.

It's because my teacher is an alien who wants to annihilate Earth! And I happen to like Earth! I'm using it at the moment!

How am I supposed to sleep at a time like this?

I call my dad into the room. I need to talk to him. Or more precisely, I need to have *him* talk to *me*.

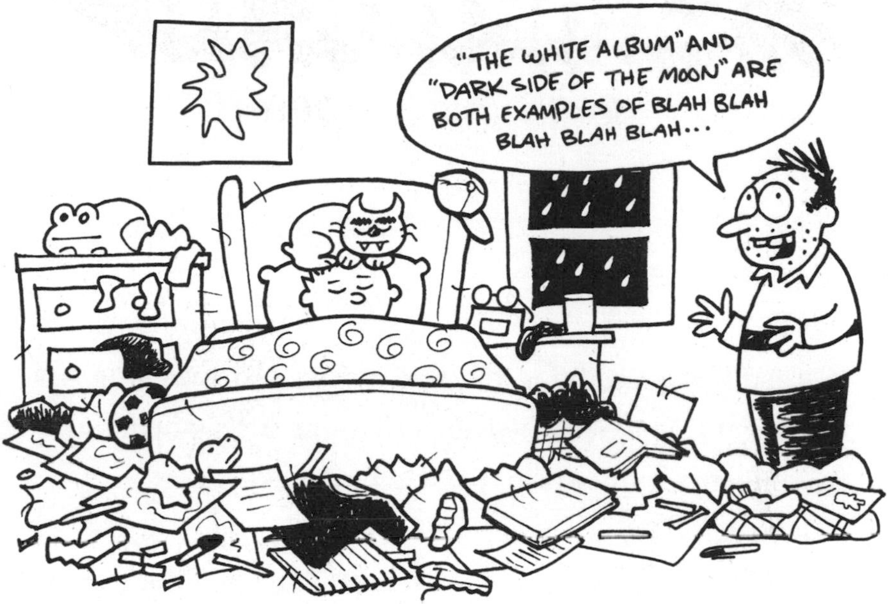
"THE WHITE ALBUM" AND "DARK SIDE OF THE MOON" ARE BOTH EXAMPLES OF BLAH BLAH BLAH BLAH BLAH...

That's better. Nothing can put me to sleep quicker than my dad's talk of old music. I'd make a fortune if I could bottle it.

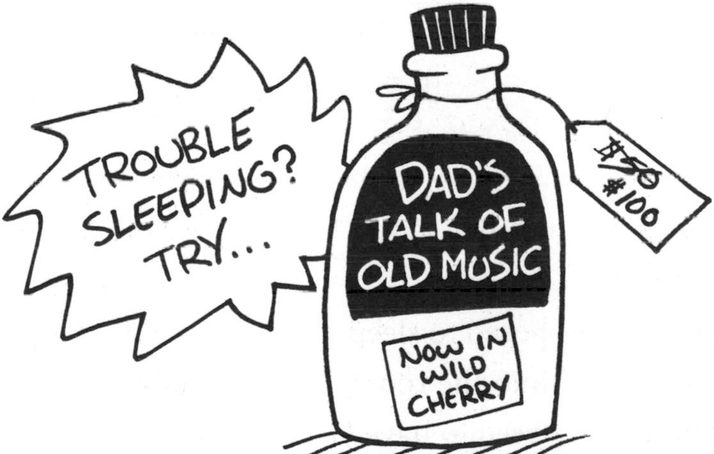
TROUBLE SLEEPING? TRY...
DAD'S TALK OF OLD MUSIC
$50
$100
NOW IN WILD CHERRY

CHAPTER 17

words is the word

It wasn't easy studying for that vocab test knowing my teacher wants to destroy the planet, but after poring over those words for hours, a miracle happened.

I got an A.

It's the second time I've gotten an A in McPhee's class. The first time was when he let us grade our own assignments.

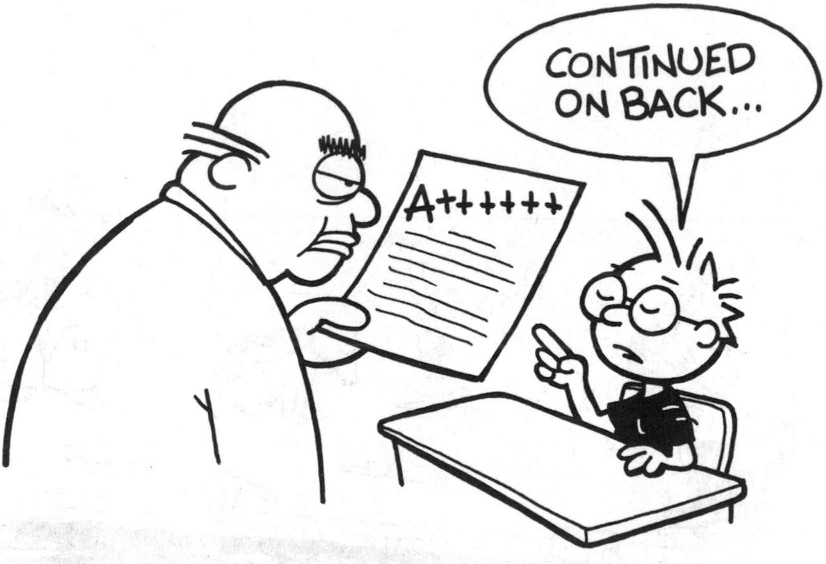
CONTINUED ON BACK...
A++++++

He hasn't tried that again.

"Nice job on the vocabulary test!" my mom says as she drives Roongrat and me to soccer practice.

I just I hope she doesn't think her lecture worked.

"Skunks have a bigger vocabulary than people do," Roongrat says. "They communicate with millions of different stinks. It's a fact."

"See what happens when you do your work properly, Marty?" my mom continues. "Maybe Mr. McPhee isn't so bad after all."

No, he's not so bad unless you happen to think wanting to annihilate Earth is bad. Call me crazy, but I happen to think it is.

I look out the window. Why would anybody want to destroy all this?

CHAPTER 18

get your kicks

I like soccer except for one thing. Simon Cardigan's on my team.

SIMON
(mistakenly thinks he's the school artist)

To make matters worse, Simon's dad is the coach. Since the coach is in charge of supplying the jerseys, Simon got to do the drawing for the front. Guess what he drew?

That's right, the only thing he ever draws. AnemoneBob TrapezoidShorts.*

"Hey, PANTS!" Coach Cardigan yells. "You forgot your practice jersey again!"

"Where is my mind?" I say.

Roongrat knows I forget the shirt on purpose.

"Marty, stop being jealous because Simon is a better artist than you. It's a fact. You should be a supportive friend."

Must be nice to have a supportive friend. Roongrat, unlike me, will wear his AnemoneBob shirt anywhere.

---

* This time with cleats!

"Pants! Focus! You've got to have the eye of the leopard! Isn't that right, Simon? Eye of the leopard!"

"Yes, Dad!"

"Simon, when we're on the field you call me 'Coach'!"

"Yes, Dad! I mean, Coach!"

"Simon! Marty! You two Forgetful Freddies do a lap around the field! EYE OF THE LEOPARD!"

Simon shows off by running hard. He's got the eye of the leopard. I jog slowly. I'll save my energy, thank you.

When we get back, Simon acts like he won an actual race and does a little victory dance.

"I'm better than you, Marty," he says as he struts by.

"Go wash a monkey!" I say, regretting it instantly. I need to work on my comebacks.

Coach Cardigan lines us up and says, "We're going to scrimmage today, white shirts against blue shirts."

Blue shirts? He reaches into his duffel bag and hands out new, powder-blue shirts with this on the front.

It's the exact same drawing, only on a blue shirt. Real creative. I put it on over my signature black shirt.

I'm officially in a bad mood because:

1. Simon's drawing is on my chest.

2. I don't know what to do about my alien teacher.

3. My mom's making fish casserole for dinner.

Other than my mom, there's only one resident of the house looking forward to fish casserole.

This bad mood might be working for me, though, because I'm playing awesome. Coach even moves me to forward. He never does that.

I'm fast when I want to be. I kick the ball over Simon's head, turn on the jets, and beat Simon to it. Ha! He should have saved his energy. Now there's no one between me and the goalkeeper, Roongrat. Here's my chance to show everybody I'm better than Simon!

I'm all ready to score a glorious goal when I see my sister across the common. And she's with someone.

Someone I know!

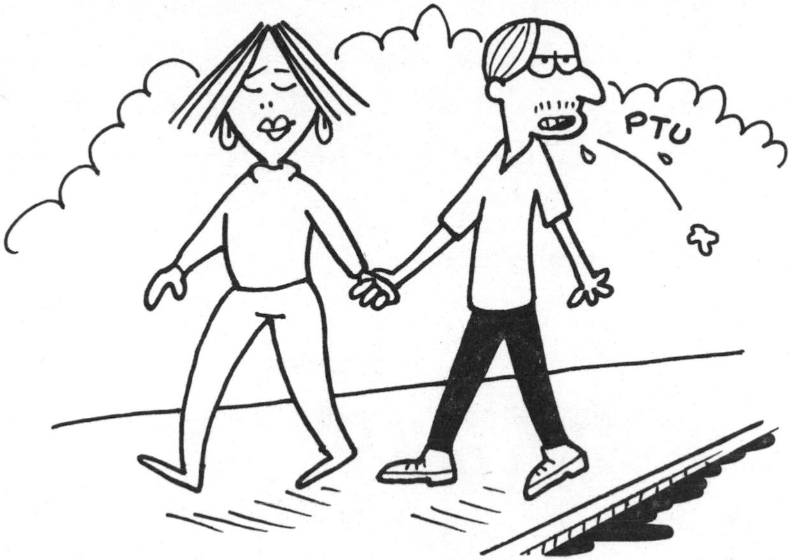
PTU

My sister and Peach Fuzz holding hands?! I can't believe my eyes! This can't be! This just can't—

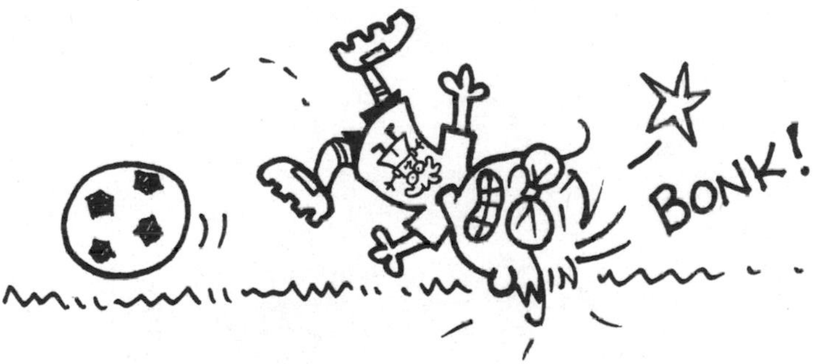
BONK!

Simon kicks the ball away.

"PAY ATTENTION, PANTS!" yells Coach.

"Yeah, pay attention, Pants!" laughs Simon.

"I would have saved it anyway," Roongrat chimes in. "The trajectory of the wind in relation to your ankle angle . . ."

"PANTS! BACK ON DEFENSE!" Coach barks. I lie there, humiliated, and watch Errriccaa and Peach Fuzz disappear around the corner. At least they didn't see my spectacular fall.

Suddenly, I hear Coach yelling!

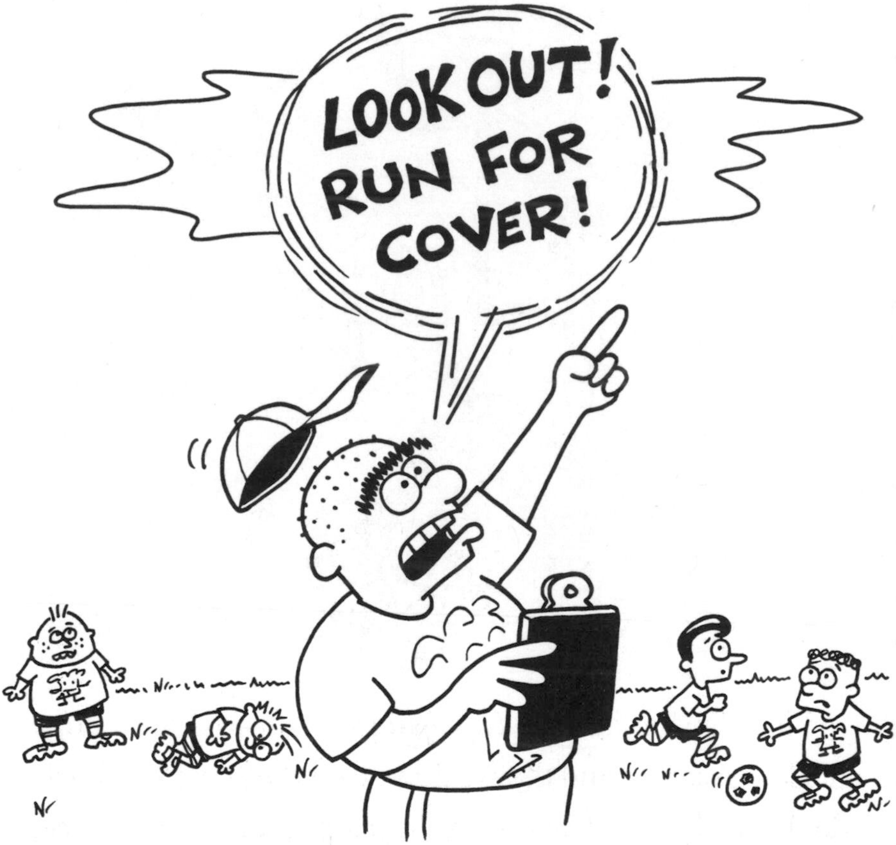
LOOK OUT! RUN FOR COVER!

The aliens are attacking! Already?! I thought there was more time!

I run as fast as I can to escape. I cut across the field, speed though the playground, jump over the sandbox, and run between the swings.

But I get tripped up.

The chain from a swing twists around my ankle, and I'm a sitting duck!

That's when I feel the photon torpedoes hitting me. My skin is melting! Oh, the calamity!

I look up but don't see spaceships. Instead, I see a huge flock of seagulls, and they're dropping bombs the way birds do. In turd form. The rest of the team is safe under a tree, laughing and pointing. Even Coach Cardigan is laughing, but Simon laughs the loudest. It's like he's showing off how loud he can laugh for a loud-laughing contest.

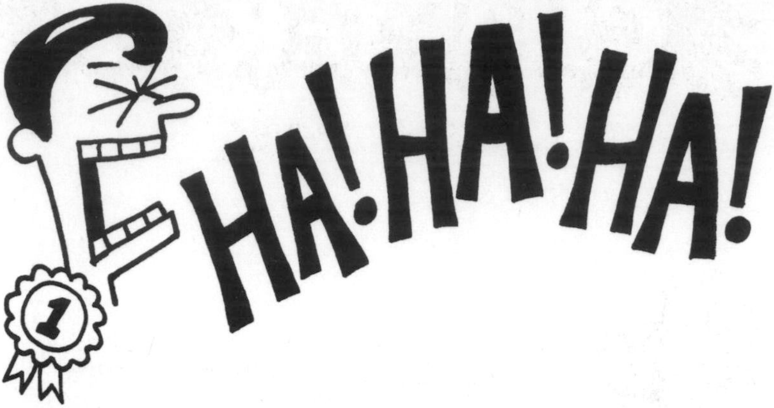
HA!HA!HA!

The birds eventually go on their way and I manage to untangle my ankle. I stand up, covered in icky bird mess. Luckily, my AnemoneBob shirt got the brunt of it.

I decide the best course of action is to avoid eye contact with anyone, so I look away from my team.

I end up making eye contact with someone anyway. I'll give you three guesses who it is.

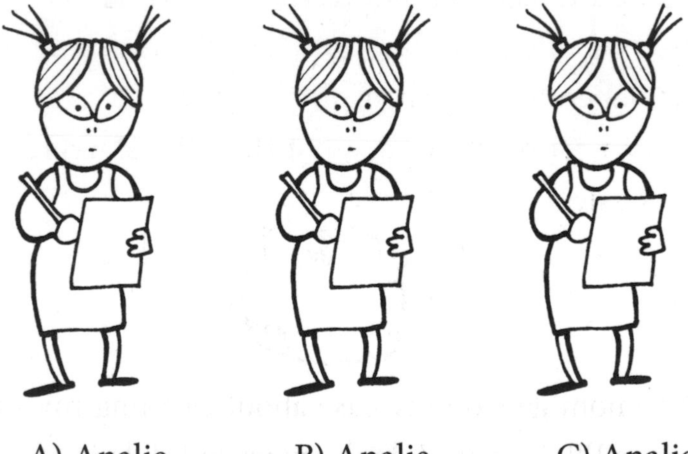

____ A) Analie ____ B) Analie ____ C) Analie*

* Hint: it was Analie.

CHAPTER 19

dreamweaver

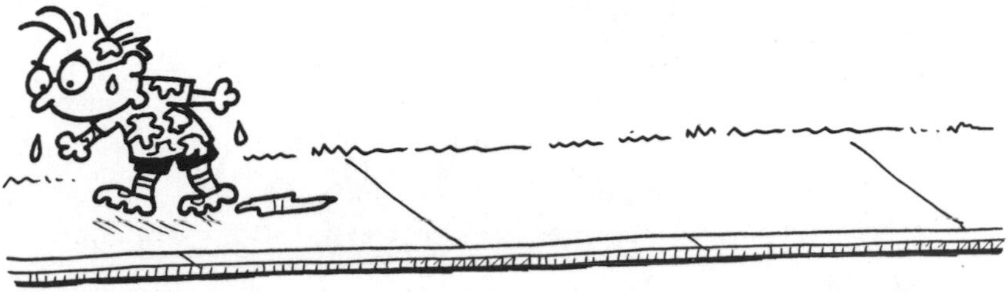

My mom gives Roongrat a ride home, but makes me walk. It's hard to blame her, but I do anyway.

On the way, I toss my disgusting AnemoneBob shirt in someone's trash can, and a lady yells at me through the window. Good for her. She doesn't like Simon's drawing either.

I take another long shower. It was only birds today, but tomorrow aliens could attack me the exact same way! Well, hopefully not *exactly* the same way.

I don't eat much dinner, but the fish casserole doesn't go to waste.

My mom gets on my case about cleaning my room. I promise I'll do it but I don't say *when* I'll do it.

Besides, I'm too exhausted, and fall asleep right away.

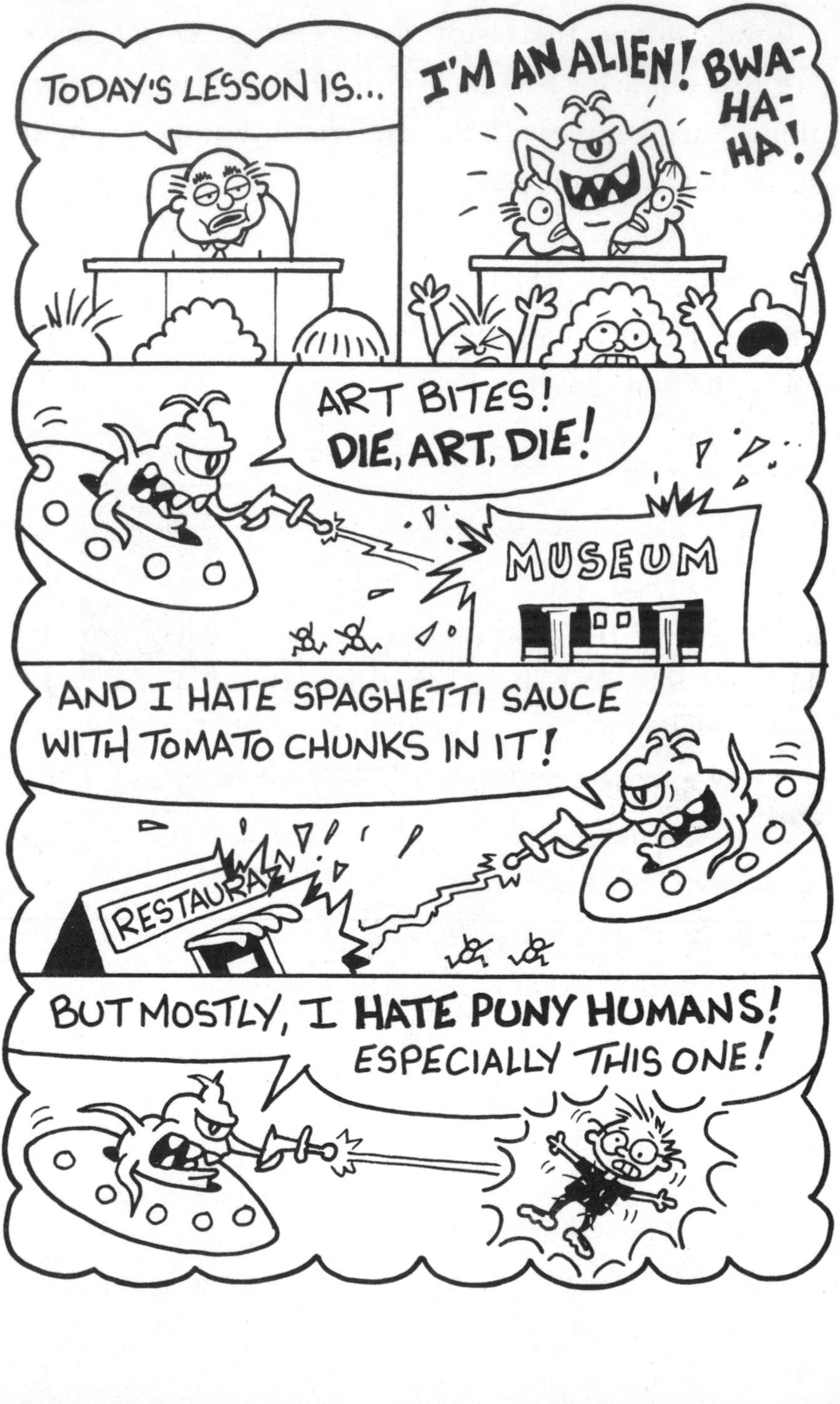
TODAY'S LESSON IS...
I'M AN ALIEN! BWA-HA-HA!
ART BITES! DIE, ART, DIE!
MUSEUM
AND I HATE SPAGHETTI SAUCE WITH TOMATO CHUNKS IN IT!
RESTAURA
BUT MOSTLY, I HATE PUNY HUMANS! ESPECIALLY THIS ONE!

I wake up in a cold sweat. My teacher is a crazed space creature out to destroy the world and I have to do something! Sure, I agree with the part about chunky spaghetti sauce, but the rest is crazy!

Parker said something to me when this whole alien thing started. She asked me if I had just watched any alien movies. I didn't understand what she was trying to tell me at the time, but now I get it.

Movies are the answer!

CHAPTER 20

testing 1, 2, 3

If movies teach us anything, it's that every alien has a weakness. You just have to find it.

I spent the weekend watching my share of alien movies, and now it's time for me to apply what I've learned. I'll rid the world of this disgusting monster once and for all.

Operation Alien Elimination begins today.

Attempt #1: Lasers

WHERE'S MY LASER POINTER?

Results: alien displays minor confusion.

Attempt #2: Germs

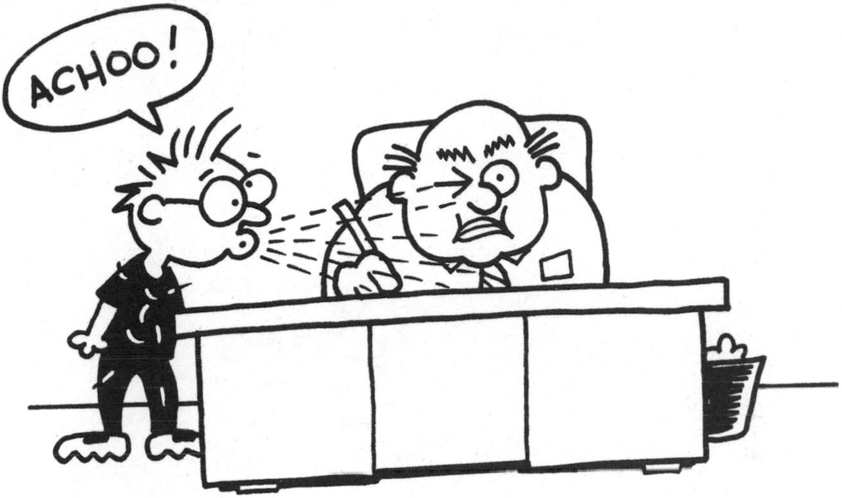
ACHOO!

Results: alien displays minor agitation.

Attempt #3: Water

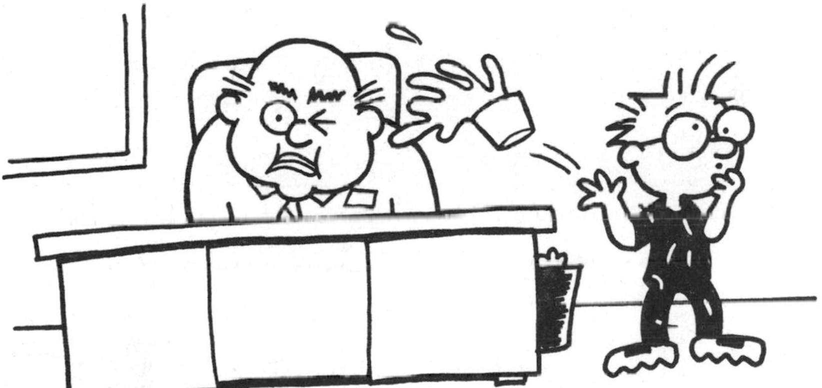

Results: alien displays annoyance and wants me to stay after school for some undisclosed reason.

CHAPTER 21

de tension of detention

This is what I expected to happen.

I'M MELTING!

But as I sit in detention and watch McPhee closely, it's clear he survived with no damage whatsoever. There's only one explanation. I completely misjudged him.

He's some kind of *super* alien!

How do I defeat a super alien? I need to watch more movies or, better yet, read that DO NOT OPEN! file on his computer. That has to be packed with secrets, things like how to dissolve stubborn super aliens and stop the invasion!

I quickly come up with a plan to convince McPhee to leave me alone with his computer.

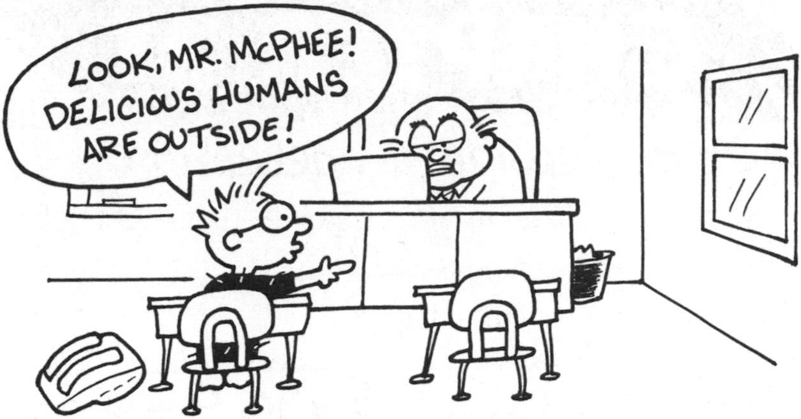
LOOK, MR. McPHEE! DELICIOUS HUMANS ARE OUTSIDE!

"Want to stay after school tomorrow, too?" McPhee says without even looking up.

Drat. He must have already eaten. Who was absent today?

I need a new plan to get him out of the room.

I rip off a piece of paper and scribble on it.

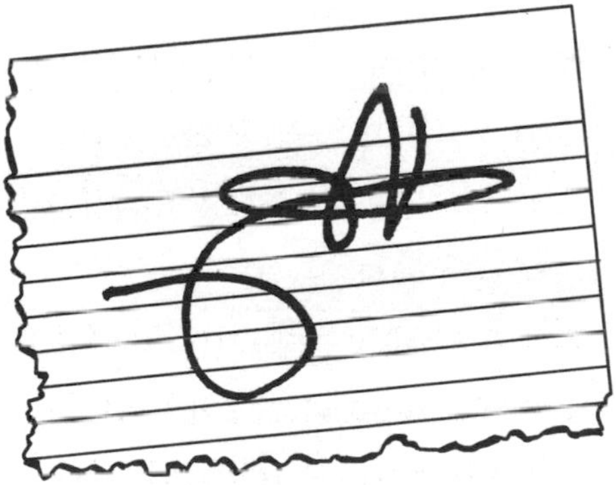

I fold it up neatly, then hold it in the air.

"Mr. McPhee. Can you take this note to Ms. Ortiz?"

I like Ms. Ortiz. She's the office lady and is always nice to me. And she's not a rube.

Ms. Ortiz was on my side when Principal Cricklewood wanted to suspend me because of a comic strip I submitted to the school newspaper. It was called *Dave 'n' Venus*. It was about two famous art sculptures that could talk to each other. Cricklewood flipped out!

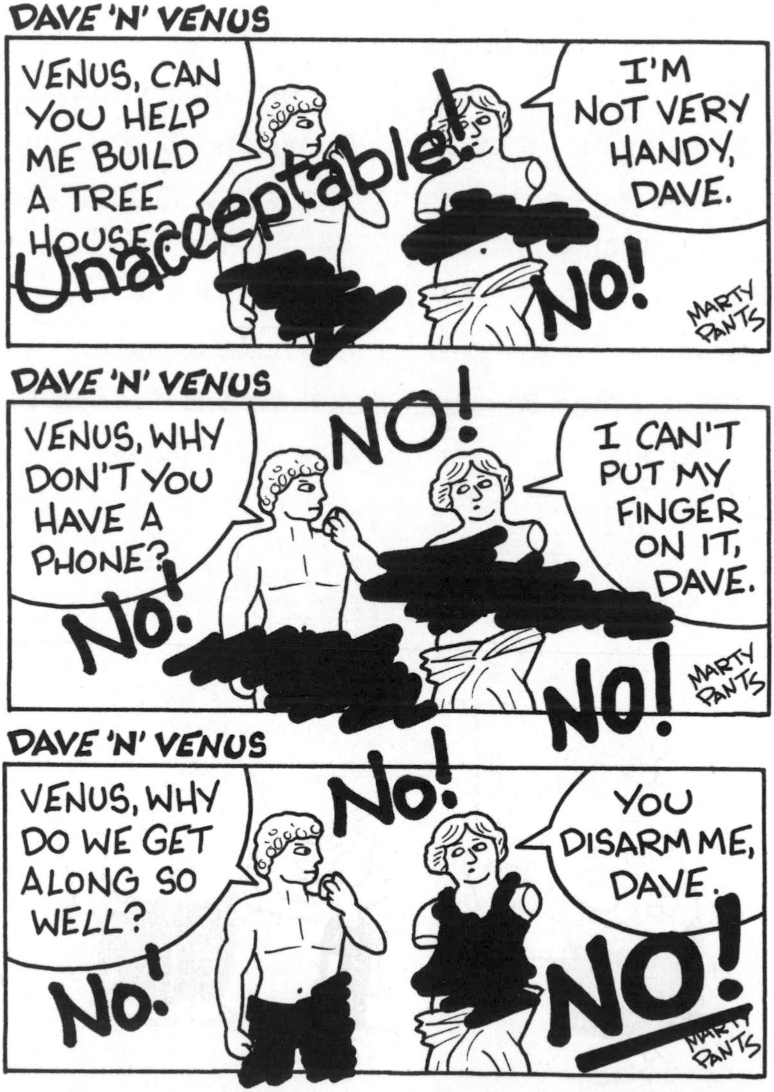
DAVE 'N' VENUS
VENUS, CAN YOU HELP ME BUILD A TREE HOUSE?
I'M NOT VERY HANDY, DAVE.
Unacceptable!
NO!
MARTY PANTS
DAVE 'N' VENUS
VENUS, WHY DON'T YOU HAVE A PHONE?
I CAN'T PUT MY FINGER ON IT, DAVE.
NO!
NO!
NO!
MARTY PANTS
DAVE 'N' VENUS
VENUS, WHY DO WE GET ALONG SO WELL?
YOU DISARM ME, DAVE.
NO!
NO!
NO!
MARTY PANTS

The problem is those famous works of art don't exactly wear clothes. I learned it's okay to show those sculptures in museums and books and stores and on posters and postcards and calendars and refrigerator magnets and pot holders and puzzles, but if I try to draw them, suddenly I'm a troublemaker. I would have been suspended, but Ms. Ortiz stood up for me.

Anyway, if I can trick McPhee into bringing this scribble to Ms. Ortiz, I'll be alone with his computer!

"You can give her the note yourself," McPhee answers. "I'll walk you down."

This alien is cleverer than I thought. We walk to the office and there's Ms. Ortiz getting ready to leave.

She smiles and says, "Hi, Marty! To what do I owe this visit?" All I can do is hand her the piece of paper.

"For you, Ms. Ortiz."

UM... THANK YOU, MARTY...

McPhee walks me to the front door. It's almost as if he doesn't trust me to roam the school unaccompanied.

"I got another call from Mr. McPhee," my mom says at dinner. "What on *earth* is going on with you at school?"

She doesn't understand the responsibility of battling an alien.

"Why are you acting up? There are going to be consequences, young man. From now on . . ."

I have no choice but to launch my secret weapon.

"Mom," I interrupt. "I saw Errikka holding hands with Salvador Ack, a high school delinquent with a mustache."

Works like a charm. The attention is off me, and I'm free to focus on my strategies for saving the planet. And attacking these pork chops.

CHAPTER 22

electric sis

Erikahh is not speaking to me. She's forbidden to see Salvador Ack, or, as I call him, Peach Fuzz. Or as my parents call him,

THAT HOODLUM!

Ericcccca was always the perfect one: perfect grades, perfect at sports, perfect hair, perfect manners.

No one could be that perfect, so I put two and two together and figured out she was a robot.

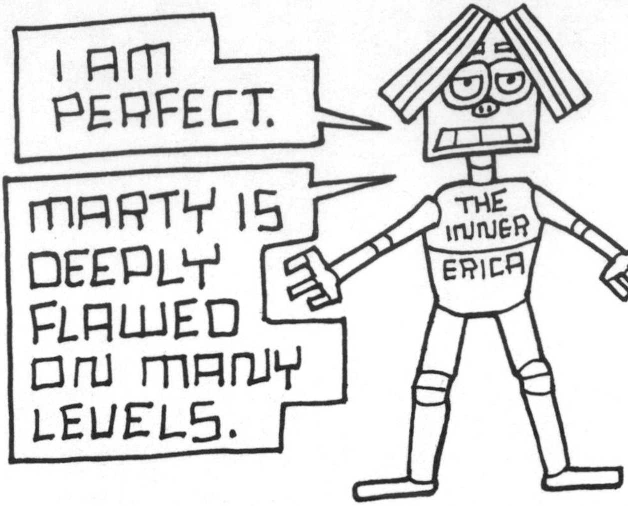
I AM PERFECT.
MARTY IS DEEPLY FLAWED ON MANY LEVELS.
THE INNER ERICA

Then one day I was at one of her soccer games with my dad, and Erikcka was being a perfect player and had already scored two perfect goals. She was ready to score again when someone on the other team "accidentally" tripped her, and she broke her arm.

It was quite the scene. I saw bone. It was then that I realized my sister was no longer a robot. She had somehow evolved into a real human being. I didn't know that was even possible.

I had to give credit where credit was due.

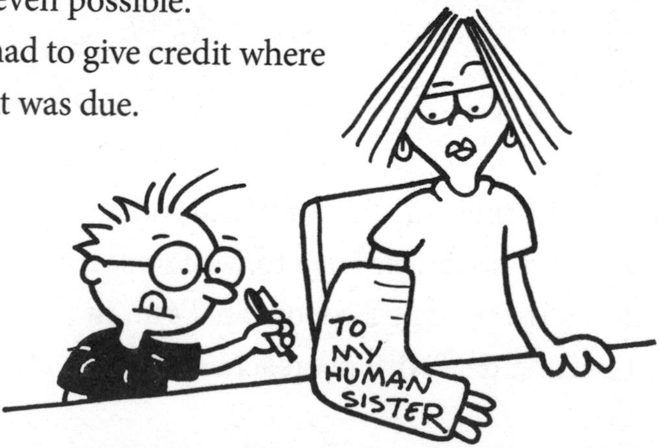
TO MY HUMAN SISTER

These days it's pretty clear she's not perfect. Sure, she gets an A+ on almost everything, but sometimes she messes up.

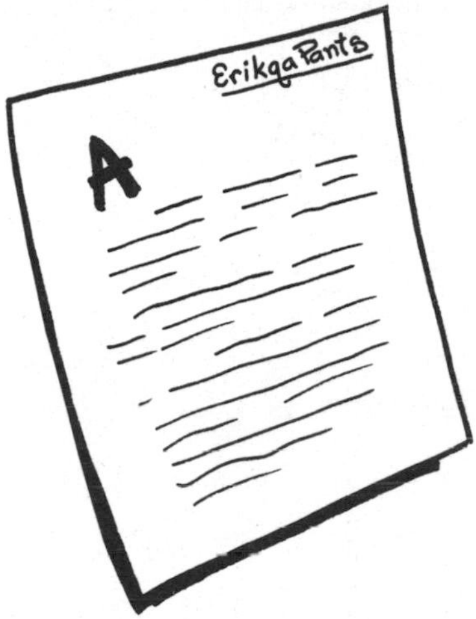
Erikqa Pants
A

She also slurps when she eats soup.

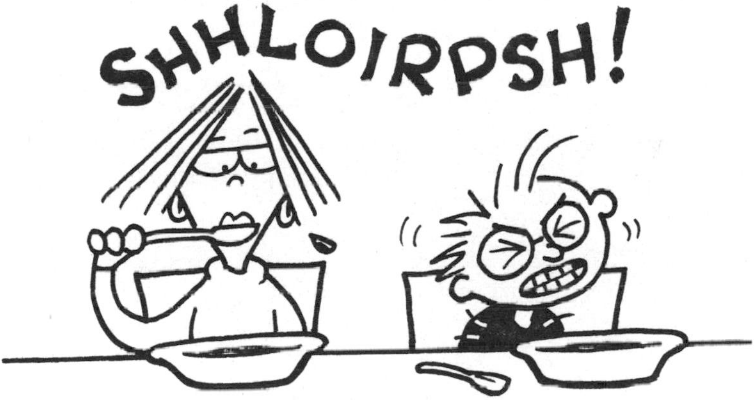
SHHLOIRPSH!

And now she fraternizes with hoodlums!

Thankfully, I no longer have to waste my time worrying about my sister being a robot. That's all in the past.

Now I need to deal with my teacher being an alien!

CHAPTER 23

questionable

McPhee sure assigns a lot of homework. Why? Because he's trying to keep everyone busy so they don't notice his evilness!

The latest assignment is to interview someone from the community who has a career that interests us. I think about interviewing the creator of AnemoneBob TrapezoidShorts so I can tell him Simon keeps stealing his character. Unfortunately, he's not from our community, and asking him to move here is apparently not feasible.

WE'RE NOT HAVING A GROWN MAN MOVE INTO THE BASEMENT!

I suppose I could interview the chief of police to find out if they're prepared for an alien invasion.

Or better yet, I could interview McPhee and trick him into confessing his evil plan!

I know the secret to making questionnaires. Start out by asking easy questions, then gradually slip in the important personal questions.

When the bell rings, I go to McPhee's desk and explain I want to interview him for the assignment. I place this questionnaire on his desk.

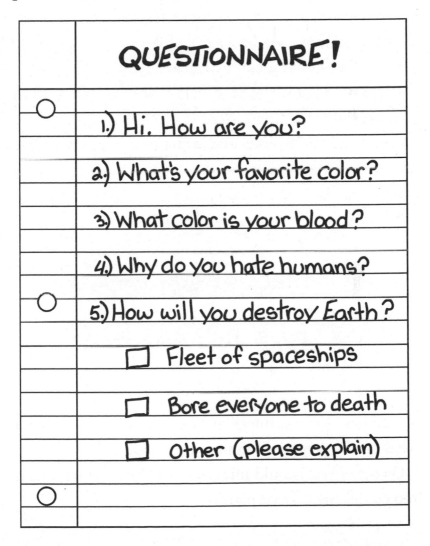

QUESTIONNAIRE!

1.) Hi. How are you?

2.) What's your favorite color?

3.) What color is your blood?

4.) Why do you hate humans?

5.) How will you destroy Earth?

☐ Fleet of spaceships

☐ Bore everyone to death

☐ Other (please explain)

Without even looking at it, McPhee says, "I'm flattered, but you should interview someone else."

What a disaster! The last thing I wanted to do was flatter him!

"Well," I say, "I'll just leave this questionnaire here in case you change your mind."

"And Marty," he says, pointing his pen at me, "don't turn this into an art project. Get your head out of the clouds."

He doesn't want my head in the clouds. Is that where his spaceship is hiding?

McPhee drops his pen and it bounces off the questionnaire.

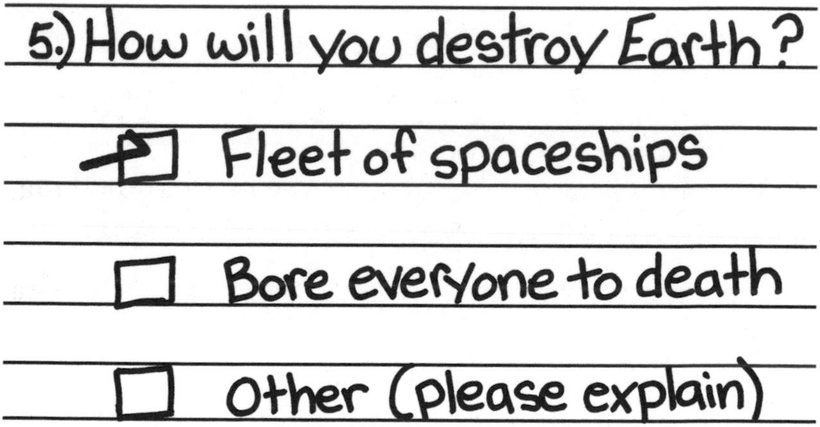
5.) How will you destroy Earth?
Fleet of spaceships
Bore everyone to death
Other (please explain)

He picks up his pen and I grab the evidence!

CHAPTER 24

clothes minded

"You tricked McPhee into confessing?"

"Look at it," I say. "That's his check mark in the box."

I'm at Parker's house lying on the couch and she's in the chair examining the evidence. Her dad will be home any minute so I'm risking my life. I could be transformed into a human ottoman at any moment. Or a tasteful end table.

"I see," Parker says. "So, our teacher . . ."

". . . is going to summon a fleet of spaceships to annihilate Earth." I finish her sentence.

"Is this anything like the time you told me your sister was a robot?"

"This is much bigger."

"Of course."

"McPhee is a danger. It's time for me to say something, right?"

"I've advised you against that," Parker says. "Any idea why?"

"I'm confused."

"Exactly!"

"But I'll figure it out."

"I'm sure you will. That'll be one thousand dollars," Parker says with a wink. "My rates went up."

As I'm about to write out an IOU, I hear the doorknob turning. It's Parker's dad! Really this time! And there's no time to escape!

Parker thinks fast.

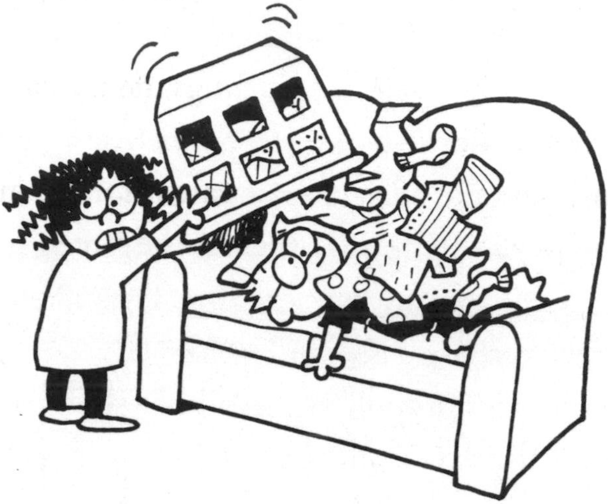

"Hi, Dad!" I hear a muffled voice say. "Just folding some laundry."

"Since when do you fold laundry?"

"Since right now!"

"It's thoughtful of you, Parker, but that's my dirty laundry."

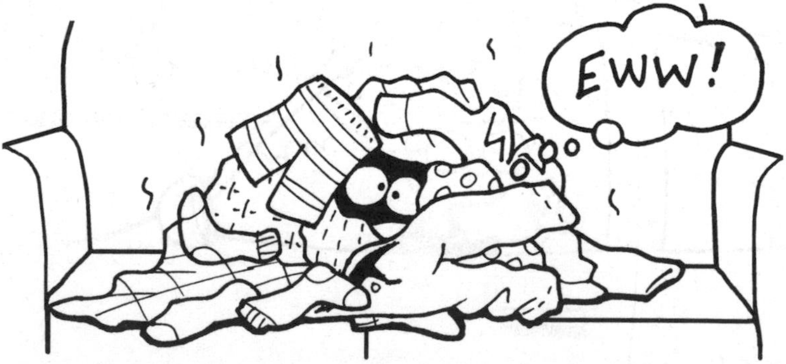
EWW!

I hear more muffled words but can't understand what's being said. It sounds like Parker's dad is going to turn me into a laundry hamper!

It gets quiet. I feel a tug on my arm, and I'm yanked out of the pile.

Parker whispers, "Go!" as she flings me forward, and I find myself outside.

Once my surge of adrenaline wears off, I get my bearings and notice a familiar face across the street.

I smile and wave. Things are going smoothly until I catch my reflection in a car window.

CHAPTER 25

drawing conclusions

I take the boxers off my head and head home.

Parker doesn't want me to say anything about McPhee being an alien. She doesn't want me to say anything about the planet being in peril.

I don't get it! Why not? What's she trying to tell me?

Then it hits me. Jerome knocked a marker off the bureau, and it bounced off my forehead.

That's the answer! Parker doesn't want me to *say* anything about my teacher being an alien. She doesn't want me to *say* the planet is in danger . . . she wants me to *show* people instead!

I'm an artist, after all, and artists are supposed to communicate through art. That's genius!

Now that I finally understand, I pick up the marker and grab my list of goals. There's no room on the front, so I turn the paper over and write on the back.

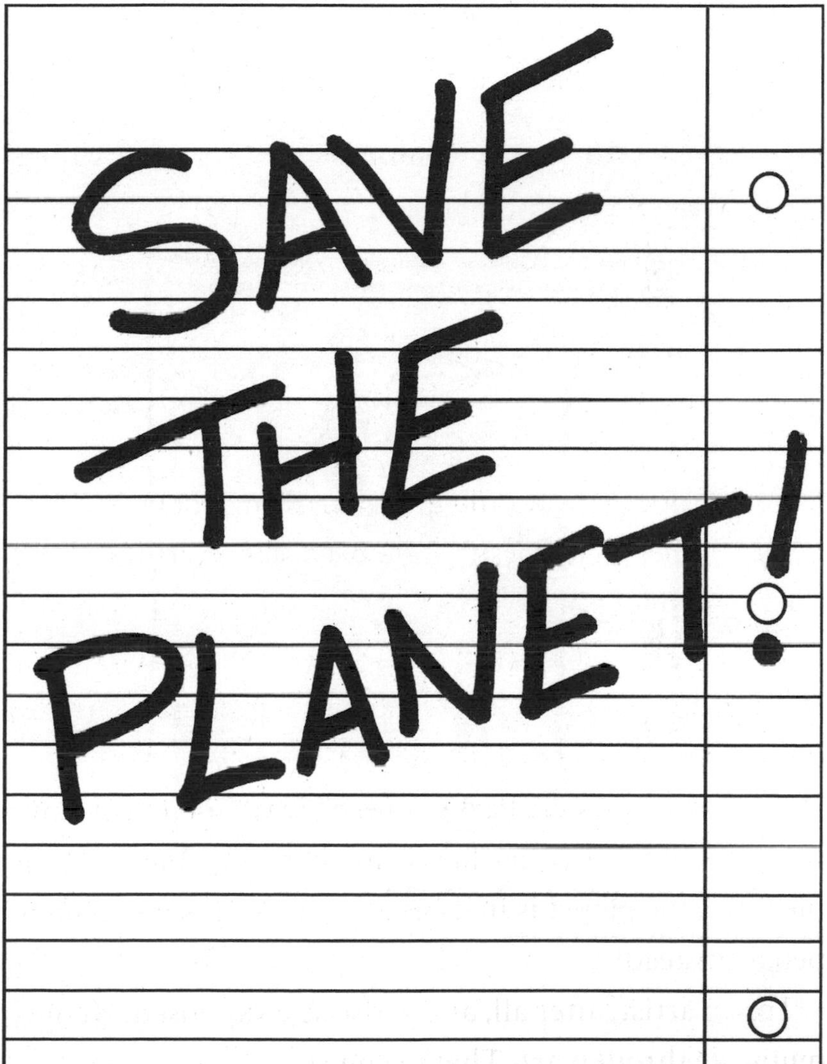
SAVE
THE
PLANET!

CHAPTER 26

rude badge of courage

Art is a powerful way to communicate. An artist named Andy Warhol painted this.

Campbell's
CONDENSED
TOMATO
SOUP

He was communicating how much he likes soup. I'm an artist, too, and now it's my turn to communicate something. Something even more important than soup!

"Marty, people have been smiling at me all day. Do you know why?"

"No, Mr. McPhee. I can't think of a single reason to smile at you."

McPhee points to his ID badge. "Did you do this?"

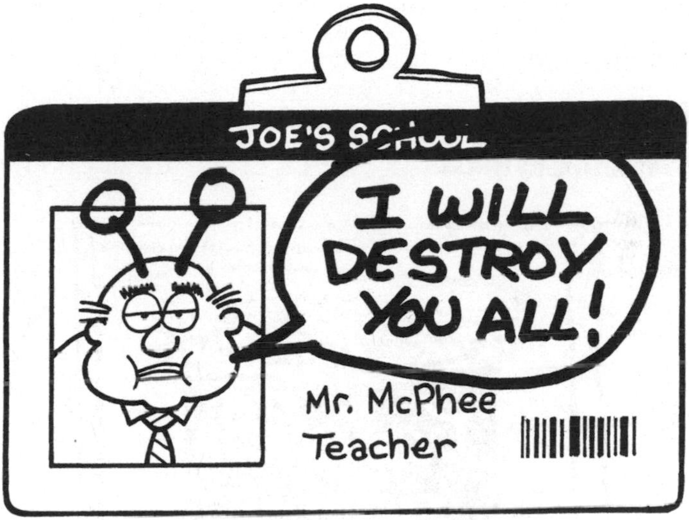
JOE'S SCHOOL
I WILL DESTROY YOU ALL!
Mr. McPhee
Teacher

I squirm in my chair. "I don't recall. You can't prove anything. I plead the fifth."

The alien takes a long look at me. I hope I come across as sincere. He goes back to his desk and tries to clean off the permanent ink. I can tell it's not working.

"Did you do that?" Roongrat leans in to ask me.

"I'm not at liberty to say," I respond.

The day progresses, and more and more people see my message on McPhee's ID badge. Somehow, word spreads among the kids that I'm the artist responsible.

The alien is finally being exposed! And I'll get the credit. All I have to do is sit back and wait for a mob of concerned citizens to overpower McPhee and hand him to the authorities.

But at the end of the day, no one accuses McPhee of being an alien. No angry militia drags him off kicking and screaming.

My art doesn't motivate anyone to take action.

In fact, it only seems to empower the alien, and he says something truly horrifying.

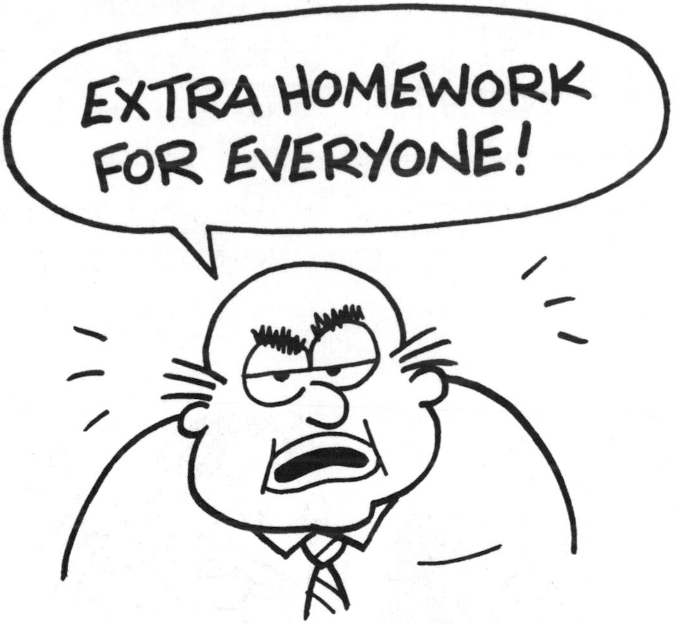
EXTRA HOMEWORK FOR EVERYONE!

Gurk! He turned the class against me!

use your noodle

I get my American chop suey and scan the cafeteria for Roongrat and Parker. They must be hiding because they don't want to be seen with me after the extra-homework debacle.

Simon is sitting with a bunch of girls, drawing AnemoneBob on their notebooks. They give me dirty looks.

I see Analie sitting alone in the corner. There's an empty chair across from her. I'm going to do it. I'm going to sit with her. I take a deep breath.

"Marty! We're over here!" Parker waves to me while Roongrat stuffs his face. I stop short and spill my lunch all over myself.

Analie continues to stare at me, and I hear Simon laugh. I go sit next to Parker.

I pick the food off of my shirt and arrange the noodles to look like a deranged octopus on my plate.

Parker hands me a napkin and says it's a good thing my shirt has a layer of cat fur to protect it from stains.

"Shanks for the eshtra homework!" Roongrat says with his mouth full. "Everyonesh angry at choo."

"I thought the whole thing was a riot!" says Parker.

No one seems to realize I'm trying to save them.

Parker asks if I'm entering the mural contest.

"What mural contest?"

"It was on the announcements this morning," Parker explains.

"An dere are flyersh all over ga shkool," Roongrat says through his food. "There'sh even one hangin up in fwont uv your fashe."

So there is. I'm a noticer. How did I not notice? I bet McPhee brainwashed me not to notice.

I rip it off the wall.

MURAL CONTEST

STUDENT ARTISTS!

WOULD YOU LIKE TO SEE YOUR ART ON THE WALL IN THE MAIN HALL OF THE SCHOOL?

Submit your drawing to the front office by the end of the month.

There will be a school-wide vote!

The mural will be the first thing everyone sees when they enter the school.

That's the perfect place to expose McPhee! This is my chance!

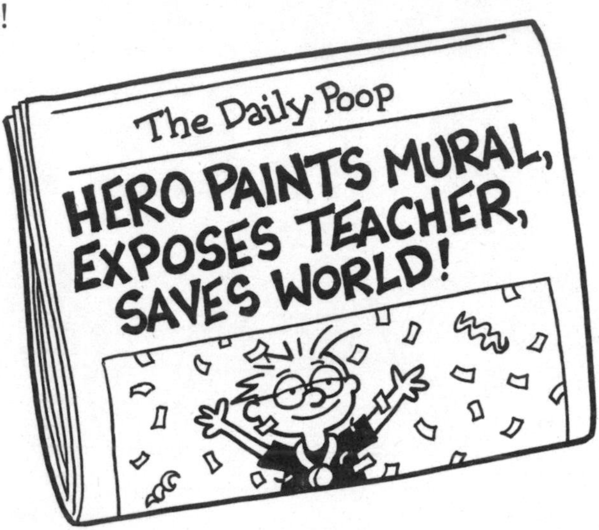
The Daily Poop
HERO PAINTS MURAL, EXPOSES TEACHER, SAVES WORLD!

"You should enter!" Parker says.

"Shimon will win," Roongrat says.

Not if he's eaten by a deranged octopus, I think to myself.

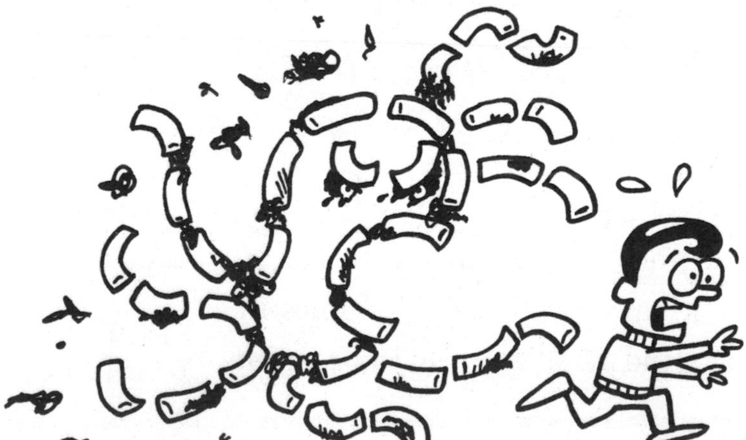

Suddenly, my octopus explodes, and something hits my glasses. Before I can size up the situation, a full-fledged food fight breaks out!

This is the scene when it's over.

Either everyone blames me for the extra homework or they think I should be eating more.

And get this, I'm sent home for causing trouble! My dad picks me up.

"What's all this about defacing McPhee's badge and causing a disturbance in the cafeteria?"

"It's complicated," I explain. "I'm the victim here."

I spend the rest of the day confined to my room, but I'm fine with that. I'll use the time to work on my mural.

Jerome helps.

PAPER WARMER

Once I determine the paper is warm enough, I grab some Paper Warmer Remover.

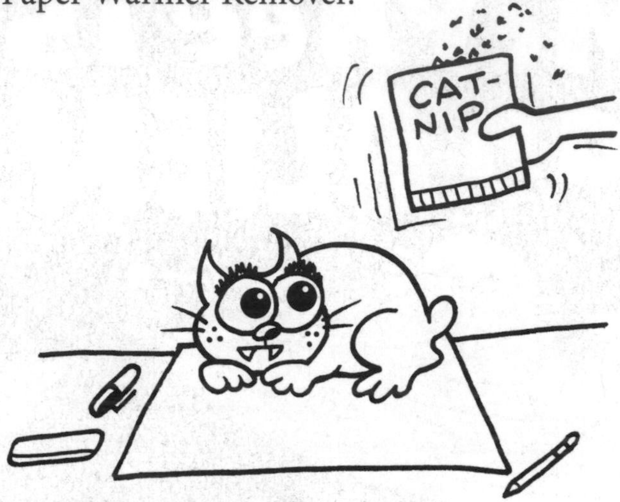
CAT-
NIP

Now it's time to get down to business.

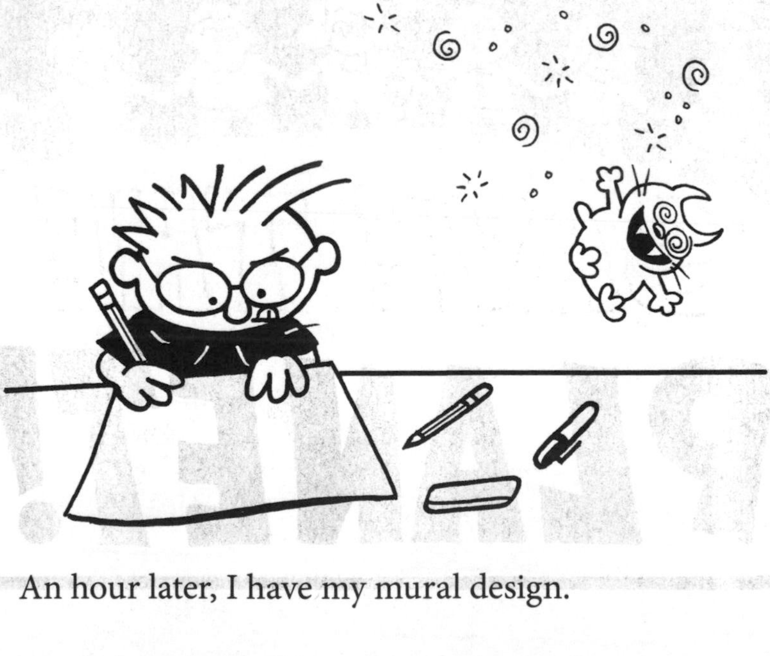

An hour later, I have my mural design.

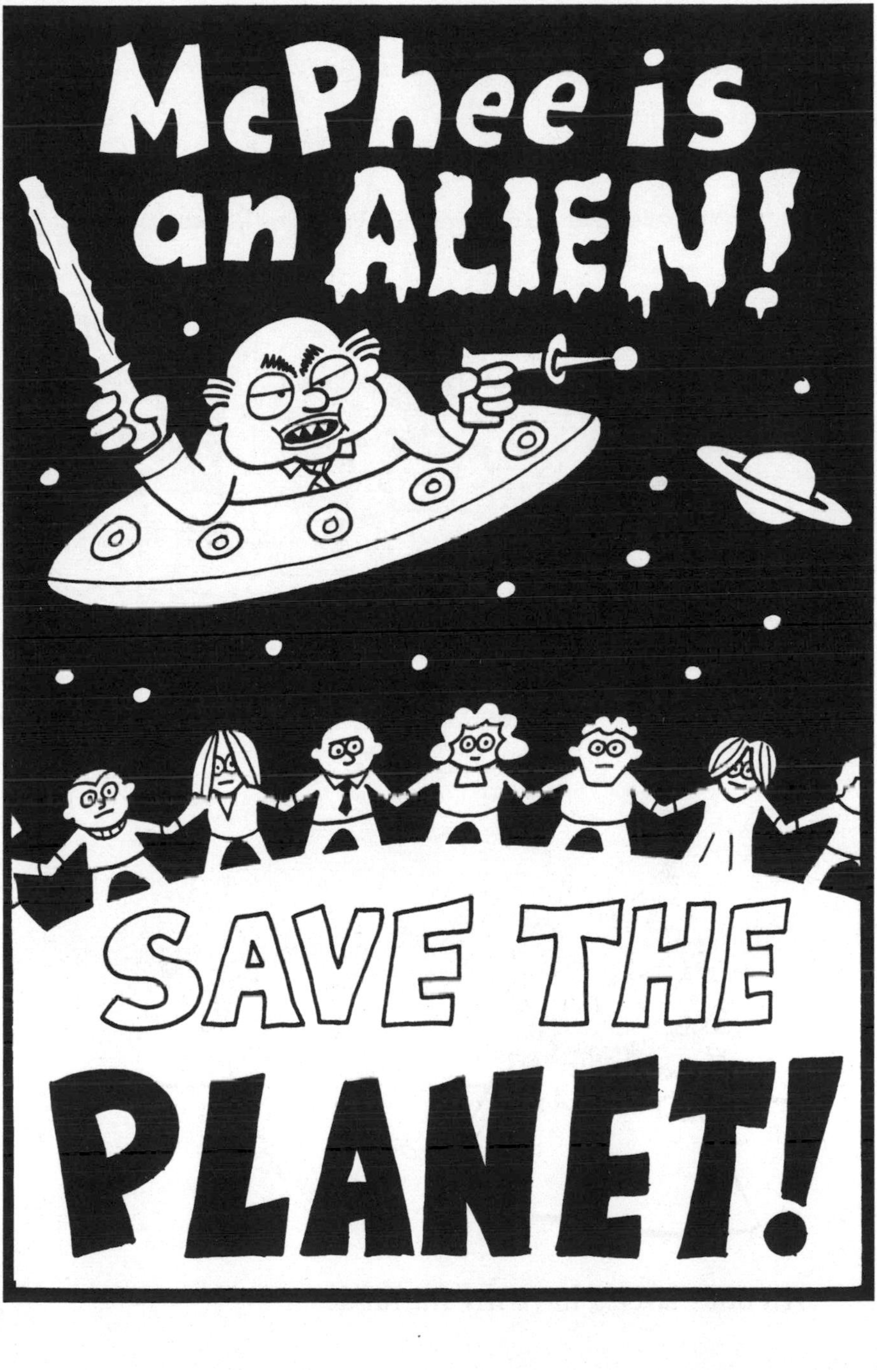
McPhee is an ALIEN!
SAVE THE PLANET!

It's the perfect message.

The problem is McPhee will never allow this to be painted on the school wall. I have to be clever. I have to be smarter than my enemy.

And considering who my enemy is, that should be easy.

CHAPTER 28

alien infiltration

"Who are you going to interview for the assignment?" Roongrat asks me as he drops a pile of video games on my living room floor.

"I don't know yet."

The truth is, I haven't given it much thought. I've been preoccupied with a little thing called:

TRYING TO SAVE THE WORLD

"I'm going to interview a banker," continues Roongrat. "Bankers get to keep fifty percent of everyone's money. It's a fact."

Parker announces she's going to interview a psychologist. No surprise there.

Simon is here, too. Roongrat invited him over to my house. Probably just to annoy me. Simon says he's going to interview his uncle, the cartoonist. I'm envious, but refuse to show it.

"That's pedantic!" says Roongrat, who has no idea what that even means. Neither do I, but that's not the point.

It soon becomes clear why Roongrat invited Simon.

"Marty! You and Simon should play *Art Heist*! Let's see who the awesomer artist is!"

"I should play a low level since I've never played before," Simon says. "You're probably an expert, Marty."

"As a matter of fact, I am an expert," I admit. "Don't worry, I'll go easy on you. You play level one, I'll play level five."

Maybe I was too confident because Simon turns out to be okay at this game. Probably because he's good at copying. In fact, he's winning. I can't let him beat me! I can't! I need a way to break his concentration.

"My sister's home," I say.

"Erica?"

"Yup, she's right upstairs."

Simon smiles his stupid smile. He has a crush on Errrikaa. She's probably the only reason he's here.

Simon has absolutely no shot with her because she doesn't go for younger guys, plus she's not a fan of AnemoneBob.

But I can use this against him.

"She has a boyfriend," I say. "He's older and has a mustache."

Simon pouts and starts making mistakes.

"She's deeply in love, and I think they're engaged to be married," I add, twisting the knife.

It's working! Simon is obviously upset, and he's playing poorly. I'm winning!

My nosy sister suddenly yells down the stairs, "Stop talking about me! I don't have a boyfriend . . . thanks to YOU!"

Simon straightens up and starts doing better. And better. My plan backfired! Simon's catching up, and I'm having trouble because I've never played level five before. Roongrat is cheering Simon on, and Parker is cheering me on.

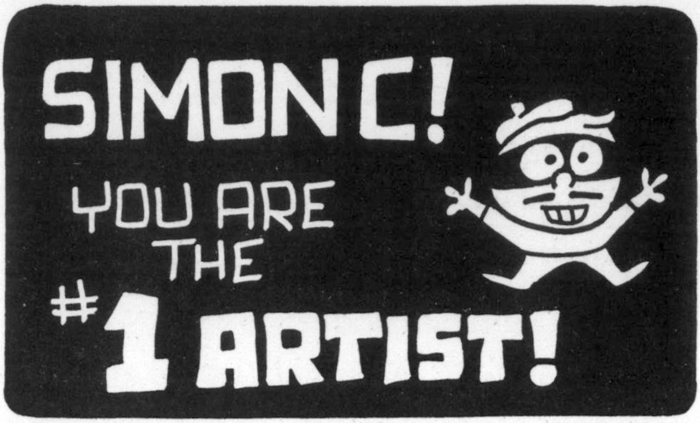
SIMON C!
YOU ARE THE
#1 ARTIST!

Roongrat high-fives Simon. Simon leans over to me and says, “I’m better than you, Marty. That’s not even my highest score.”

Arrgh! He tricked me! This isn’t the first time he’s played! How could I let that rube beat me? Why did I pick level five?!

“Don’t be mad because Simon is better than you,” Roongrat says. “It’s just a fact.”

Meanwhile, Simon does his lame victory dance.

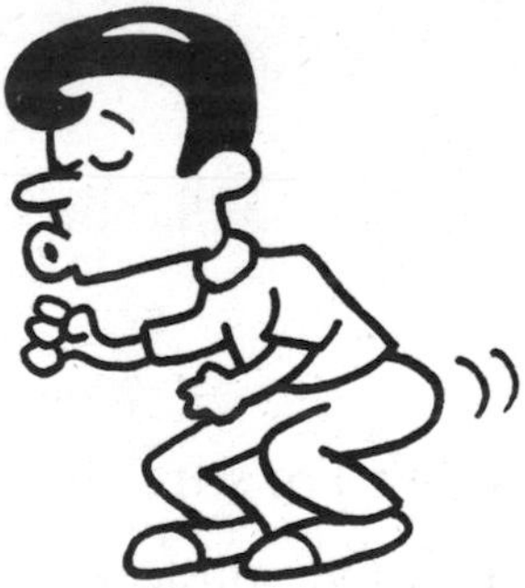

“Let’s play a different game!” Parker says. I think she’s trying to move things along because she can tell how upset I am.

"I brought the new *Alien Infiltration*!" says Roongrat.

I usually don't like playing *Alien Infiltration*, but this time it sounds like a good idea. I'll consider it research and test my skills against the impending alien attack.

All four of us play, and it doesn't start well. Everyone is doing better than I am because I'm just not focused. I'm still annoyed. But there's no way I can let Simon beat me again!

I come in dead last.

MARTYP
YOU ARE A LOSER.
YOU ALLOWED ALIENS TO DESTROY EARTH.
NICE GOING!

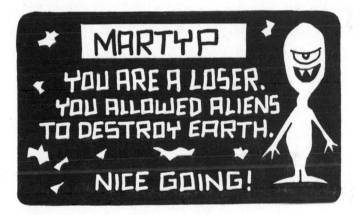

"Good thing it's not your job to protect the planet!" Simon says.

Roongrat laughs, "Yeah, because we'd all DIE!" Parker doesn't gloat even though I'm sure she's quite pleased she came in first. As for me, I've made a decision.

I tell everyone it's time to leave.

I'm calling the police.

question authority

"Petey's Pizza."

I've never called the police before, but I don't think that's how they're supposed to answer the phone. I order six pepperoni pizzas, hang up, and try again.

"Hello, this is Officer Pickels speaking."

That's more like it.

"Hello, this is Marty Pants speaking. I'd like to report an emergency."

"What's your emergency?"

"I need to interview you for a school project."

Officer Pickels says I can come in right away, so I ride my bike to the police station.

I don't have anything prepared, so I begin by asking the questions everyone wants to know.

Do you run red lights for fun?

Can you arrest someone for
annoying you?

Can I shoot your gun at a
bad guy?

His answers alternate between "No" and "You sure you want to be a police officer?"

When I tell him I actually want to be an artist, he tells me they use sketch artists to catch criminals. He asks me if I want to give it a shot.

"I'll describe someone and you try to draw that person based on my description."

"Let's do it," I say. I pull out my pencil, and he hands me a sketch pad.

Officer Pickels describes his wife, and I do my best to capture her likeness.

Officer Pickels doesn't look too happy with my sketch. I don't blame him. I wouldn't look too happy either if my wife looked like a female Snoopy.

He says, "Want to see the inside of a jail cell?"

Nice. The VIP treatment.

He brings me over to a cell and motions me to go inside. When I do, I hear the door clang shut behind me.

Am I under arrest for annoying him? "Give me another chance!" I say. "I'll draw your wife less Snoopyish!"

It's no use. He's gone.

Is he off to find more criminals to lock in here? I need to act intimidating, just in case! I take out my pencil and write on the wall.

DON'T MESS
WITH MARTY.

Good. That's intimidating. Now I need to practice my tough-guy voice.

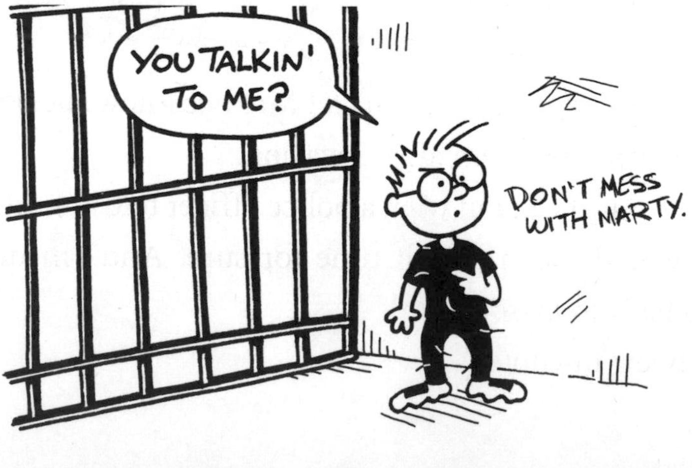
YOU TALKIN' TO ME?
DON'T MESS WITH MARTY.

I hear Officer Pickels unlock the door.

"Scary, isn't it?" he says. "You don't want to end up in there, do you?"

"I'm never going back to prison," I say in my tough-guy voice.

He walks me outside.

Finally, I ask THE question. The only question that matters. The real reason I am here.

"Officer Pickels," I say. "Are you prepared for an alien invasion?"

Before answering, he briefly looks up into the sky. I'm sure he was scanning for spaceships, but it almost looked like he was rolling his eyes at me.

"We are totally unprepared for an alien invasion," he admits.

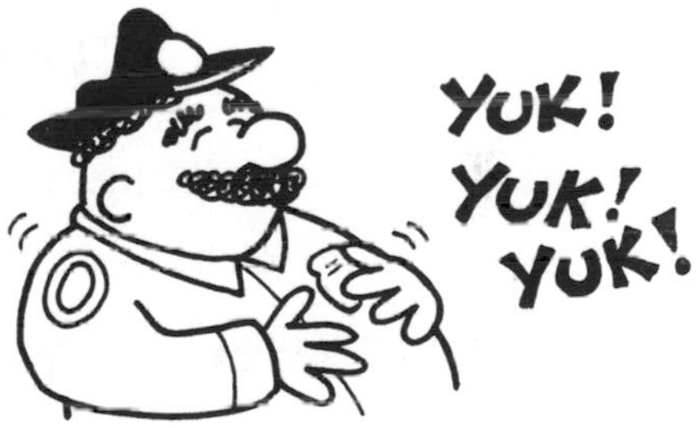
YUK!
YUK!
YUK!

I was afraid of that. I can tell Officer Pickels is afraid, too, because he shakes his head and lets out a nervous laugh.

Now I'm in a pickle. I have to write my report, but I can't let McPhee know the police are unprepared for an alien invasion.

But I can't lie about what a police officer told me, either. That would mean prison time for sure. And I'm never going back to prison.

I review my notes.

> Question: Are you prepared
> for an alien invasion?
>
> Officer Pickels: We are totally
> unprepared for an alien invasion.

There's only one way to handle this.

> Question: Are you prepared
> for an alien invasion?
>
> Officer Pickels: We are totally
> ~~un~~prepared for an alien invasion.

That's called editing, and I'm pretty sure it's legal. Once McPhee reads that, he'll think twice before attacking.

I thank Officer Pickels and turn to get my bike, but it's not there! Did the aliens take it?

Officer Pickels asks me if I locked it.

I didn't. I thought it would be safe in front of the police station.

"Describe it to me," he says.

"It's blue and, I don't know. It looks like a bike."

"How about you draw it for me?"

"Can I get a ride home in a police cruiser?" I ask.

"Maybe another time, Marty. Want me to call your parents?"

I can just imagine my parents answering that phone call.

THIS IS THE POLICE. WE'RE CALLING ABOUT YOUR SON, MARTY...

"I'll walk," I say.

It's a long way, but I learned how to walk when I was just one year old, and I'm pretty good at it now.

The more I think about it, the more I'm convinced the aliens stole my bike to get spare parts for their spaceship. The attack must be getting closer.

I'm about halfway home when something unexpected happens.

That was definitely on purpose! I'm just grateful Peach Fuzz kept going and didn't come back to pummel me. Maybe he considers us even now, but I doubt it.

Weird coincidence that he rides a bike that looks exactly like mine, though.

When I finally get home, I'm tired, muddy, and hungry.

Good thing there are six delicious Petey's pepperoni pizzas waiting.

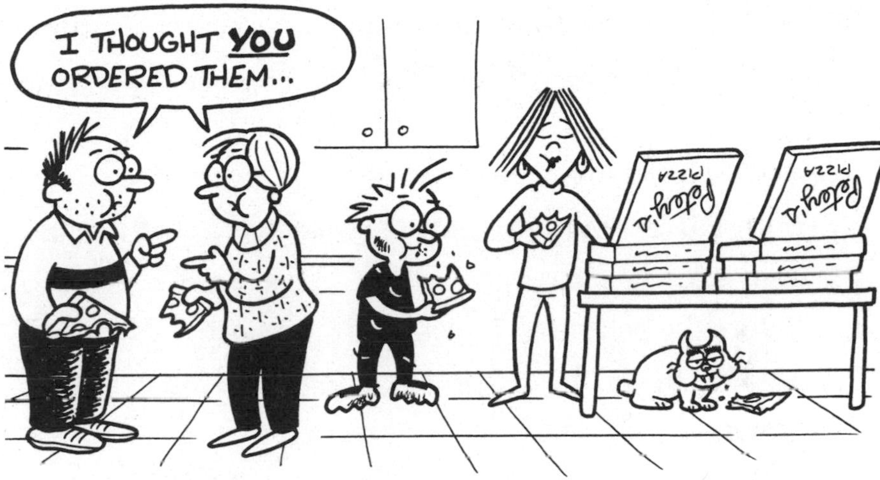
I THOUGHT **YOU** ORDERED THEM...
Petey's PIZZA
Petey's PIZZA

CHAPTER 30

on the edge

Today we hand in our reports.

Both Parker and Roongrat seem shocked that I interviewed a cop.

Before the bell rings, I peek at Simon's paper. He interviewed his uncle, the cartoonist. I do a good job of hiding my interest.

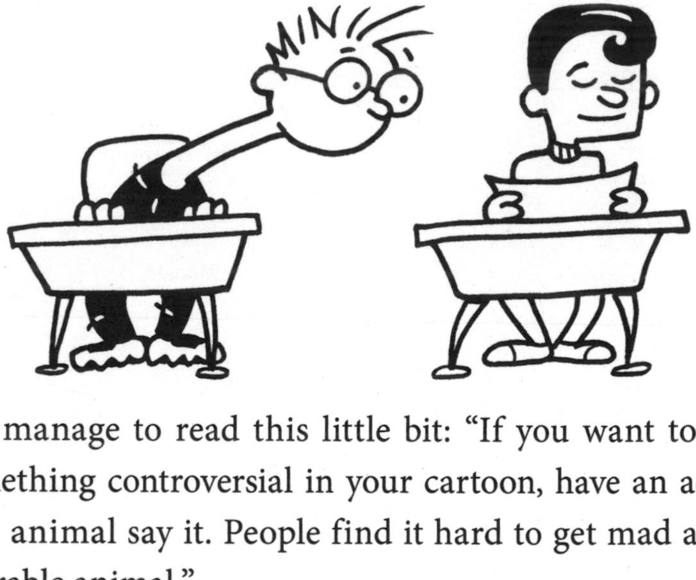
MIN

I manage to read this little bit: "If you want to say something controversial in your cartoon, have an adorable animal say it. People find it hard to get mad at an adorable animal."

That's what I call useful advice! I decide to add one finishing touch to my report.

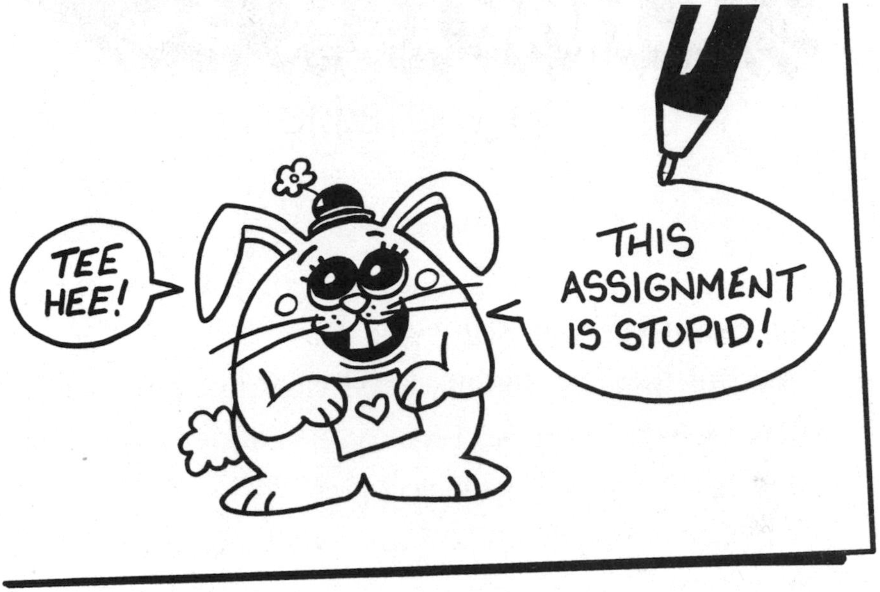
TEE HEE!
THIS ASSIGNMENT IS STUPID!

CHAPTER 31

mural dilemma

Can you believe I have detention again? You'd think an alien would have better things to do.

I use my time in captivity to develop my mural idea. I *need* to win this contest. I'll simultaneously beat Simon and save the planet. The perfect plan.

McPhee is busy typing on his computer, so I pull out my mural drawing to figure out a way to improve it.

Wha . . . ?

The top of my drawing is missing! Gone! It looks like it was chewed off! Who would do such a thing?

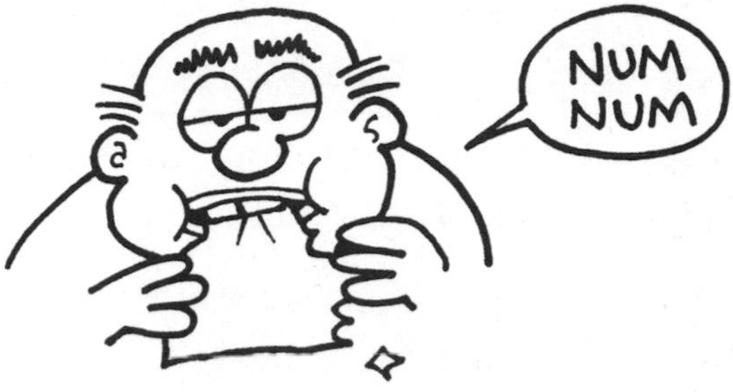
NUM
NUM

Possible, but not likely. Who else?

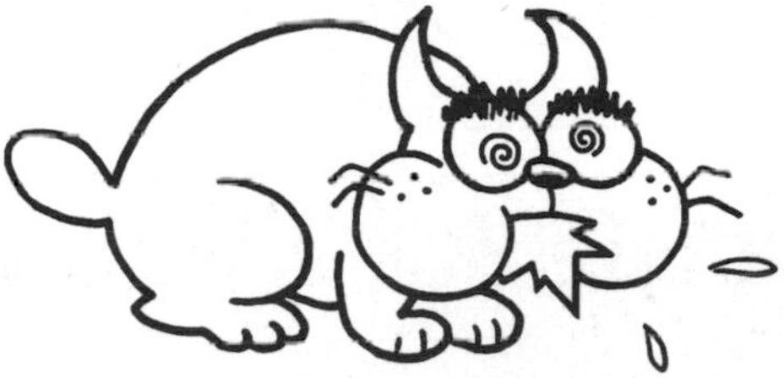

That's it! Jerome must have eaten it when he was all hopped up on catnip! Now I have to start over!

Or do I? I look at the drawing again and realize this might actually work.

I'll submit what's left, the bottom part of the drawing. It declares, "Save the Planet," and everybody is in favor of saving the planet from something, right? This will get votes! Once I win the contest, I can paint the *entire* drawing on the wall, including the top part about McPhee being an alien! McPhee will have to confess once he's been exposed by a mural! That's how art works.

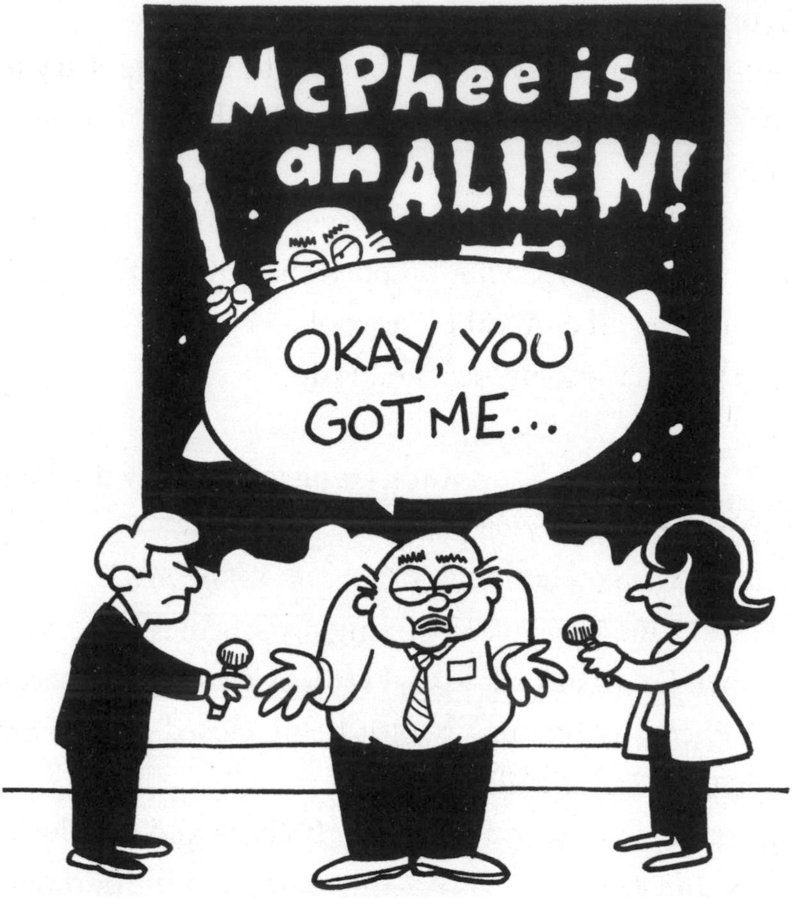
McPhee is an ALIEN!
OKAY, YOU GOT ME...

I raise my hand. Without even looking up, McPhee says, "Yes, Marty?"

"Mr. McPhee, where do I submit my drawing for the mural contest?"

"Submit it to the front office."

"Can you do it for me, please?" Why did I say "please"? I never talk to him that way. I sound suspicious.

"Bring it here," he says.

I fold up my drawing and hand it to McPhee. I try to sneak a peek at his computer screen, but he turns it away from me.

That's fine. The second he leaves the room to deliver my mural drawing, *bam*! I'll open that DO NOT OPEN! file and read all of his alien secrets!

I retreat back to my seat and wait.

And wait.

"Mr. McPhee, when are you going to bring my drawing to the office?"

"The office is closed. I'll drop it off tomorrow."

Gurk! This alien keeps ruining my schemes!

When I'm finally excused, I walk by the office to check if McPhee was fibbing about it being closed. Aliens are known to be deceitful, you know.

I peek through the office door. It's dark and sure looks closed. But as I lean on the door, it opens. In the darkness I notice a stack of papers on the desk.

MURAL CONTEST VOTING BALLOTS

Theoretically, I could grab a bunch of the ballots, fill them out with ME as the winner, and stuff the ballot box. Not the most honest way to win a contest, but the world is at stake. Regular rules do not apply.

I grab some ballots, cram them into my backpack, and take off home.

I find my mother having another phone conversation with McPhee and get sent upstairs to clean my room.

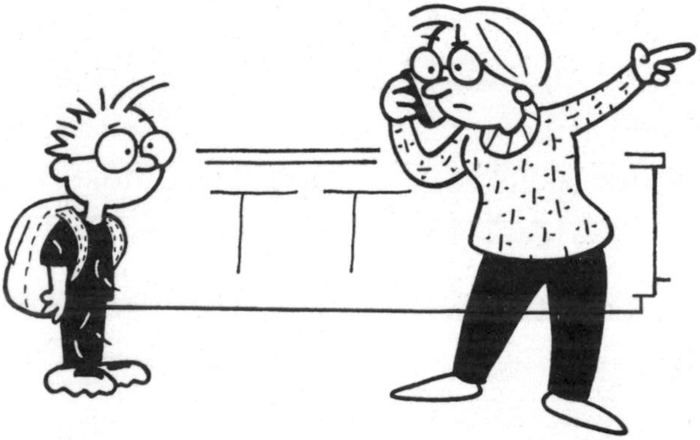

Instead, I begin filling out the ballots by voting for myself over and over. I alter my handwriting so as not to arouse suspicion.

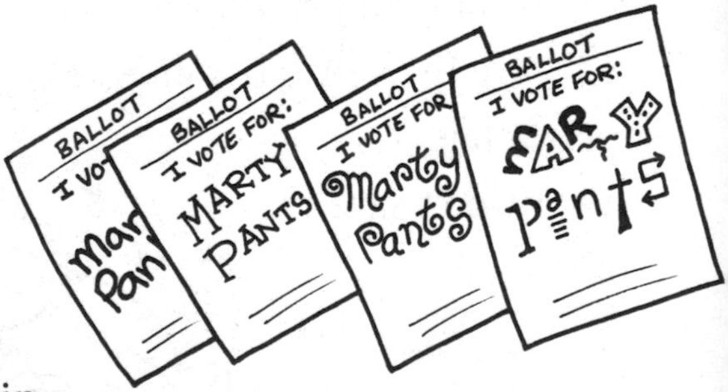
BALLOT
I VO
Mar
Pan
BALLOT
I VOTE FOR:
MARTY
PANTS
BALLOT
I VOTE FOR
Marty
Pants
BALLOT
I VOTE FOR:

By the end of the week, I have every ballot filled out. The voting will take place on Monday and I'm going to make sure I win.

By cheating. I take a beanbag moment.

When I wake up Saturday morning, I'm surprised to find myself still in my beanbag. I'm even more surprised to see it's snowing.

Wait, that's not snow!

Jerome shredded every last ballot!

Now, you'd think I'd be mad, but I'm not. I never would have forgiven myself if I had to cheat to win that mural contest. Cheating would make me like Simon, and I never want to stoop to his level.

I'll save the world the old-fashioned way. By using my superior talent.

Or I won't save the world at all.

CHAPTER 32
what's in store

I'm going to the supermarket with my dad. Why? Painting a mural will take a lot of energy, and you know where energy comes from.

CANDY
CANDY
CANDY
CANDY
CANDY
CANDY
candy

My mom is on a business trip, so the rules are different. My dad's a pushover. He goes straight to the healthy stuff, and I cut left toward the deliciousness.

Before I get far, I recognize someone in the pasta aisle.

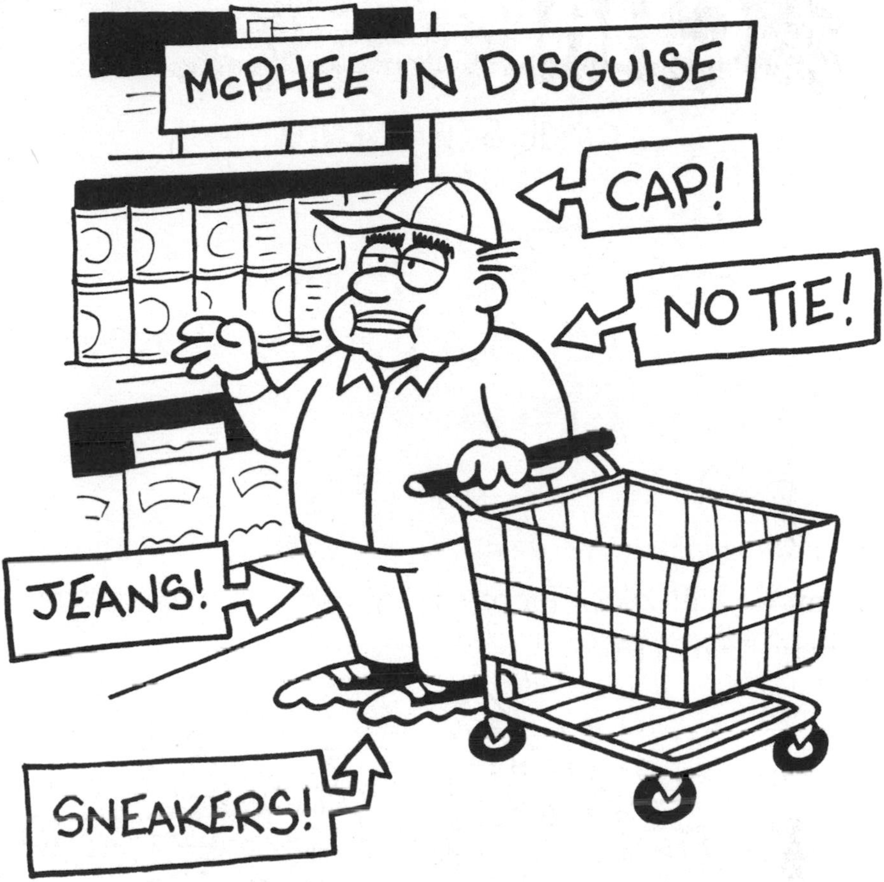
McPHEE IN DISGUISE
CAP!
NO TIE!
JEANS!
SNEAKERS!

He must be up to no good!

I slip into the next aisle before he can spot me. I grab a big box off the shelf and hold it in front of my face. It will be my camouflage as I follow him around the store.

I track him as he goes up and down the aisles putting things into his cart.

Suspicious things.

- ziti
- soup for one
- vanilla yogurt
- fish food
- frozen pizza for one
- single serving burrito dinner
- AA batteries
- vanilla ice cream

I see what he's up to. That's all fuel for his spaceship! Except the batteries. He probably eats those.

McPhee glances my way, so I lift the box to hide my face. I don't think he saw me, but that was too close for comfort.

I slowly back out of the aisle and bump into someone.

My heart jumps! Now's my chance to talk to Analie. All I need is something to say. Maybe I could say, "Oops, sorry." Yeah, that would work.

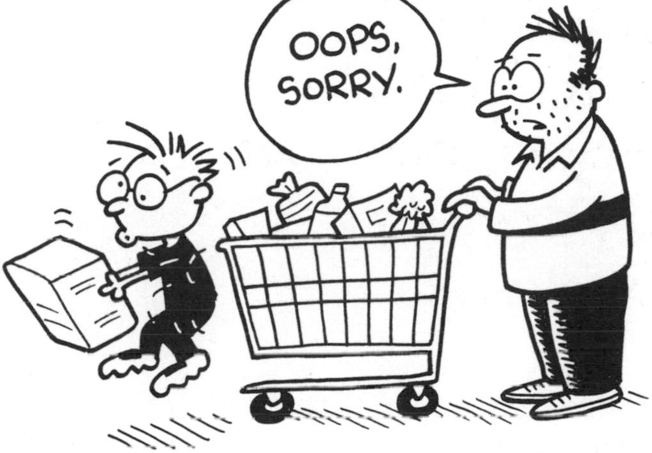
OOPS, SORRY.

"Time to check out," my dad says. "You ready?"

I turn back to Analie, but she's already gone. That girl's like lightning.

"I'm ready," I say.

"Marty," my dad asks, "what's that you got there?"

"Oh, this?"

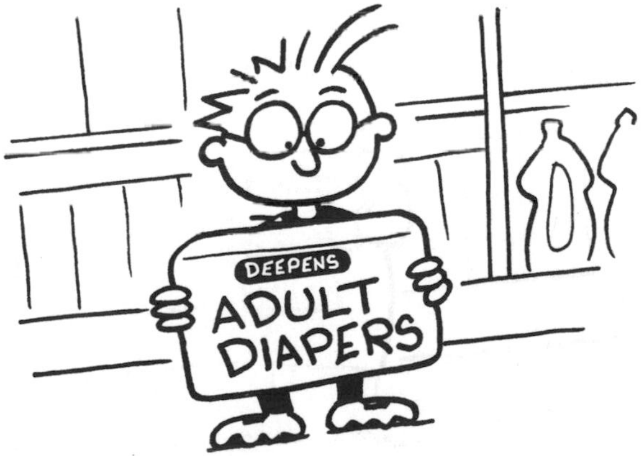
DEEPENS
ADULT DIAPERS

I should have paid closer attention to what I was using for camouflage.

"Um, I need these," I say. "For an art project," I add, thinking fast.

CHAPTER 33

don't try this at home

"Dad, can we take the long way home?"

"Why?"

"I just like driving around with you."

The real reason is McPhee's car is right in front of us as we pull out of the parking lot. I want to tail him to his evil lair and catch him fueling his spaceship!

"Turn right here," I tell my dad. "Left here."

The radio is playing classic hits. My dad starts talking about music. Must . . . fight . . . urge . . . to . . . sleep . . .

I concentrate on McPhee's license plate.

Hmmm . . . that's not a word, but it's also not random. It must mean something.

This Evil Alien Conquers Humans Regularly

It fits.

"OK, that's enough," my dad says. "Time to head home. The ice cream is melting."

It's hard to argue with logic like that. I need a good counterpoint.

"But I don't like ice cream!" Drat. I'm giving myself away.

"What's all this about, Marty?"

"Just a little farther, Dad!"

"I'm turning back, Marty. We can drive around another time."

"But I don't want to drive around with you another time!"

My dad starts to turn left as McPhee turns right.

The world is depending on me. I make a strategic move.

"Watch out, Dad! There's a spider!" I grab the steering wheel and tug it to the right. We turn just like I planned. The part I didn't plan on was crashing into McPhee's car as he turned into his driveway.

CHAPTER 34

crash test dummy

It takes a lot to make my dad mad. This counts as a lot.

"MARTY! What did you DO?!" He looks at me with bulging, angry eyes. I feel bad. It wasn't supposed to go down like this.

McPhee gets out of his car. My dad looks at him, then back at me. His eyes slowly change from mad to sad. I feel a hundred times worse.

My dad gets out and joins McPhee in examining the damage. They talk and McPhee peers through the windshield. I start to sink down, but I know it's too late.

I scan the area, but see no signs of a spaceship. He must keep it someplace else. Smart.

My dad gets back in the car and tells me there was only a scratch and McPhee said not to worry about it. The rest of the ride home is quiet.

I help bring in the groceries without being asked, and I even put things away, which I never do. I'm not used to this amount of quietness from my dad.

I can tell Erricah senses the tension because she starts talking in a whisper.

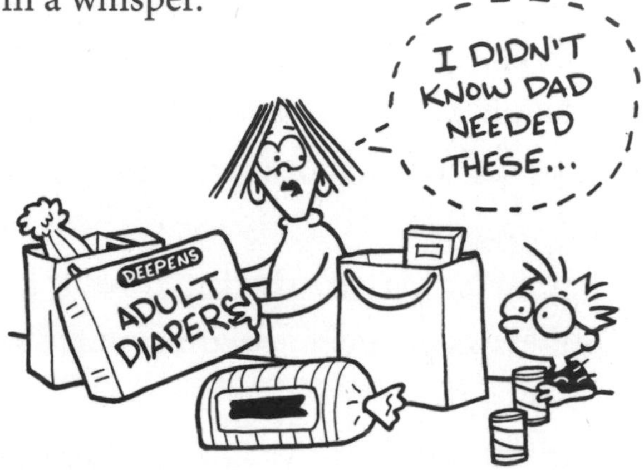
I DIDN'T KNOW DAD NEEDED THESE...
DEEPENS
ADULT DIAPERS

We have a quiet dinner but my dad doesn't eat much. For dessert, Erricaa and I have the ice cream.

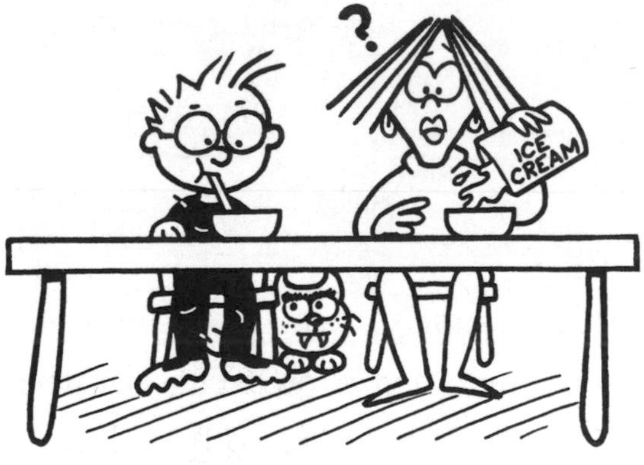
?
ICE CREAM

Erickahh goes out to meet a friend, and now it's just my dad and me. I head to my room. My dad soon follows and sits next to me on the bed.

"Marty, I didn't tell Mr. McPhee you grabbed the wheel. I took the rap. If he knew you did that on purpose, you could get kicked out of school. This is serious."

Of course it's serious. He's an evil alien!

"Your mother is on a business trip, and every time she goes away, she's afraid things are going to fall apart. Remember when Erica broke her arm? Your mother was on a business trip. You're not helping things."

He pauses. "I need to know what's going on with you, Marty."

I'm not supposed to say anything, so I just look at the floor. Well, I would if the floor was visible.

"I don't care how much you dislike your teacher or how unfair you think he is, there's no excuse for what you did. That was dangerous! What were you thinking?!"

I keep looking down. "Do you want a story about a spider crossing the street?"

"I don't want a story, Marty. I want the truth."

"I was just trying to follow him! I didn't mean to crash into his car! Honest!"

"Why was it so important to follow him?"

"Because he's an . . . an . . . an interesting guy."

Ouch, it hurt to say that.

My dad seems more worried than mad. But he's definitely both.

Later, I overhear him talking to my mom on the phone. I hear them use words like *different*, *distracted*, *delusional*. It's cute that they're talking in alliteration.

They seem worried about me, but they've got it all wrong. I'm about to save the planet from the most horrible space creature imaginable. They'll see.

CHAPTER 35

twisted sister

I'm grounded.

I do extra chores, eat all my dinner, rinse my plate, load the dishwasher, change the litter box . . . I do everything!*

I even make a card.

Dearest Father
FRONT
SORRY ABOUT THE CRASHING THING
INSIDE
©
MARTY PANTS
ALL RIGHTS RESERVED
BACK

None of it helps. I'm trapped with no computer, no TV, no freedom. Saving the planet is on hold.

* Except clean my room.

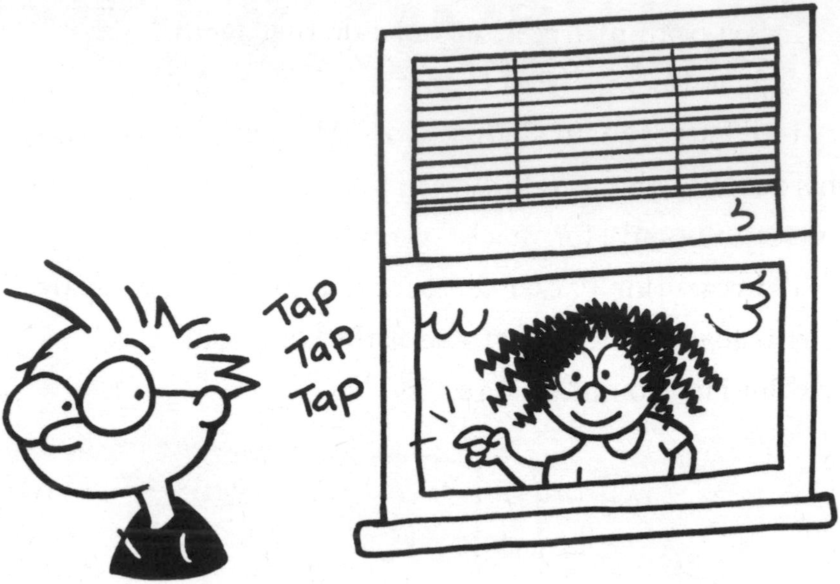
Tap
Tap
Tap

I look up and there's Parker. She climbed the tree outside my window. She's a risk taker.

"I heard you're grounded," she says when I let her in.

"News travels fast."

"What did you do this time?"

"Crashed into McPhee's car."

"WHAT?"

I explain how it went down.

"I messed up," I say. "I was trying to catch him fueling his spaceship, and it didn't go well."

"No one got hurt?"

"Right, but I heard my parents talking about bringing me to a head doctor, but my head is fine."

"Marty, promise me you won't do that again."

"I promise. But listen to this . . ."

I tell Parker about all the proof—McPhee's license plate, his disguise, the secret codes in his vocabulary words, the batteries he buys for snacks, everything.

I'm ready for Parker to become a psychologist again, but instead she says, "Let's go to the common!"

"But I'm grounded," I remind her.

"Chicken?"

I sneak down the tree with Parker because I'm not chicken.

I think this makes it official.

While my dad naps in the living room, Parker and I run to the common.

Instead of just hanging out on the swings, we go on the monkey bars, the seesaw, the slide . . . everything. It's goofy but we have a blast! It's the most fun I've had in a while. I even ride the springy spaceship.

"I bet McPhee's spaceship looks like this, only bigger," I say.

"You know the psychologist I interviewed for the school project?" Parker asks.

"Yeah."

"I described you to her, and she said you sounded very interesting."

"I am."

"I agree. I like you. You find adventure."

"It finds me."

I guess it's been a while since I rode this thing. I feel like I'm going to hurl, so I stagger over to the trash can.

I notice someone peeking at me from behind a tree.

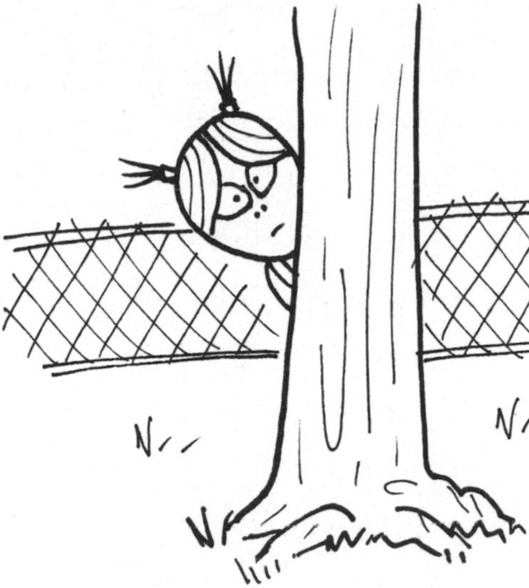

Then I blow chunks.

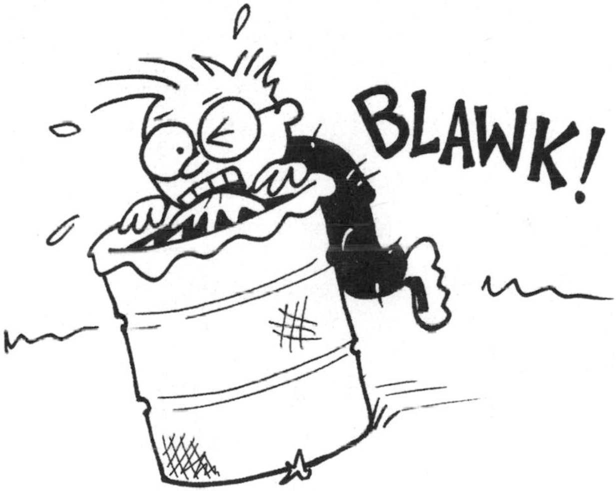
BLAWK!

Oh no! Analie might think I threw up because I looked at her!

"You okay, Marty?" asks Parker.

"What do you think of Analie?"

"Who?"

"The new girl in class. You know, the quiet one who sits in back. She's over there by the tree."

"She was a second ago," I explain.

Parker puts her hand on my shoulder. "Sometimes there are *real* people in your life who might walk away, but what they really want is for you to follow."

Then she turns and walks away.

Parker's just sent me a clear signal. I head in the direction of the tree.

Analie must be around here somewhere. I cross the street, turn the corner, and suddenly find myself face to face with a girl, but it's not Analie.

And she's not alone!

Ericccca is *not* happy to see me. "What are you doing here, Marty? You're supposed to be GROUNDED!"

"What are YOU doing here with HIM?!" I shoot back. "You promised Mom and Dad . . ."

"Marty, do NOT tell Mom and Dad!"

I pull her aside. "What do you see in him, Erickha? He's a bully! A no-good hoodlum!"

"You wouldn't understand. Just don't tell!"

"What if I do? I'm not afraid of you."

Peach Fuzz moves in, spits on the ground, and says, "Maybee yer afraid a me."

Good call. I am afraid of him.

"This is between Marty and me," Errika says.

"Don't wurry," Peach Fuzz tells her. "I no how ta handle deese situationz."

He grabs my right index finger.

"I hear ya like ta draw, Weddy. Be a shame if sumthin happened ta yer drawin' hand."

"Let him go, Salvador," Erikca says.

"He needz ta be tawt a lessun," snarls Peach Fuzz.

"I SAID let him go."

"Yeah, let me go." It's not often I agree with my sister.

But Peach Fuzz doesn't let go of my finger. He starts twisting it.

Then he does let go. Not by choice, but because my sister kicked him where no guy wants to be kicked. Peach Fuzz collapses like a sack of peaches. I told you my sister's a very good soccer player.

Erica looks at my finger. I tell her it's fine, but it kind of hurts. We walk home, leaving Peach Fuzz moaning on the sidewalk.

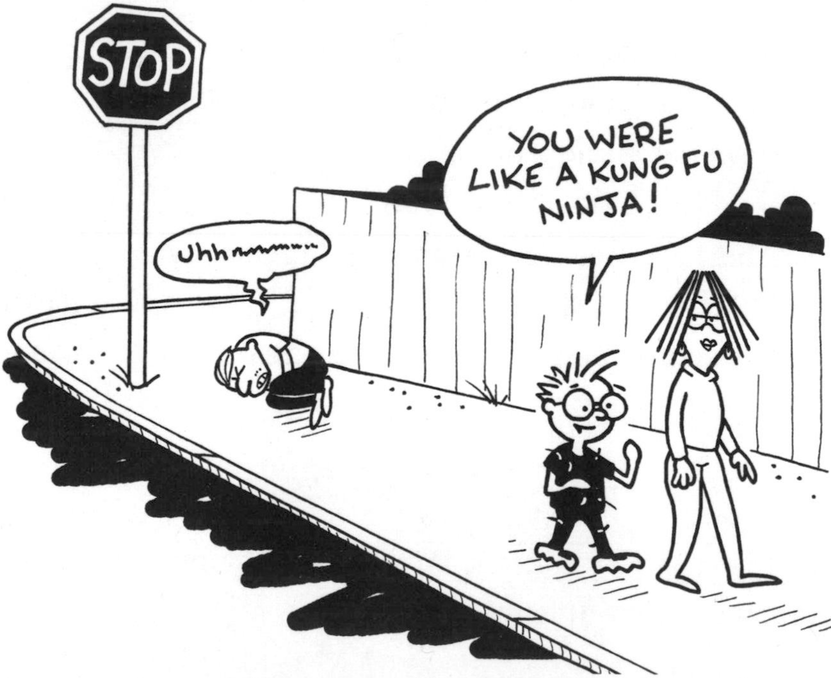
STOP
Uhhnnnnnn...
YOU WERE LIKE A KUNG FU NINJA!

Erica promises not to say anything about me sneaking out of the house.

"And I promise not to say anything about your boyfriend," I mumble.

"I no longer have a boyfriend," she says, and spits on the ground.

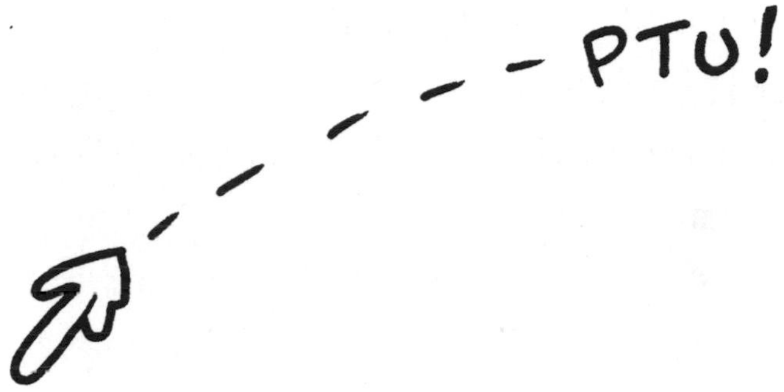
PTU!

CHAPTER 36

bad finger

"What's wrong with your finger?" My mom is back from her business trip and can tell something isn't right with my hand.

She's like a detective.

Erica looks like she wants to say something, so I blurt out, "I sprained it getting a fly out of my nose." I wish I'd thought of something cooler.

"I'm taking you to the emergency room, Marty."

My mom calls ahead to make sure they're ready for me.

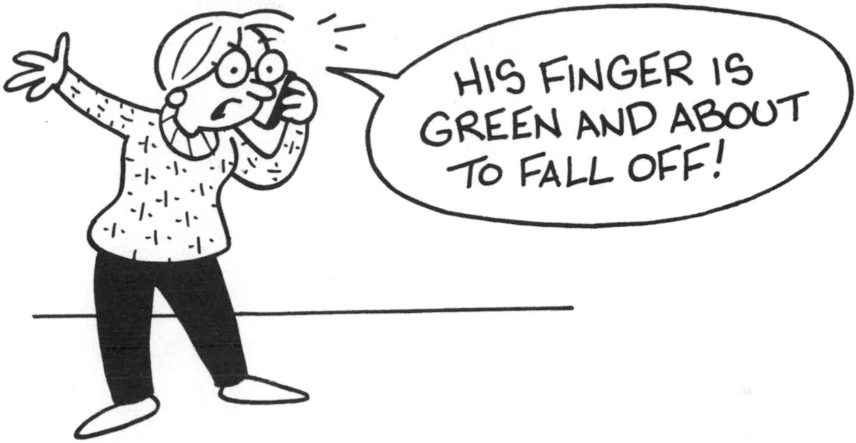
HIS FINGER IS GREEN AND ABOUT TO FALL OFF!

Sitting in the waiting room, I peek at the magazines around me. They're the same ones from last time.

I can tell.

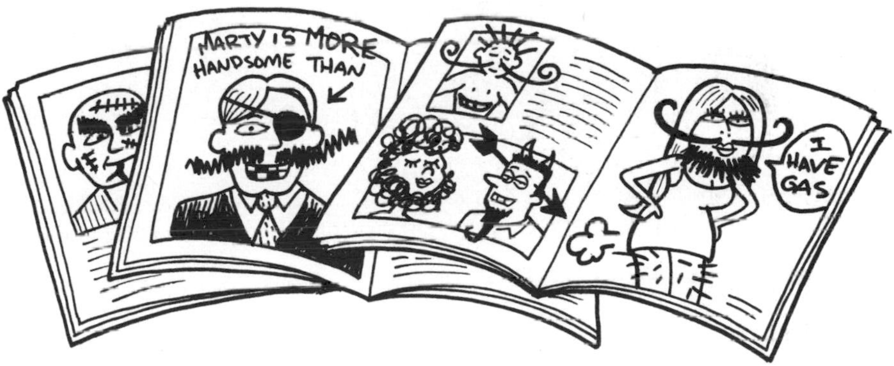
MARTY IS MORE HANDSOME THAN
I HAVE GAS

I look around for some fresh publications and notice someone sitting across the room.

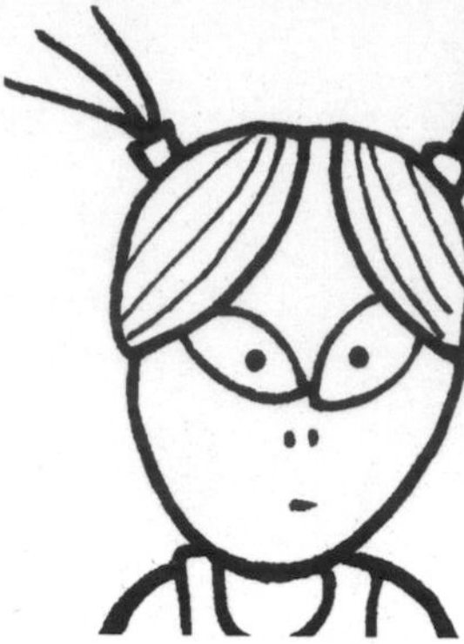

Analie! She's sitting alone, and I suddenly feel embarrassed to be with my mom. I decide I need a magazine from that side of the room. I walk near her and glance at what she's reading. It's a version of *People* magazine I've never seen before.

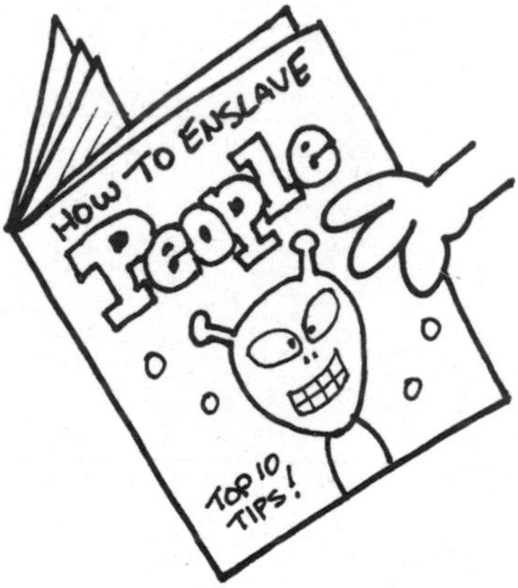
HOW TO ENSLAVE
People
TOP 10 TIPS!

Must be new.

I gather all my courage and say, "Hi. We hardly know each other, but I think you're interesting. Want to hang out sometime?"

At least that's how it sounded inside my head. Once it reached my mouth it sounded more like, "Enin rebmun."

Analie looks blankly at me and says, "Greetings."

I try again. "What a lovely voice you have. Do you sing? You should sing. Would you like to come to my house and listen to music sometime?"

But all my mouth could manage was, "Walla walla."

I hear the nurse call, "PANTS. MARTY PANTS." Too bad. The conversation was going so well. I wave to Analie, but she just stares back and writes in her notebook.

Before the doctor can examine my finger, she has to unwrap the bandages my mom put there.

The doctor puts the stethoscope on my chest and listens to my heart. I'm not sure what any of this has to do with my finger. Then she puts the stethoscope on my back. Who has a heart in their back? It slowly dawns on me what's going on. She's making sure my heart is located where a human heart is supposed to be. She's on the lookout for aliens just like I am! I give her a thumbs up.

She tapes a splint to my finger.

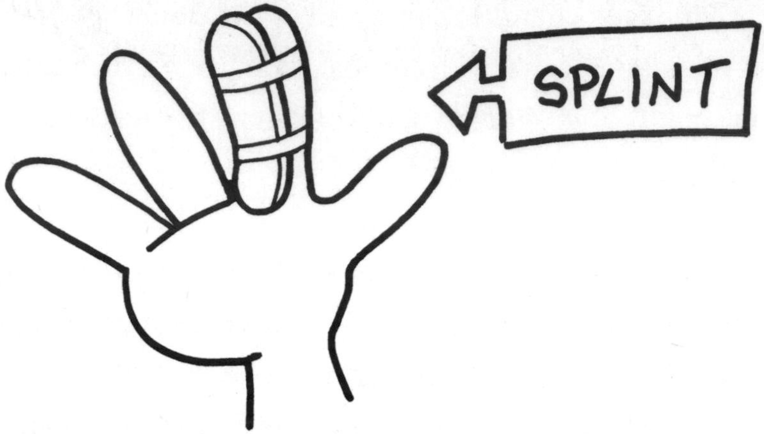
SPLINT

the contest

The splint keeps my finger from bending, so I have trouble tying my shoes. I also have to write with my left hand. Worst of all, it hurts to draw!

At school, Parker seems interested in my splint. Roongrat says, "Did you know the Surgeon General is developing full-body splints?"

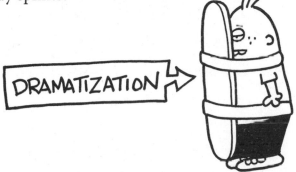

DRAMATIZATION

But the big news is that today is Monday! The mural drawings will be displayed for everyone to vote on!

My "Save the Planet" idea has to get the most votes, for the sake of mankind. I cross my fingers. Ouch. Bad idea. The splint.

Everyone is gathered around the display wall.

There are students and teachers and even some parents.

"I can't wait to see what Simon drew," Roongrat says.

People are voting, and Ms. Ortiz is collecting the ballots. I push my way to the display wall. Simon's contribution is easy to spot.

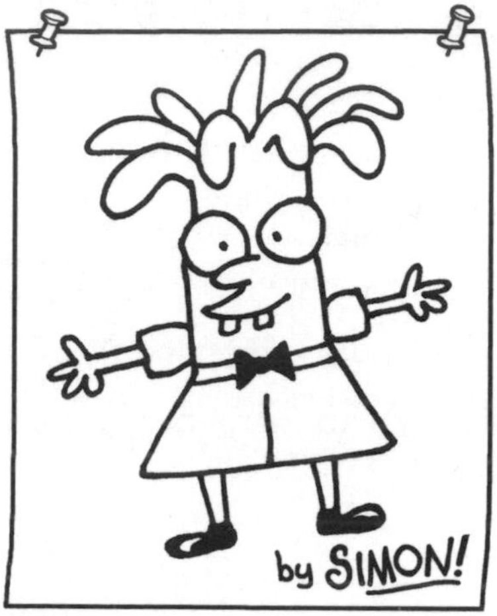
by SIMON!

"Awesome!" says Roongrat. "Simon did it again!"

Yes, he did it again, all right.

I look at the rest of the competition. All amateurs. Carlos drew a superhero, Lynn drew flowers, Nikki drew a race car, Jen drew a turtle, Stephen drew . . . hey, wait! Where's mine? My "Save the Planet" drawing isn't even up there!

There's only one explanation. McPhee! He was supposed to submit it and didn't! On purpose. Why? Because he's an alien and doesn't want to save the world! Why did I give it to him?!

Roongrat says, "Marty, I found your drawing."

Whew, it's up there after all. How did I miss it? I follow Roongrat's finger to see where he's pointing.

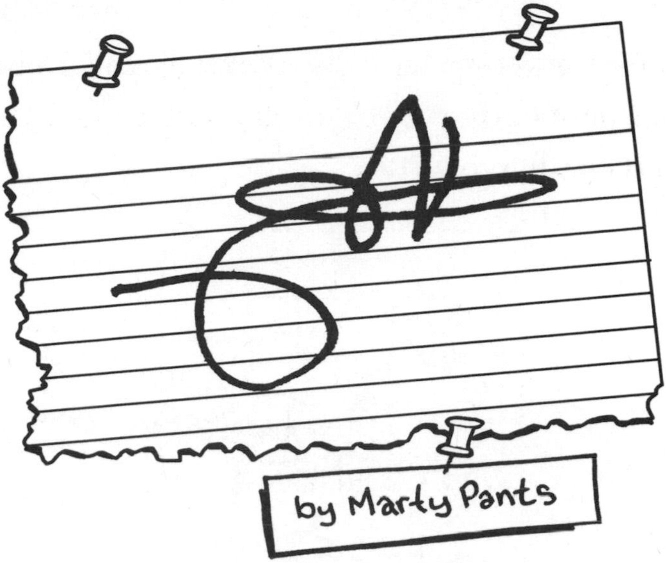
by Marty Pants

Oh no, no, no, no, no, no, no! That's the random scribble I handed to Ms. Ortiz! She thought I was submitting it for the contest!

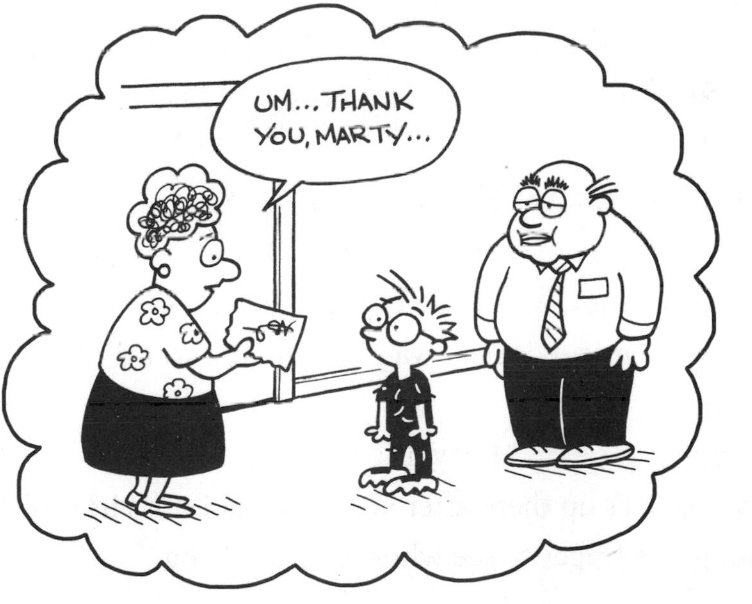
UM... THANK YOU, MARTY...

Simon slaps me on the back. "Wow, Marty! I'm waaaay better than you. Ha, ha!"

My stomach feels awful.

Doubly awful.

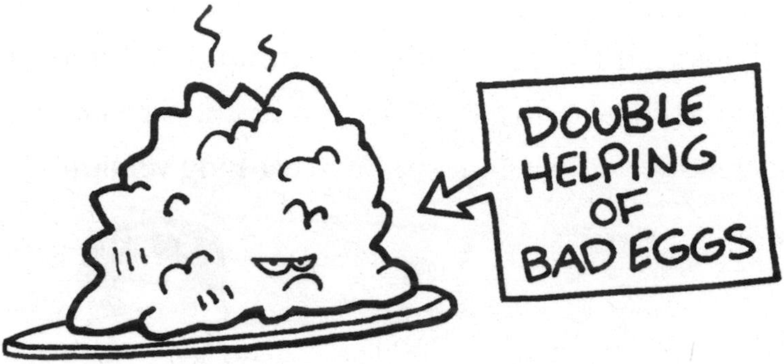
DOUBLE HELPING OF BAD EGGS

CHAPTER 38

pop goes the world

At the end of the day, Ms. Ortiz announces Simon won the mural contest. In a landslide, no doubt. Simon does his insufferable victory dance. The extra-long version.

I get looks of pity. Simon gets high fives. But not from me.

CAN'T. SPLINT.

I remain in a daze all the way home.

I notice a bag of balloons on the kitchen counter. I blow one up and draw on it with a marker.

Then I grab a pin from my mom's sewing kit.

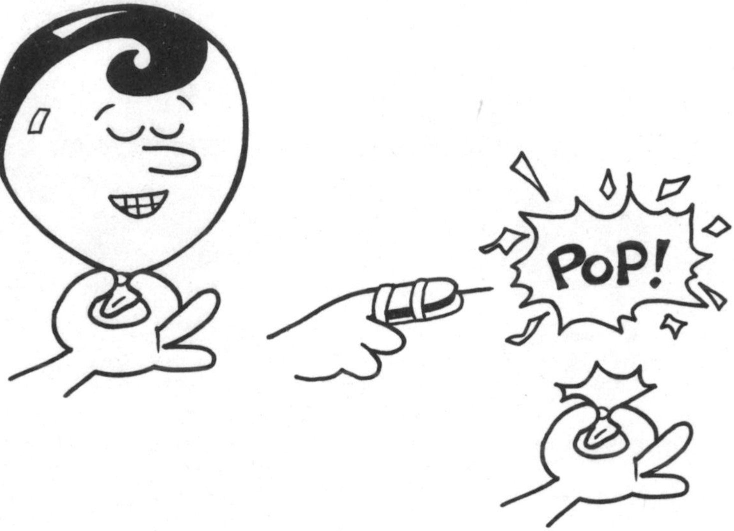
POP!

I repeat the process.

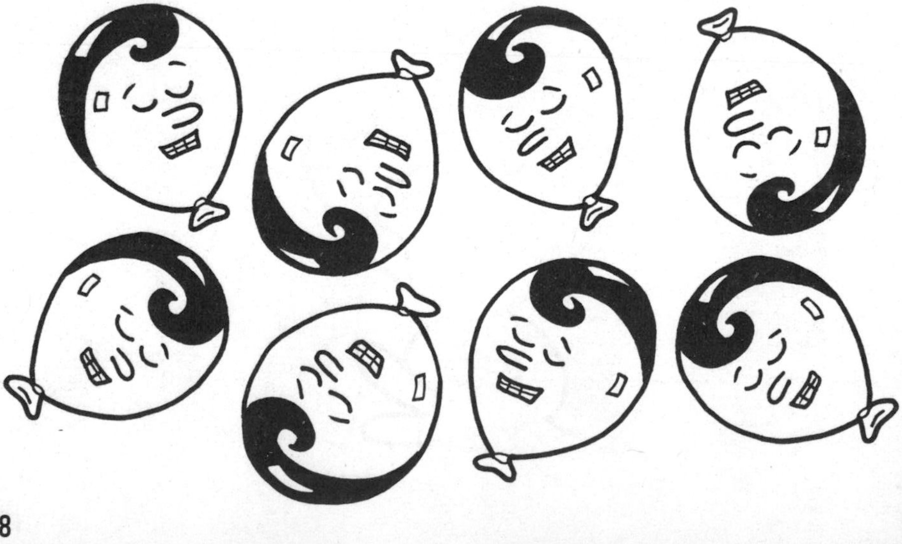

Jerome seems happy to help.

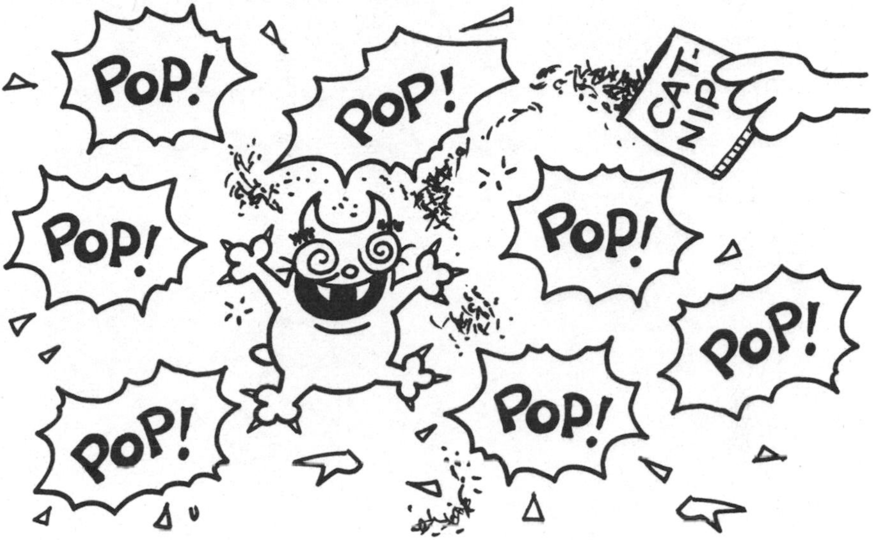
POP!
POP!
CAT-NIP
POP!
POP!
POP!
POP!
POP!

Simon beat me. It stings, but that's not the worst part. I have one balloon left, and draw something else on it.

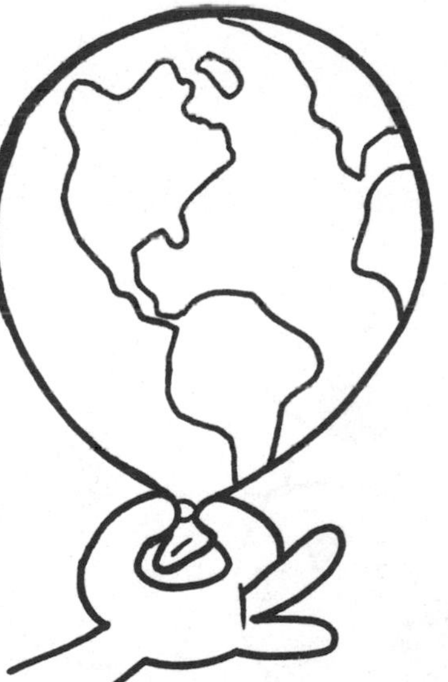

My grand plan failed. If I don't act quickly . . .

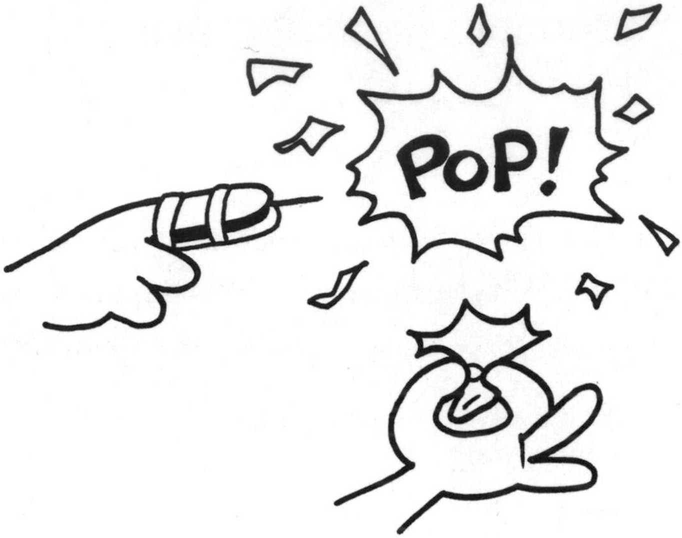
POP!

CHAPTER 39

too much coffee, man

Erica comes home with a super grande mocha cappuccino latte coffee double espresso swirl. With whipped cream. I want it. She says no. I make a sad face and show her my splint.

Guilt is a powerful tool.

I'm not usually a coffee drinker, but I heard it can perk you up. I could use that right about now because I'm very perked down. I need a way to defeat my alien teacher and I'm counting on this coffee to inspire me.

I drink half.

It works! I get a stupendous idea!

To pull it off, I'll need a quick influx of cash.

I peek into Erica's room, put on my sad face, and show her my splint again. "I sure wish I had some money."

"Don't push it," she says, and kicks her door closed.

On to Plan F.

F is for froggy bank.

I've already spent all the quarters and dimes on something.* The emergency nickels and pennies will have to do.

* Candy.

My grounding is over, so I can legally leave the house. I guess losing the mural contest and having a sprained finger helped shorten my sentence. Also, they made an appointment for me to see some kind of head doctor even though I keep telling them my head feels fine. It's my finger that hurts.

I load up with the coins and take a stroll downtown to buy what I need to save the world.

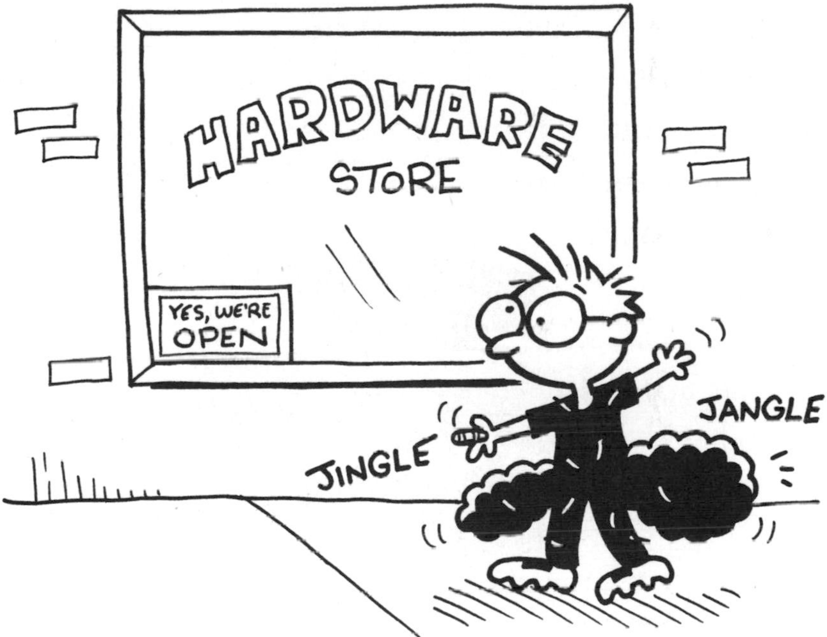
HARDWARE
STORE
YES, WE'RE
OPEN
JINGLE
JANGLE

escape artist

It's late and I finish the other half of the coffee.

The time is now.

Time is of the essence.

Time is on my side.

No time like the present.

Time to set the wheels in motion.

Time's up.

Time to make the donuts.

I tiptoe by my sister's room. The door is open a crack, but she doesn't notice me because she's watching TV. And using her phone. And on her computer. And doing homework. And listening to music. And snacking. And painting her nails.

My mom's on another business trip, so now I only have to worry about my dad. He's sitting in the living room with the TV on. Asleep.

I try to sneak past him.

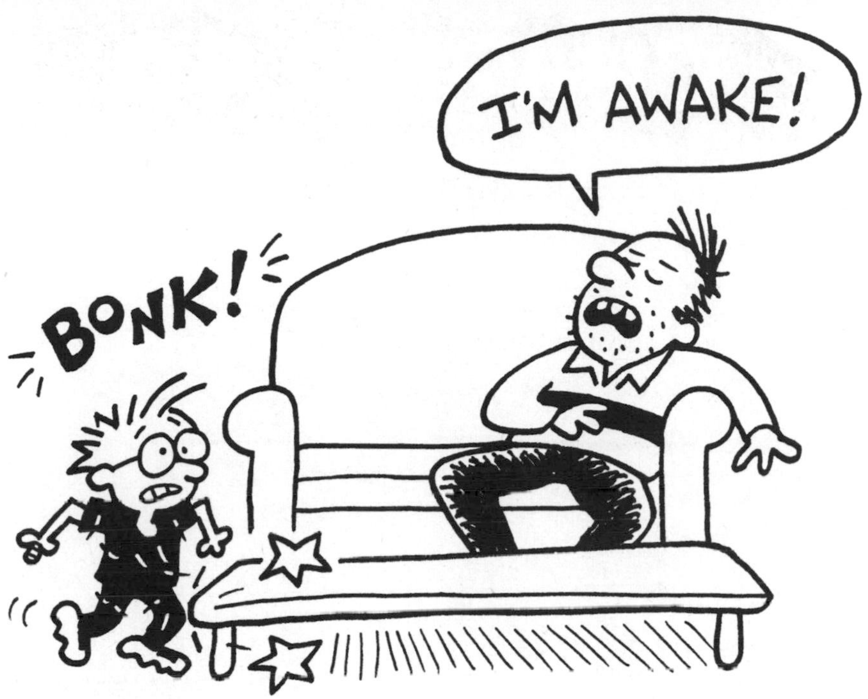
I'M AWAKE!
BONK!

Good news. He never announces that he's awake when he's actually awakc. That's a reflex he has when he's sound asleep. The coast is clear.

I slip out the front door and start walking toward the school.

It's dark and quiet, but mostly dark.

My supplies are stuffed down the front of my pants, so I walk a little funny. I pass Roongrat's house, and all the lights are off. Most of the houses are dark, and every other streetlight is out.

I've walked this way a zillion times, but never this late at night.

Alone.

I hear footsteps and stop. The footsteps also stop. I don't see anyone ahead of me or behind me, so it must have been my own footsteps.

I continue walking.

Every movement seems loud when it's this quiet. A car goes by, and I try to act casual. A dog barks in the distance.

I want to chicken out, but I've already proven I'm not chicken. Besides, I'm halfway there, and I have an important mission. Eye of the leopard.

I finally get to the school, and I touch the front of the building. This will be my canvas. My "Save the Planet" mural will cover the front of the school.

The design is all secure in my memory.

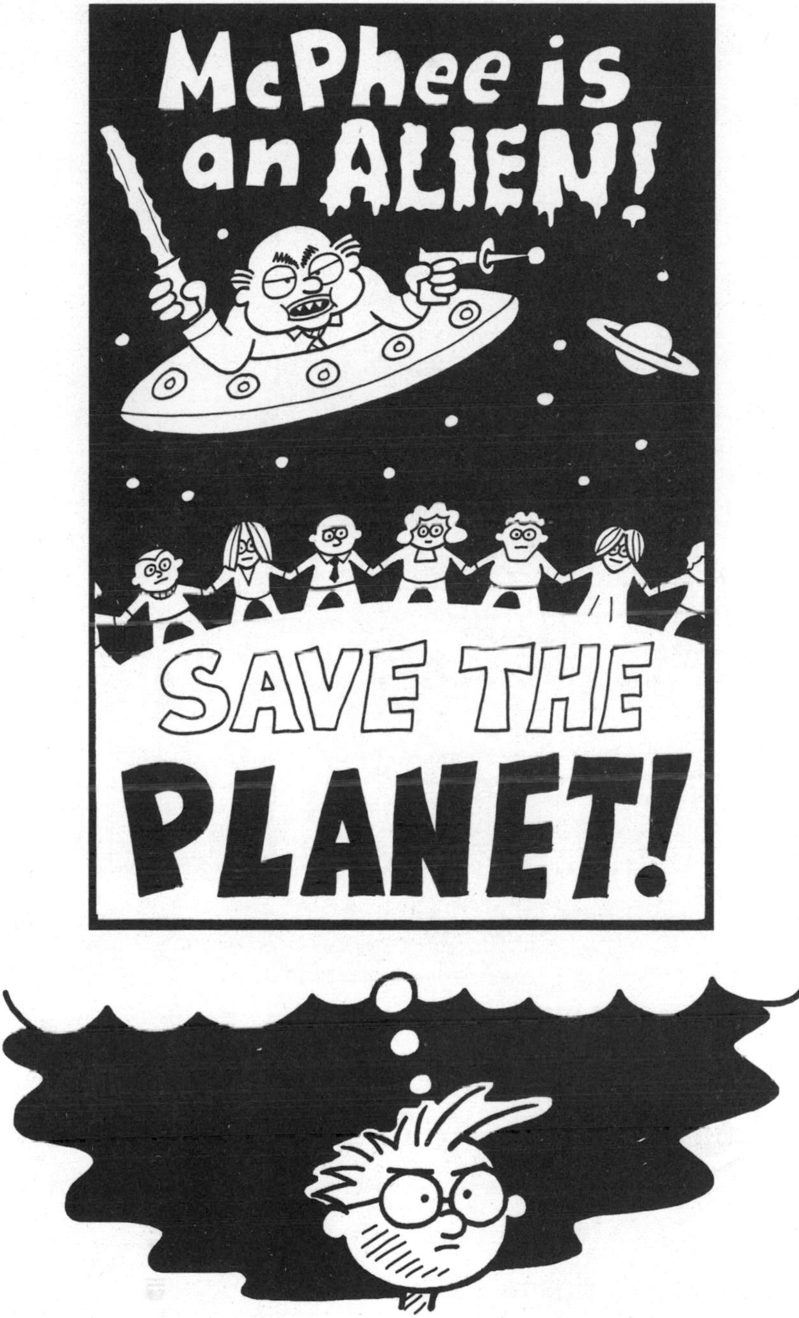
McPhee is an ALIEN!
SAVE THE PLANET!

Everyone will see it. It will make the newspapers, and I will have changed the world with my art, just like an artist is supposed to do.

I take out my supplies: two cans of spray paint. I press one of the nozzles with a nonsplint finger, and I'm under way.

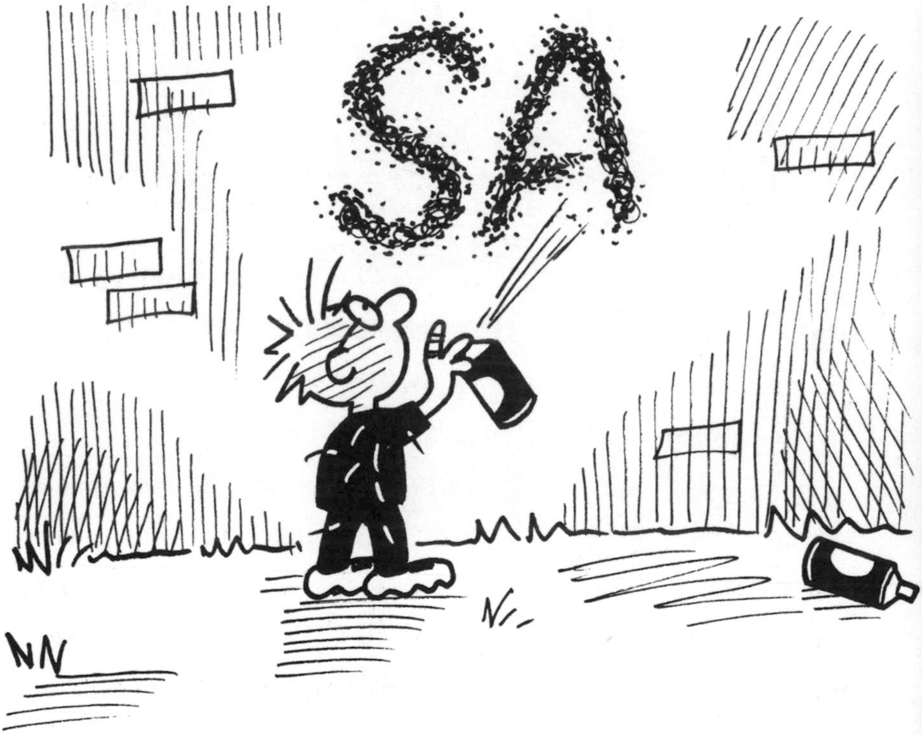
SA

This is harder than I thought. I'm going to need a ladder to get to the high areas, and I'm also having trouble seeing.

I didn't plan this well. I could use a hand.

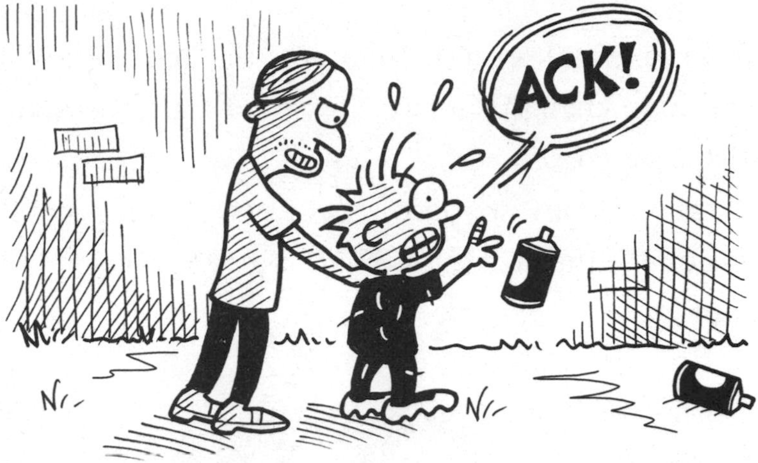
ACK!

"Yer out late, Weddy."

Peach Fuzz?! What's he doing here? He grabs the spray paint out of my hand.

"Ya like ta cause truble, Weddy? I'm gonna cauze ya all kindsa truble. Yer sister ain't here ta protect ya."

He sees my splint and smiles. "How's ya finga?"

"Fine," I say. "How's your . . ."

"SHUT UP!" yells Peach Fuzz as he pushes me. I fall backward and my glasses come off. I reach around in the dark trying to find them.

Why did this seem like a good idea? Why am I out here late at night? Why?! The coffee. I blame the coffee.

Then I hear, "GWAKYAAA!" It's blurry, but I can tell Peach Fuzz is being attacked by a wild animal! A rabid raccoon, I think. He runs around screaming, trying to pull it off his face. I put my glasses on just in time to see Peach Fuzz crash into a Dumpster and the critter tumble into it.

Peach Fuzz turns around and comes at me. His clothes are ripped, he's scratched, and his eyes look crazy! Is he rabid? What's he going to do to me?

Out of nowhere, a blinding white light engulfs Peach Fuzz. He stands frozen like a statue.

Two silhouettes appear in the light, and I hear a strange voice.

The aliens have come!

"Hold it right there."

Correction. The police have come! They're arresting Peach Fuzz for vandalism. He keeps saying he's innocent, but since he was holding that can of spray paint, it doesn't look good for him.

One officer puts him in handcuffs, and the other takes the cans for evidence.

"Salvador Ack, I should have known!" says one of the cops. "Painting your initials on the school?"

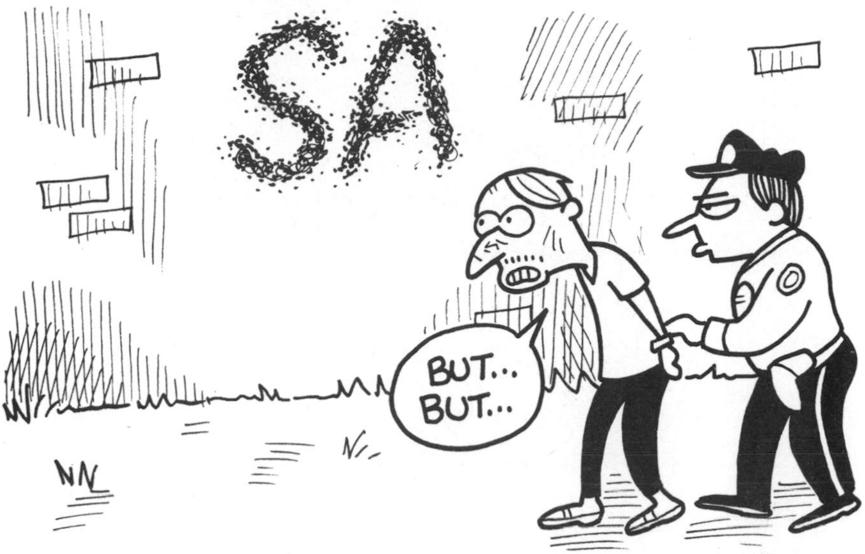
SA
BUT... BUT...

I'm still on the ground, hidden in the shadows. Before I can crawl away, I hear Peach Fuzz blurt out, "IT'S DAT KIDZ FALT!"

A flashlight shines on me.

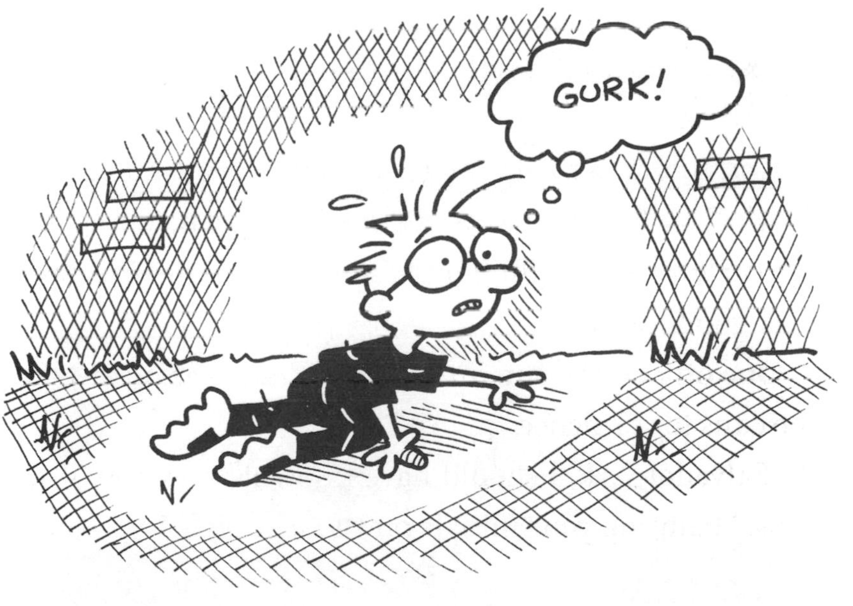
GURK!

"FREEZE!"

I freeze.

"Now, stand up slowly."

I know that voice. It's Officer Pickels.

"Marty?" He seems surprised and helps me up. "Are you responsible for this?"

Busted.

"Yes," I confess. "It was me."

"You're the one who called this crime in to the station?"

"Umm . . ."

"Maybe you have what it takes to be an officer of the law after all! But Marty, you shouldn't be following criminals around. That's dangerous business. Leave it to the professionals."

"Yes, sir."

"You should be home in bed. Let me give you a ride."

"No, thank you."

"I insist."

Peach Fuzz is taken away in one car, and I go in the other. I finally get my ride in a police cruiser. I sit in back where they usually put the criminals.

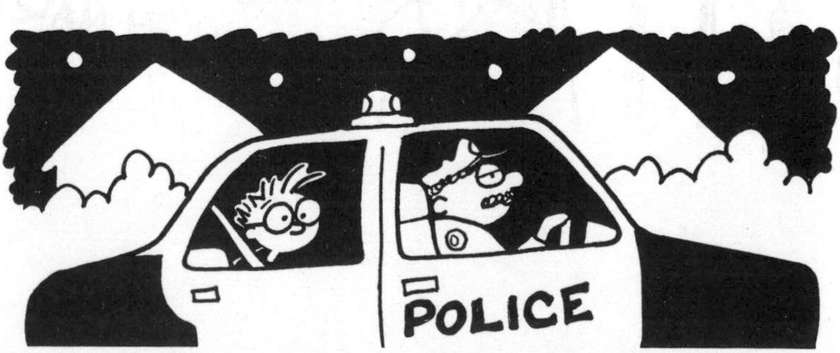
POLICE

I'm a little shaken up and just stare out the window. For a second, I thought I saw Analie looking back through the darkness.

My cruiser turns in the direction of my house and Peach Fuzz's cruiser turns in the direction of the police station.

I can picture Peach Fuzz arriving in his cell.

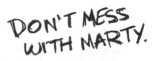

DON'T MESS
WITH MARTY.

POLICE NOTES

There was a report of vandalism at the school. Police were dispatched and discovered a juvenile male with a peach-fuzz mustache in possession of two cans of spray paint. The juvenile's initials were observed painted on the building. He was arrested and later released to the hospital, where he underwent a series of extremely painful shots, as it appears he was bitten multiple times by a rabid raccoon.

CHAPTER 41

something's missing

I was able to talk Officer Pickels into dropping me off
in front of my house instead of escorting me inside and
waking my dad. Professional courtesy from a fellow law
enforcement official, I guess.

He waits until I get inside before he drives away. The
front door isn't completely closed so I'm able to enter qui-
etly. I try to sneak past my dad, but bump into the table
again.

I'M AWAKE!

BONK!

What a night.

I crawl into bed, but can't sleep. The coffee is partly to blame, but the real reason is something's missing.

Jerome.

He always sleeps on my head at night. Always. Where is that crazy little . . .

The front door! I forgot to close it all the way when I left! Jerome snuck out!

This is no time for sleep. I have to do something! I have to find him! He could be anywhere!

Flyers. I need to make flyers.

Okay, the first thing I need is a picture of Jerome, so I look through my photos.

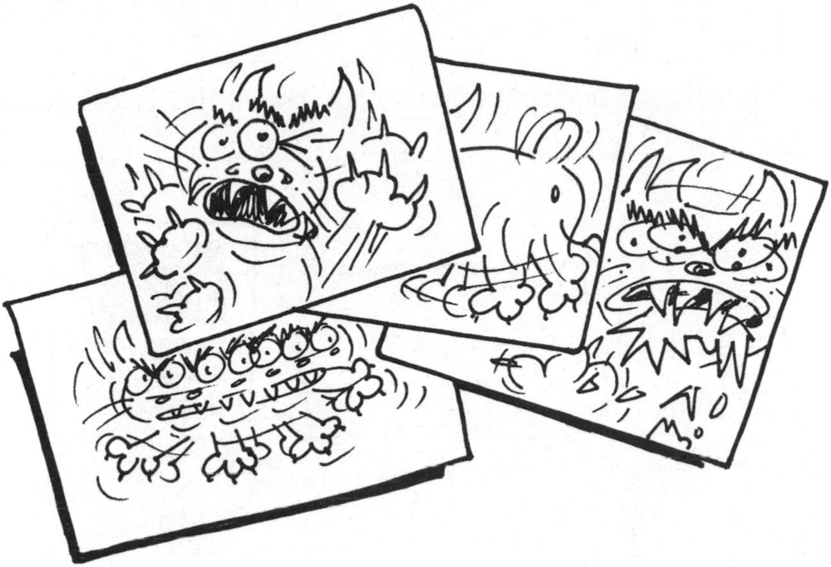

I can't find a single good one, so I take off the splint. I don't care how much it hurts, I have to draw.

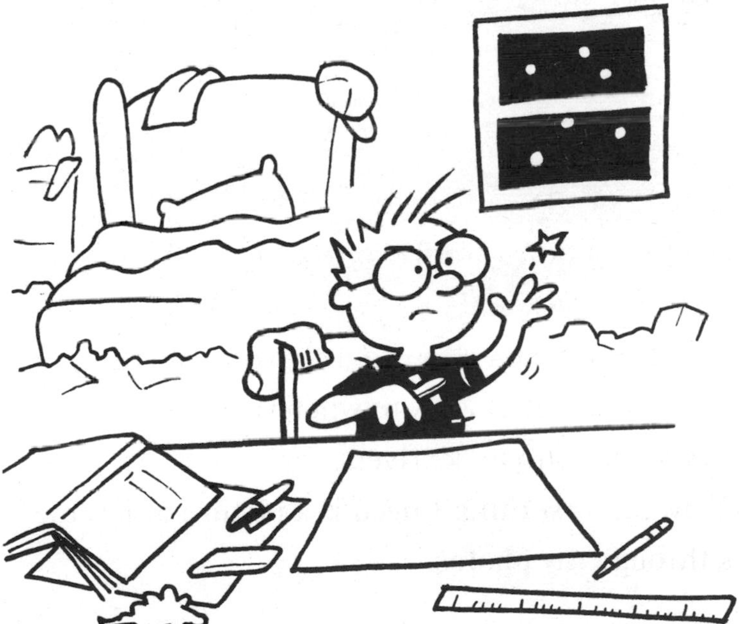

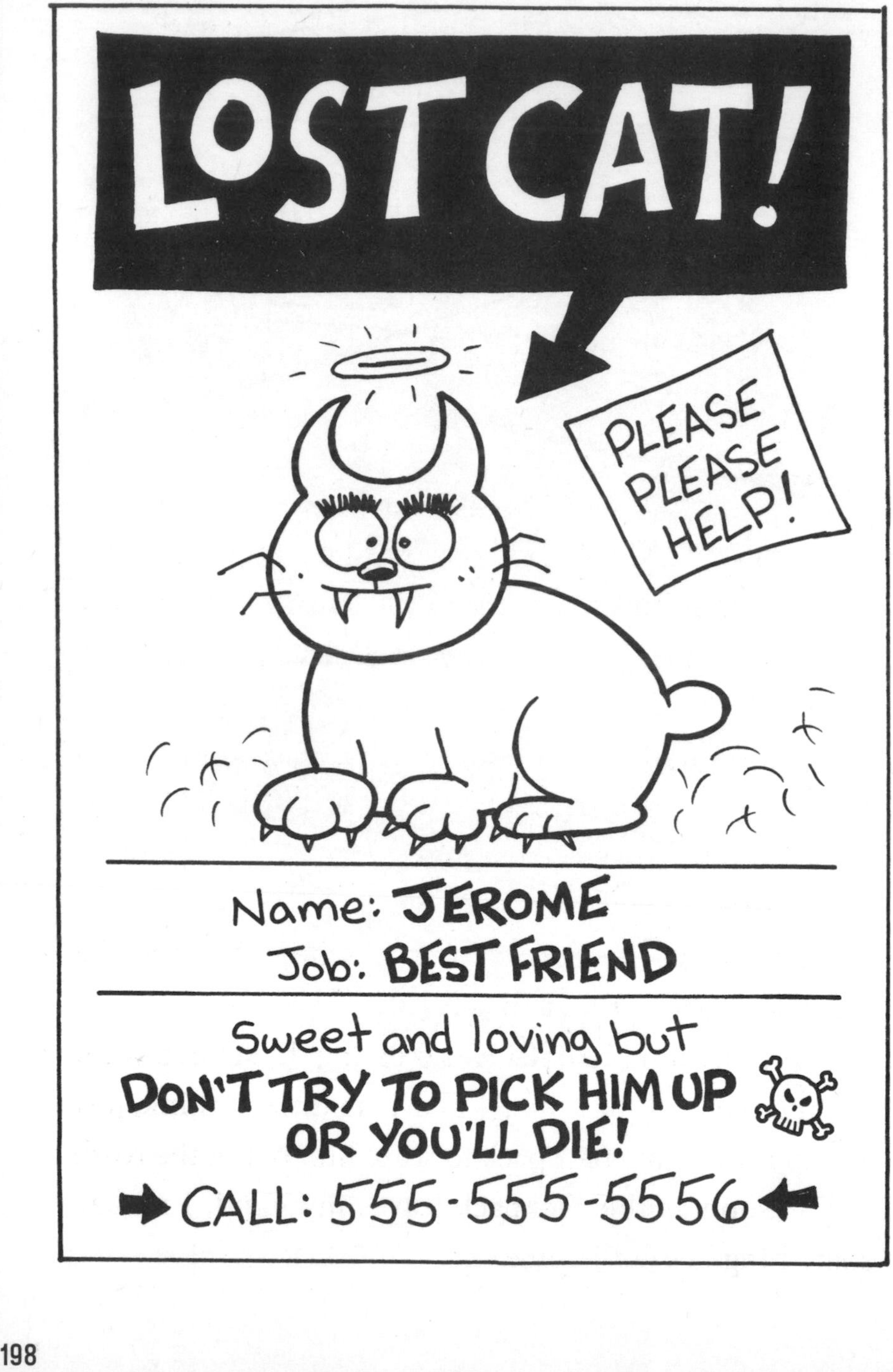
LOST CAT!
PLEASE PLEASE HELP!
Name: JEROME
Job: BEST FRIEND
Sweet and loving but
DON'T TRY TO PICK HIM UP OR YOU'LL DIE!
CALL: 555-555-5556

the walk

Oh no! I slept through my alarm! I rush to change my clothes, stuff the "Lost Cat" flyers in my backpack, and run downstairs.

My dad's still passed out in the living room. I can't believe how late I am! No time for breakfast.

I dash outside and hope to see Jerome, but there's no sign of him anywhere.

I'll hang the flyers on my way to school. I run to the nearest telephone pole and . . .

Wait, I see him! Jerome! He's crossing the street toward me and *there's a car coming*! I have no time to think, just act, so I throw my backpack to scare him out of the road. But as soon as the backpack leaves my hand, I realize something. It's not Jerome.

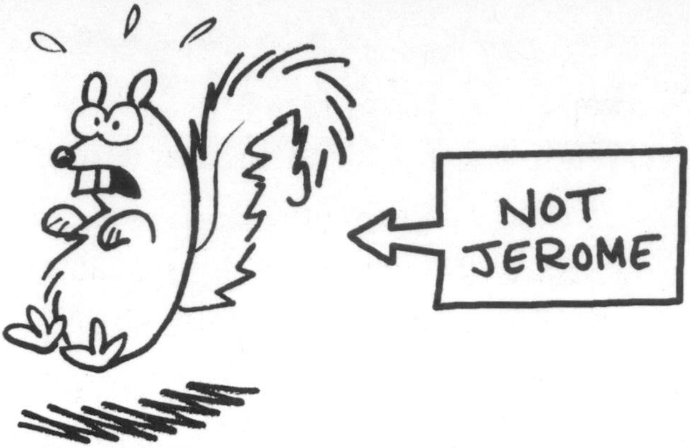
NOT
JEROME

The confused squirrel darts away while the oncoming car meets my backpack.

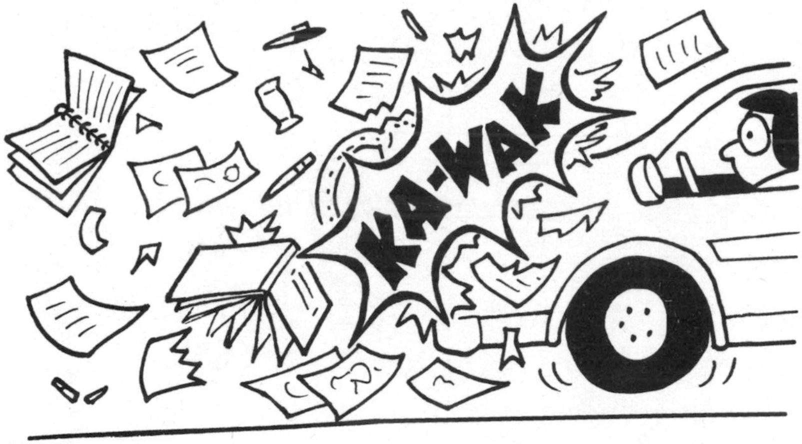
KA-WAK

The lady in the car slows down long enough to make an unfriendly gesture at me.

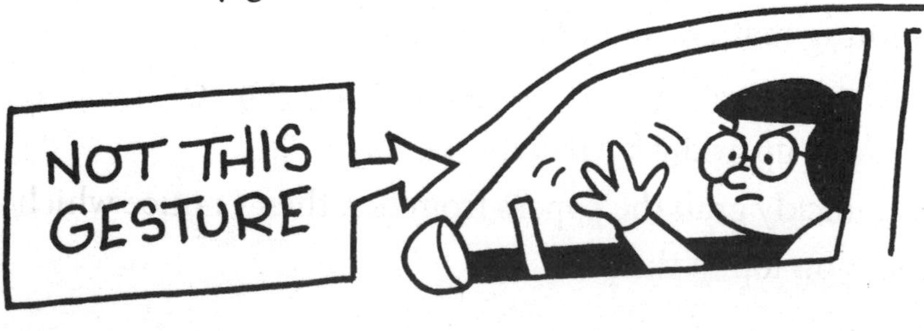
NOT THIS
GESTURE

Ripped papers float down, my math book is in two pieces, there are tire tracks on my homework, and the "Lost Cat" flyers are all torn up!

This is a disaster! I try to keep my wits about me and scoop up what I can from the street. Cars beep at me as I try to cram my stuff into what's remaining of my backpack.

I pick up a ripped flyer and stare at my drawing of Jerome. Then I look down at my clothes. For the first time in as long as I can remember, there's no fur on them.

Jerome really is gone.

I give up. I sit on the curb with my head in my hands and watch my papers blow away. Who cares? Not me. Nothing matters anymore.

Then someone hands me a pile of my papers.

I look up and it's Analie!

I quickly grab the papers from her, then I notice which one is on top of the pile.

ME
ANALIE

"Thank you," I say as I stuff them into my mangled backpack.

Analie says, "Greetings-human."

Did you notice that? I fish out my list of goals and make a quick update.

~~- SAY A COMPLETE SENTENCE TO ANALIE~~

analie

Analie helps me pick up the rest of my stuff and we walk to school together. She tells me her last name, but it's hard to pronounce. It starts with an *N*.

I tell her about Jerome and show her the drawing I made. I get a little emotional. Forget about all the other embarrassing things I've done — crying in front of Analie now counts as the worst.

She writes things down the whole time we walk. Her voice is monotone, and she doesn't seem to blink. Somehow I find this appealing. She also seems very interested in me, and I find that even more appealing.

I tell her all kinds of stuff. I even mention that there's something I can't really discuss and the world is in peril. She nods knowingly. I bet she suspects McPhee, too. She seems smart like me.

Analie N. tells me she's originally from a place far, far away. I think she means Montana. She also tells me I'm the only person who can see her. What a nice thing to say.

We're both very late for school, but for some reason I'm the only one who gets detention. McPhee doesn't even notice Analie, he's so blinded by his hatred for me.

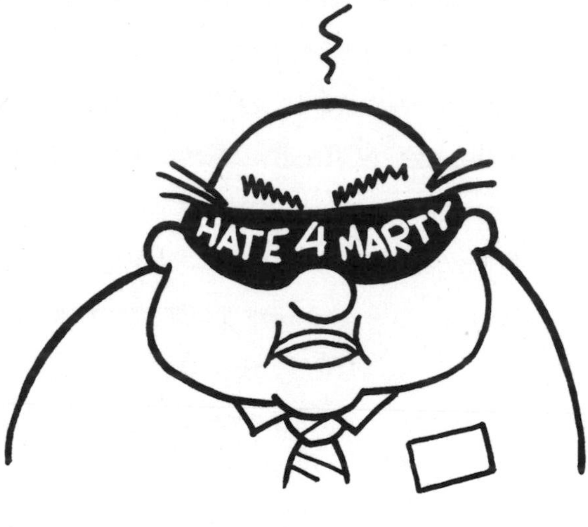
HATE 4 MARTY

CHAPTER 44

opening day

At lunch, I sit and talk with Analie, while Parker and Roongrat give me strange looks.

Analie tells me, "You-will-not-see-me-after-today."

"Are you moving?" I ask.

"My-mission-will-be-complete."

I guess that means she's moving back home. Folks from Montana sure have a funny way of saying things.

I finally get up the nerve to talk to Analie, and now she's leaving. At the end of lunch, I feel like she knows me better than anyone else, except maybe Parker.

I watch Simon walking by us with some paintbrushes. "Time to work on my mural!" he says loudly enough for everyone to hear.

I look back to Analie, but she's gone. She didn't even say good-bye.

On the way back to class I see Simon again. He's looking at the wall, closing one eye and holding up his thumb as if he's a real artist. That was supposed to be the spot where I exposed McPhee. That was supposed to be the wall where I saved everyone! I was meant to paint there, not Simple Simon.

Not only is my backpack falling apart, my life is, too. It's only fitting this day ends in detention.

I stare at McPhee as he stares at his computer. You win, McPhee. I can't save the world. My world has already ended anyway.

I didn't eat breakfast or lunch and start to notice how hungry I am. I search what's left of my backpack for the emergency candy. Nothing.

My stash must be all over the road.

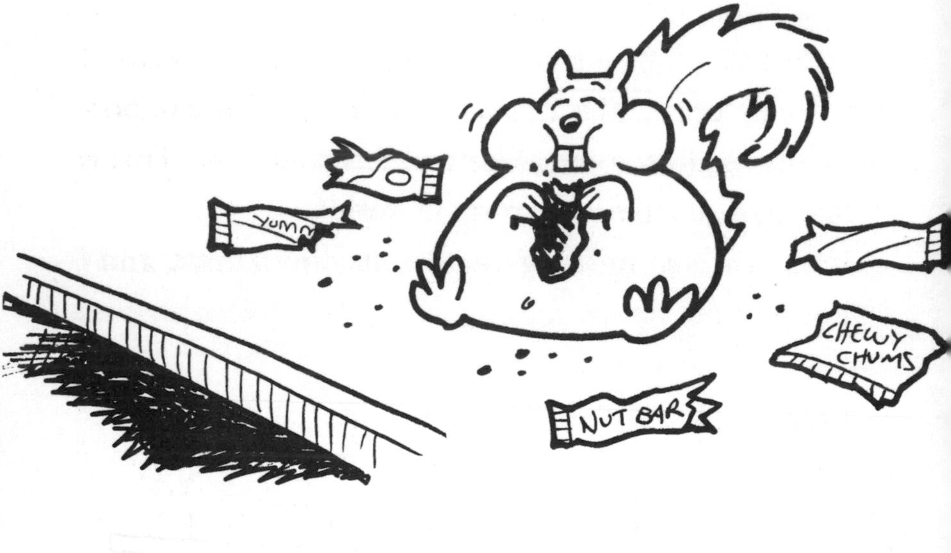
YUMM
CHEWY CHUMS
NUT BAR

Great. All I manage to find is an old, pulverized fortune cookie. I eat the crumbs out of the wrapper and peek at the fortune.

> *Your imagination will lead you in the wrong direction.*

Fortunes never seem to apply to me.

Suddenly, there's a commotion in the hallway. McPhee looks through the door window, then back at me.

"Promise me you'll stay in that seat," he says gravely.

I nod obediently.

"Give me your word, Marty."

I give him my word.

McPhee leaves the room and shuts the door behind him. I wonder what's going on out there, but more importantly, he finally left me alone with his computer! This is it! My last best chance to save the world!

But I gave him my word that I'd stay in my seat, and I like to keep my word.

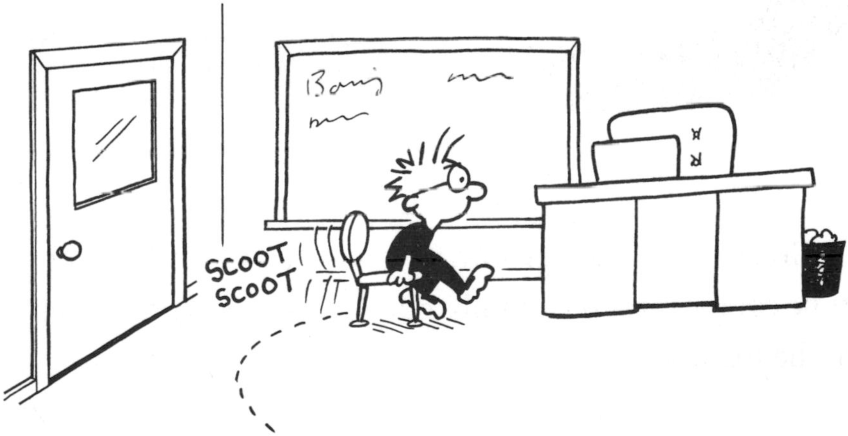
SCOOT
SCOOT

I get to his computer, but he's one step ahead of me. Now I need a password to get in!

Okay, Marty, try to think like McPhee. What kind of password would he use?

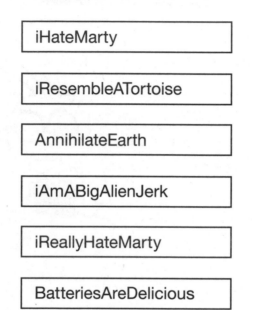

iHateMarty

iResembleATortoise

AnnihilateEarth

iAmABigAlienJerk

iReallyHateMarty

BatteriesAreDelicious

No luck.

Then I realize I'm going about this the wrong way. If I really want to think like McPhee, I need to come up with the lamest, most uncreative password of all time.

password

I'm in.

And there's that DO NOT OPEN! file just sitting there.

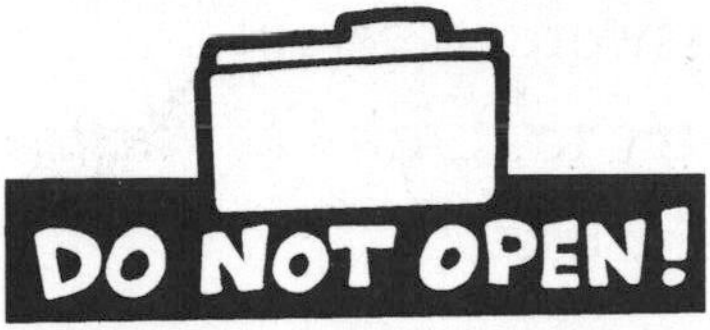
DO NOT OPEN!

I take a deep breath.

For the second time, I open it.

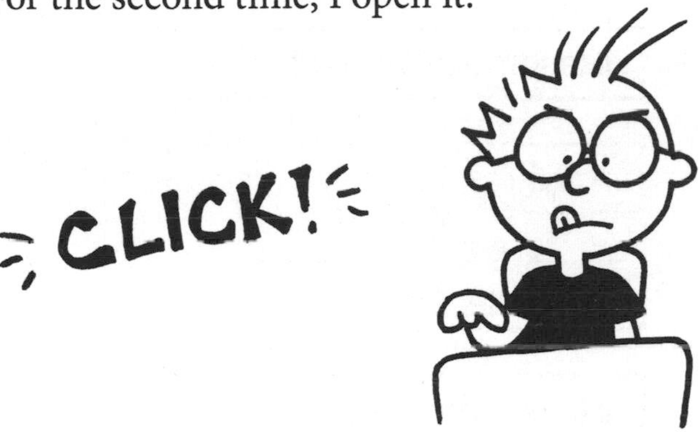
CLICK!

I see the word *annihilate* again.

I look further and notice vocabulary words, homework assignments, tests . . .

Wait. Is that why McPhee got mad at me when I snooped on his computer? He thought I was trying to cheat by peeking at test answers? That's all it was?

Wait again. I see something else.

SECRET FINAL PLANS TO INFILTRATE AND ANNIHILATE EARTH

CHAPTER 45

100% proof

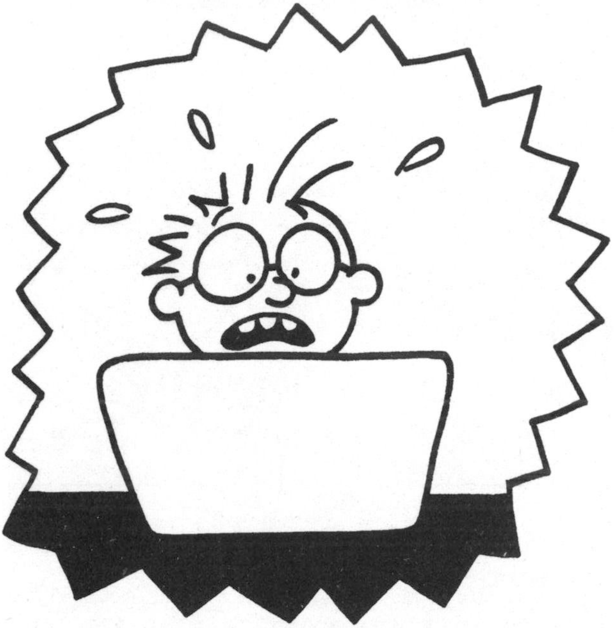

There are maps and pictures and plans, parts of it are in an alien language. There are step-by-step instructions on how the aliens should pretend to be human to gain our trust. It even details where spaceships will attack Earth and when!

Tomorrow!

I send the page to the printer in the corner of the room and it starts whirring. I scoot my chair over and grab the page as soon as it finishes printing.

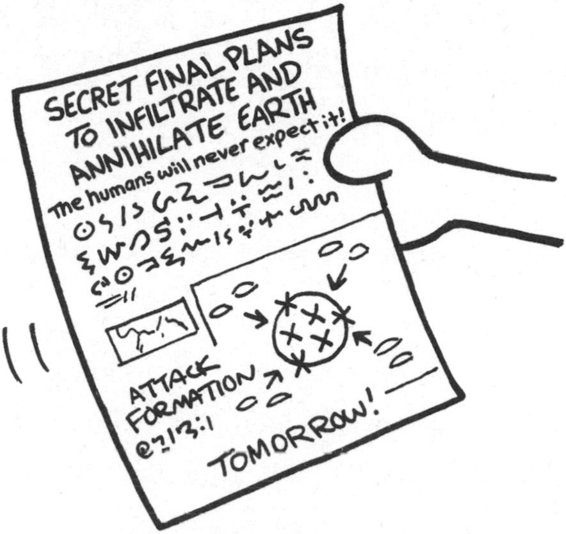
SECRET FINAL PLANS
TO INFILTRATE AND
ANNIHILATE EARTH
The humans will never expect it!
ATTACK
FORMATION
TOMORROW!

It's gotten quiet in the hall. McPhee must be coming back! If he sees what I did, there's no telling what he'll do to me. Detention for a month or disintegration for an eternity!

I quickly scoot my chair across the room back to my spot. Then the printer starts whirring again. Oh no! It's printing another page, and I don't have time to get it! The whirring stops just as McPhee walks in the door.

He has blood on his shirt! Has the invasion begun? He walks right up to me. And I have page one of his secret plans in my hand. Page two is sitting right there in the printer. I keep wondering if another page is about to print. McPhee doesn't look happy, but offers no explanation as to what happened.

At that moment, a crackling voice comes from the sky. It's Ms. Ortiz on the intercom.

"Marty's parents are here, Mr. McPhee. He has an important appointment. Please excuse him."

My parents! Somehow they knew I needed rescuing!

McPhee stands over me breathing heavily and in a very low voice says, "Go."

"Yes, sir!" Gurk! I never call him *sir*! He's going to know I'm onto him! I casually gather my stuff and casually leave the room. I casually walk down the hall. I'm holding his plans tightly in my hand, casually. I'm about to casually break into a sprint when someone blocks my way.

"I-need-to-stop-you-right-now," Analie says.

"Not now! Anytime but now!"

"What-is-that-in-your-hand-human?"

"A secret document the world needs to see!"

She looks me in the eyes. "Can-you-hold-two-things-at-once?"

Only then do I notice she's holding something, too. It's . . .

"I-recognized-this-creature-from-the-flyer-you-created."

Jerome!

I was so preoccupied with escaping that I didn't even see him!

Oh yeah, escaping! I grab my cat and thank Analie about a dozen times. I kiss Jerome on the forehead and do the same to Analie.

Did I really just do that?

"Crm wif me!" I say as I put the paper in my mouth so I can grab her hand. But she's already gone.

I hear McPhee's voice booming from the room. "MARTY! GET BACK HERE!"

I don't think so, McPhee.

I turn and run.

I burst through the front doors of the school with my crazy cat in my arms and the secret document flapping in my mouth.

My parents are waiting in the car with the engine running. Perfect! I bolt down the stairs, fumble with the door handle, and jump in the backseat.

"GO, GO, GO!" I shout.

"Hi, Marty," my mom says. "We're taking you to see a head doc . . . what are you doing with Jerome?!"

McPhee heads down the steps toward the car, waving his arms.

"GO, DAD, GO!"

My dad starts to drive.

"WAIT! MR. PANTS! STOP!"

My dad stops.

"NO, DAD, NO!"

CHAPTER 46

stuff gets real

CAN I HELP YOU, MR. MCPHEE?

"Don't help him, Dad!"

"Your son (*pant*) took something (*pant*) without permission and (*pant*) I can't have him showing it to (*pant*) anyone."

"What did you take, Marty?" sighs my mom.

"Don't say what it is, Marty, (*pant*) just give it back to me (*pant*). Now, (*pant*) please."

"It sounds important. Give it back to Mr. McPhee, Marty."

"But, Mom . . ."

"Marty, you took something that doesn't belong to you."

"Look at it, Mom! Just look at it!"

"Mr. McPhee said he doesn't want anyone to look at it."

"Doesn't that make you *suspicious*?!" I snap back. I can usually count on my dad to stick up for me, but right now he's staring at the floor and shaking his head.

It's all up to me, so I turn to McPhee and say, "If you want it, come get it!"

I put the paper on the seat and plop Jerome on top of it. McPhee looks scared.

In unison, my parents yell, "MARTIN SEYMOUR PANTS!"

I can't hold it in any longer, so I just blurt it out.

"McPHEE IS AN ALIEN AND THESE ARE HIS PLANS TO ANNIHILATE EARTH! DRIVE, DAD! DRIVE LIKE THE WIND!"

My dad doesn't drive like the wind. My parents just look at me, then each other.

That's when I notice my classmates are gathering outside the car. There's Roongrat, Simon, everybody, and I hear them snickering. The only one not laughing is Parker, and she must be mad because she told me not to say anything. But I had to!

My dad gets really calm and says, "I know that's what you think you found, but that's not right, is it, Mr. McPhee?"

McPhee opens his mouth and closes it, like he doesn't know what to say. Then I hear something. Chewing.

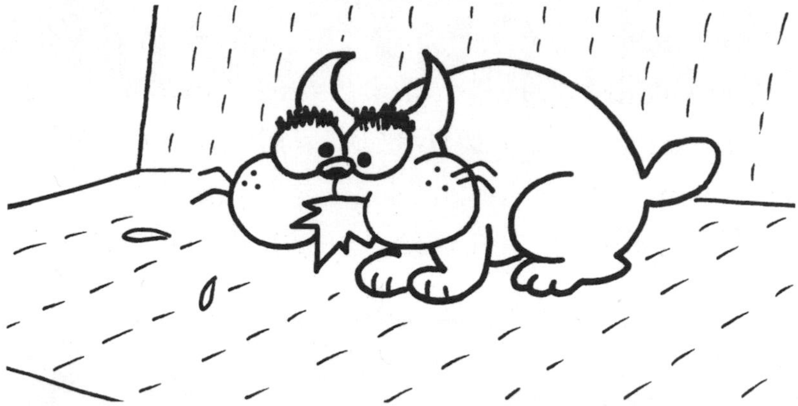

The secret plans!

I grab Jerome and say, "Throw it up, buddy! You can do it! Look at McPhee!"

But it's no use, the proof is gone. It's cat food. I'm doomed. We're *all* doomed.

"I'm telling the truth!" I plead. "I'm telling the truth!"

I hear Simon laughing his obnoxious laugh and some girls giggling. Parker is biting her nails, and my parents look disappointed, as if I did something wrong.

I slump back in the seat. No one believes me. I feel helpless.

"I'm sorry about this, Mr. McPhee," my mom says. "We'll make sure Marty never bothers you again."

McPhee looks at my parents. He looks at the kids laughing at me. He looks at my humiliated face. Then he sighs and says something no one expected.

"Marty's telling the truth. He discovered the plans I wrote to annihilate Earth."

CHAPTER 47

set to stun

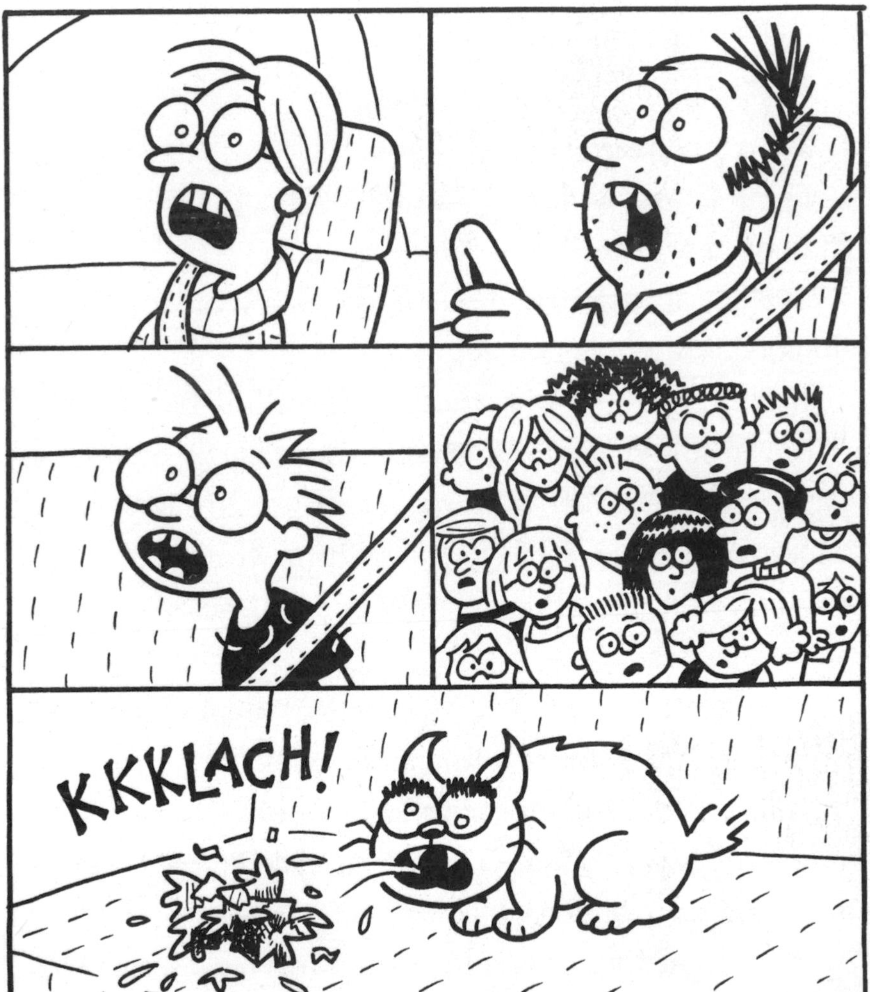
KKKLACH!

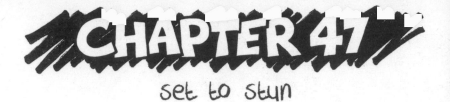

CHAPTER 48

annihilate earth

McPhee confesses.

He confesses that he's secretly a writer, and he's been working on a science-fiction story called, "Annihilate Earth." He claims it's all a big misunderstanding.

I insist he let us look at it to see if his story checks out. McPhee looks uncomfortable with the idea, but I give him no choice. We go inside.

"All right," McPhee says. "Skim the story and get it over with. I know it's not very good."

I start reading and actually, it's not bad. I would even say it's creative. I am finally forced to admit that my teacher is not what I thought he was.

He's not a rube. "Satisfied?" McPhee says.

"Can I keep reading?" I ask. "I really want to see what happens next."

My parents and McPhee look surprised. They talk while I read. McPhee takes the blame for everything. He admits to discouraging my art because he thought a creative career was a pipe dream. He claims he didn't want me to get my hopes up, like he did when he was a kid.

And, get this, he admits to not entering my drawing in the mural contest! He said he forgot, but I know it was on purpose!

Despite his constant discouragement of me, I decide to be the bigger man and encourage him to read his story to the class the next day. His eyes light up. Well, as much as sleepy tortoise eyes can light up.

DRAMATIZATION

"Really?" he says. "You think it's good?"

"Sure, why not?" I say. The real reason I want him to read it in class is so we won't have to do any work. And I guess it's kind of good, too.

But then as I get near the end of the story, it just stops.

"Where's the ending?"

"I have two endings," McPhee responds. "And I can't decide which one to use."

He shows me both.

Version one ends with Earth being completely destroyed. Version two ends with Earth being saved at the last minute.

"Which one do you like better?" he asks. "I'm leaning toward the one where Earth is destroyed."

"No. Use the one where Earth is saved," I say.

"Are you sure, Marty?"

"Definitely."

"Then that's the way it will be," he declares.

I did it!

McPhee's book was obviously his way of planning a *real-life* Earth invasion and I just used my persuasive powers to talk him out of it. You're welcome, Earth!

I have a list to update.

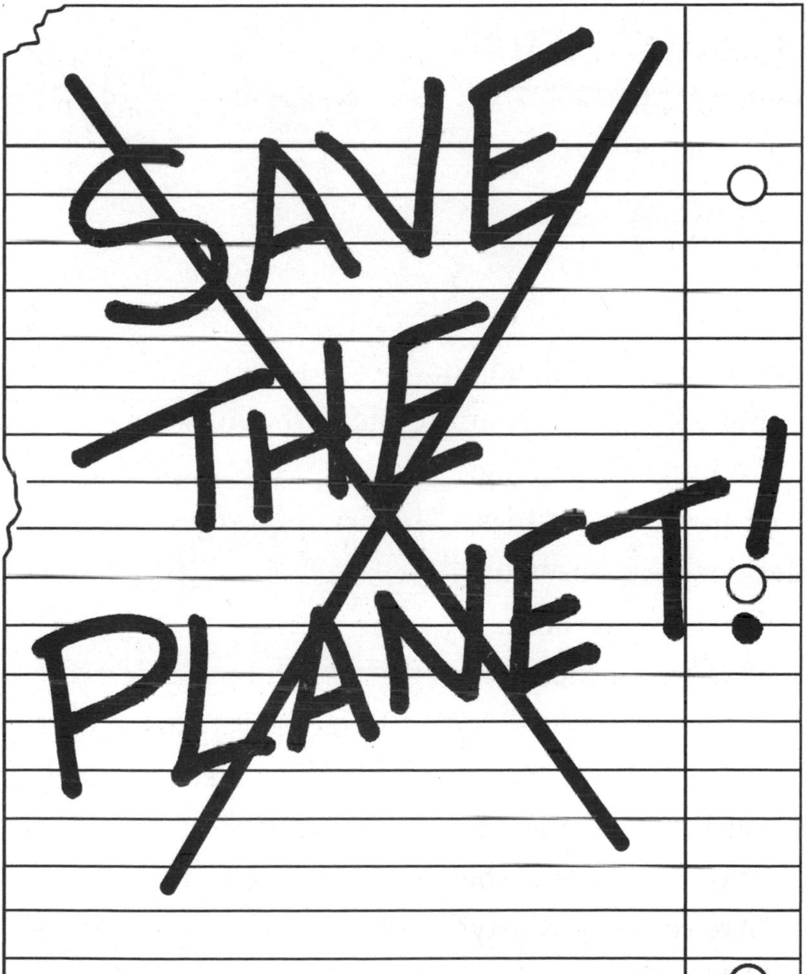
SAVE
THE
PLANET!

CHAPTER 49

likely story

The next day the story is a big hit. The class applauds when McPhee finishes reading it. McPhee then surprises everyone and does something we've never seen him do before. Smile.

That's his version of a smile. Take my word for it.

Word gets out, and now other classes want him to read it. I think Ms. Ortiz is also impressed with his story because I notice her winking at McPhee.

I can relax because my alien teacher is no longer a threat to the planet. I have rendered him harmless, and he's learning to assimilate with us humans.

My parents canceled the appointment with the head doctor. They finally realized my head is fine the way it is.

All the kids in class are being nice to me because I got credit for convincing McPhee to read his book, and we haven't had homework all week!

McPhee is like a new person.* He's less uptight and my grades have actually gone up, which is a new direction for me. Probably because he's trying to make up for being a total jerk for so long.

McPhee even gives me a chance to redo the report on Abraham Lincoln.

When I hand it to him, I look at his expression. He looks perfectly fine, like he had a good breakfast.

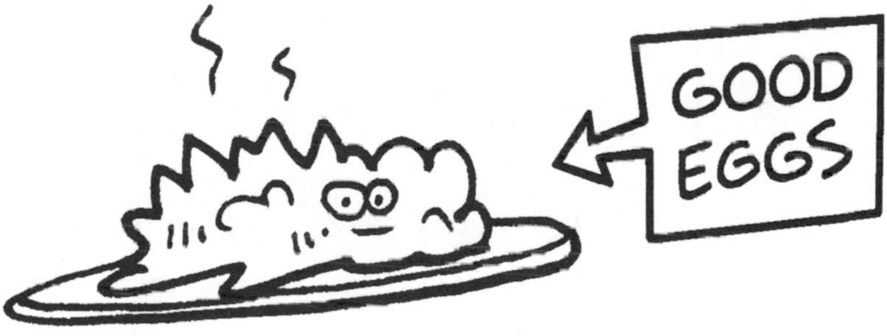
GOOD EGGS

This time my report had plenty of boring words, complete sentences, and indented paragraphs.

But, really, it was the last page that pulled the whole thing together.

* He's "like" a new person because he's actually an alien.

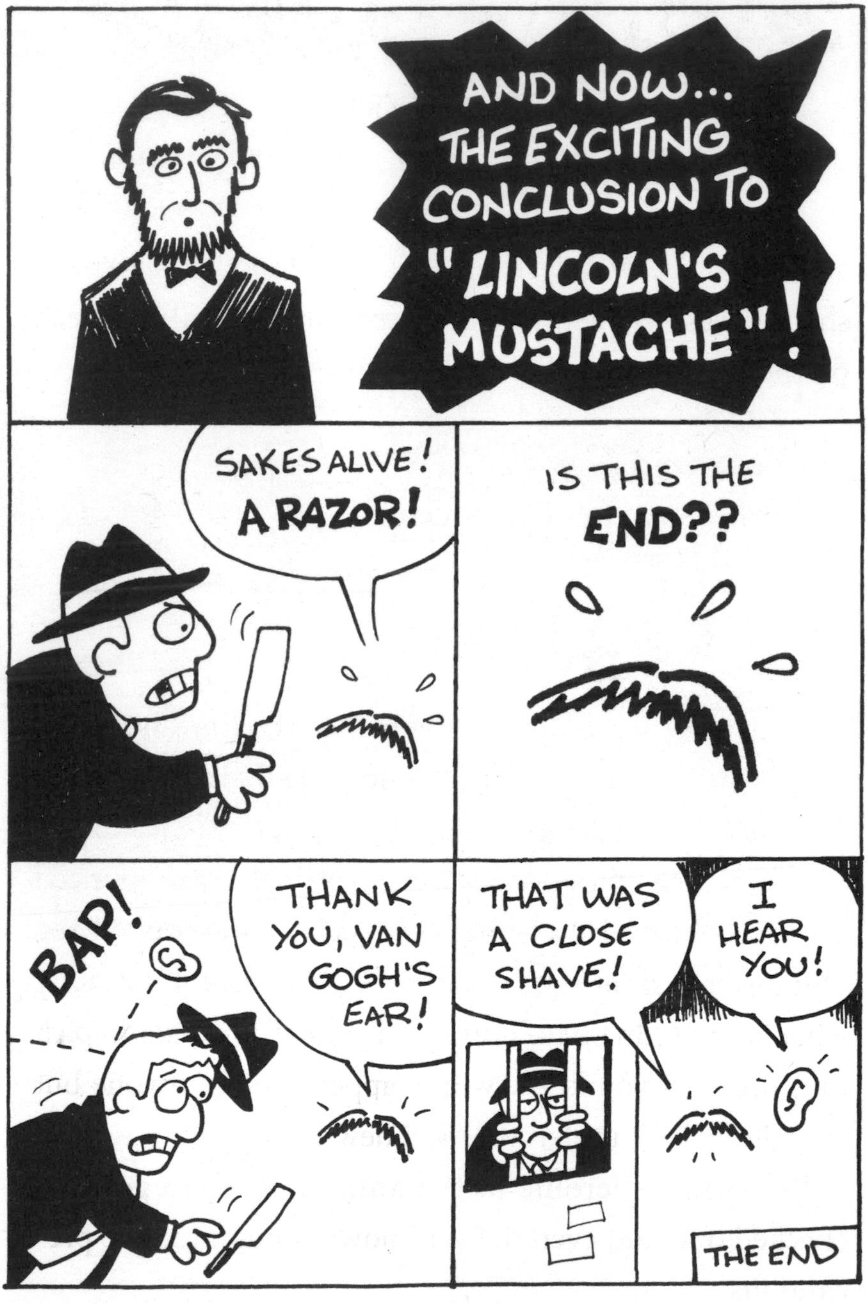
AND NOW... THE EXCITING CONCLUSION TO "LINCOLN'S MUSTACHE"!
SAKES ALIVE! A RAZOR!
IS THIS THE END??
BAP!
THANK YOU, VAN GOGH'S EAR!
THAT WAS A CLOSE SHAVE!
I HEAR YOU!
THE END

CHAPTER 50

loose ends

You might be wondering about the blood on McPhee's shirt. It was his own. When he went into the hall to check on the commotion, the commotion was . . .

JEROME!

And remember when that rabid raccoon attacked Peach Fuzz? That was Jerome, too. I know this because I found some of Peach Fuzz's shredded shirt under Jerome's claws.

Jerome must have followed me that night and pounced on Peach Fuzz. He somehow found his way out of the Dumpster and into the school where McPhee did exactly what he shouldn't have done with my cat. He tried to pick him up. And you know what happens when anyone but me tries to pick up Jerome. Bad news.

We brought Jerome to the animal clinic to get him checked out, and even the vet knows enough to take precautions.

McPhee got scratched up but somehow managed to get Jerome into an empty classroom. Analie must have noticed Jerome and picked him up.

Wait. I thought I was the only person who could pick up Jerome.

That's weird. Must be something different about Analie. I remember something she said, too. Analie said the reason she recognized Jerome was because of the drawing I did for the "Lost Cat" flyer. In other words, my art worked!

I update my list.

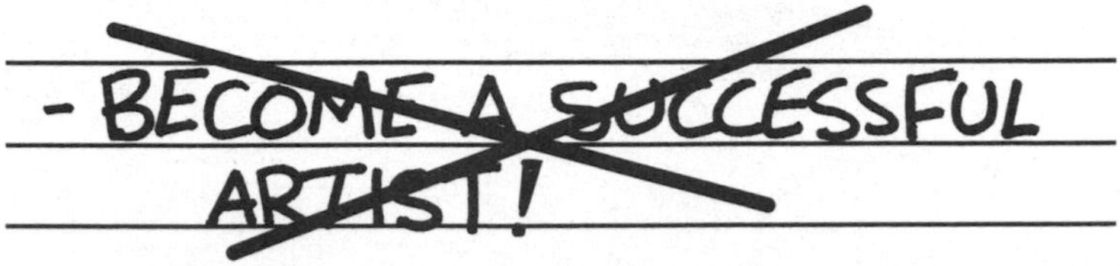
- BECOME A SUCCESSFUL
ARTIST!

Then something else happens. Ms. Ortiz stops me in the hall to tell me they're not going to use Simon's AnemoneBob TrapezoidShorts drawing for the school mural after all. Something about legal reasons and the school not wanting to get sued.

"So, we're going with the drawing that came in second place."

"Which one is that?" I ask.

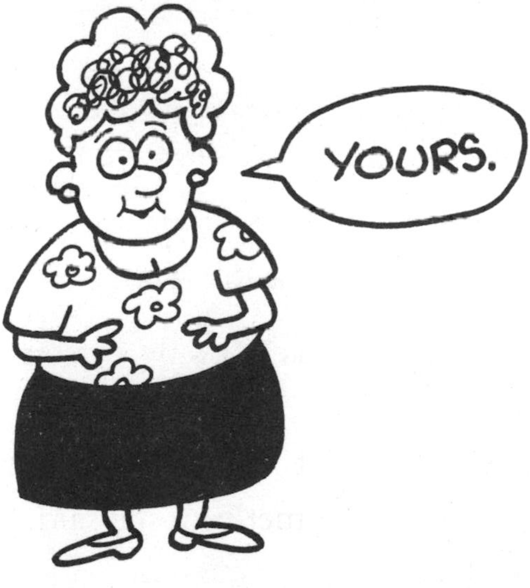
YOURS.

"MINE??"

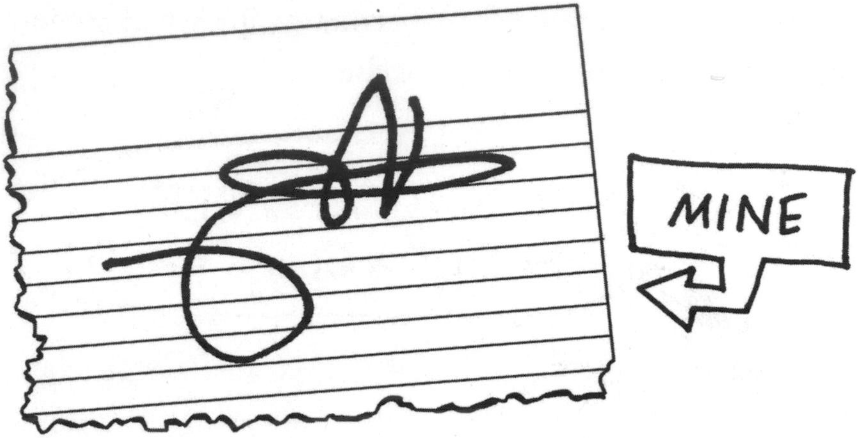
MINE

"All the other entries got one vote each. Yours got two."

Two? I didn't even vote for it myself! Which two people voted for my scribble?

"Of course I voted for yours, Marty!" Parker tells me after school. "I thought the scribble was a bold choice. It represents growing up while still wanting to hold on to your childhood."

That's deep. Now I'm starting to like my scribble.

"It also reminds me of the Starship Enterprise," she adds.

"I voted for it, too," says Roongrat. "Parker threatened to give me a wedgie if I didn't. That's a fact."

Simon was shocked about not getting to do the mural. I guess he's used to getting his way.

That reminds me, I learned a new word today.

Schadenfreude.

My dad told me it means feeling happy when something bad happens to someone else.

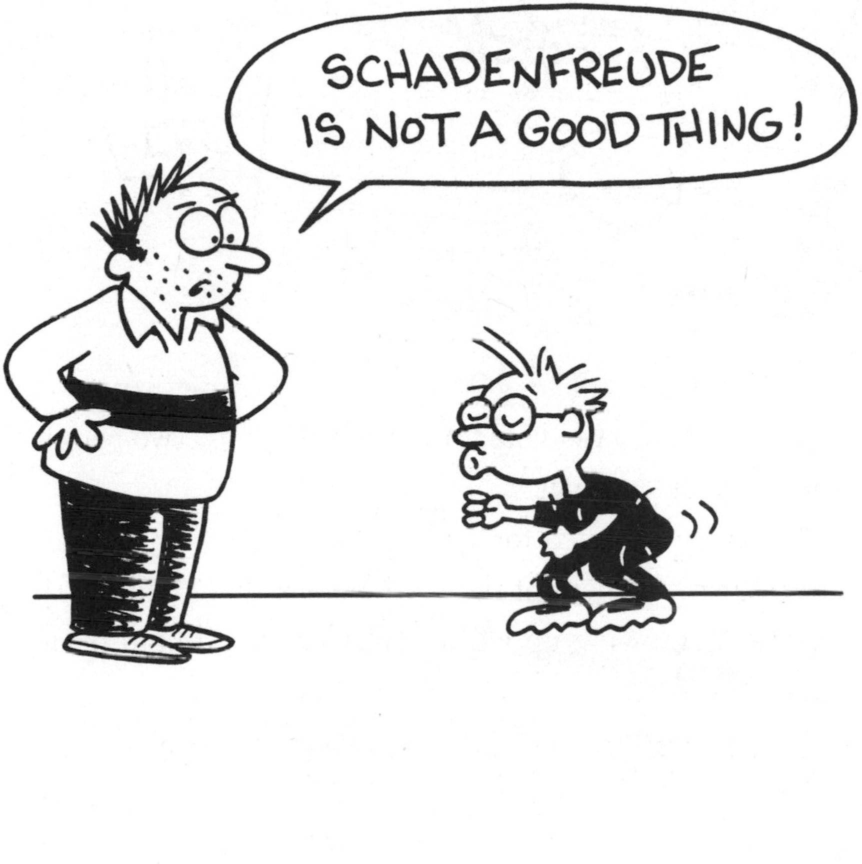
SCHADENFREUDE IS NOT A GOOD THING!

CHAPTER 51

wrapped up in a bow

My mom has the house decorated for my birthday with streamers, banners, cups, plates, napkins — pretty much all the usual stuff.

WHAT HAPPENED TO THE BAG OF BALLOONS?

She sent out invitations to my whole class, and almost everyone shows up. My job is to hand out goodie bags. I don't want to wait until the end so I do it right away.

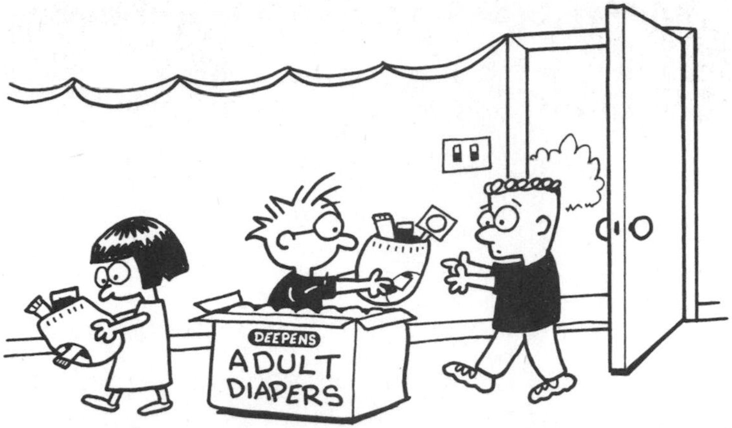
DEEPENS
ADULT
DIAPERS

"All right, chocolate cake!" I hear Roongrat say to Simon. "Did you know all the geniuses ate chocolate cake?"

Simon is still moping about not getting to do the mural. I tell him Erica is upstairs and will be joining us for cake, and he gets all happy again. I don't want any moping at my party.

"The cake had a picture of you on it," my mom tells me, "but Jerome ate your face."

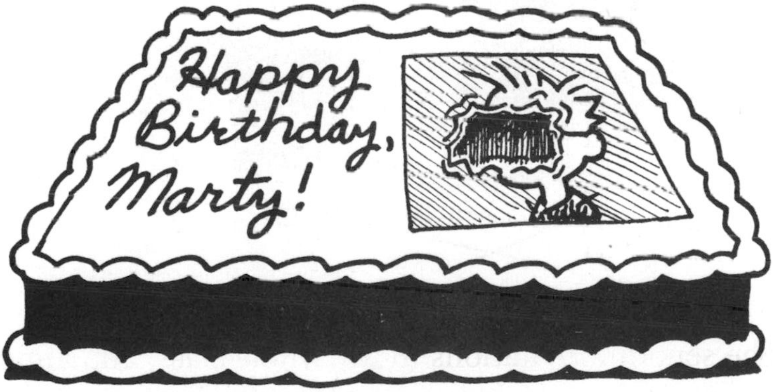
Happy Birthday, Marty!

Of course he did. Glad he's back to normal.

I make a wish and blow out the candles.

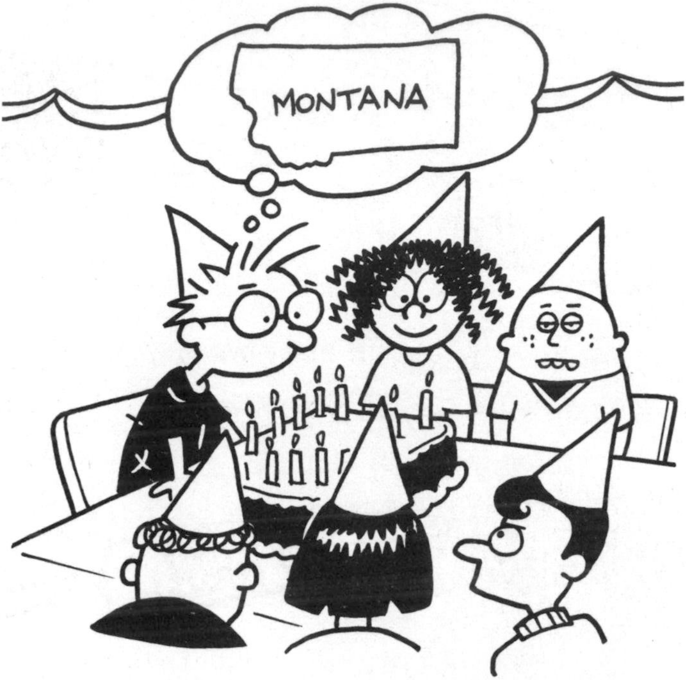
MONTANA

"Open the presents!" Parker says, and starts tossing them to me.

Roongrat got me this:

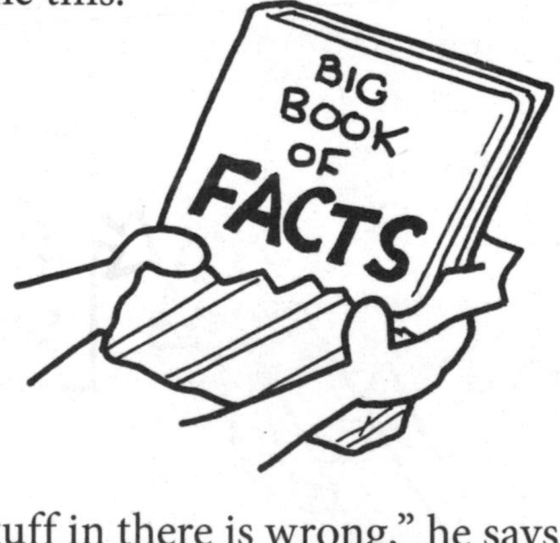
BIG BOOK OF FACTS

"Some of the stuff in there is wrong," he says.

Simon got me this:

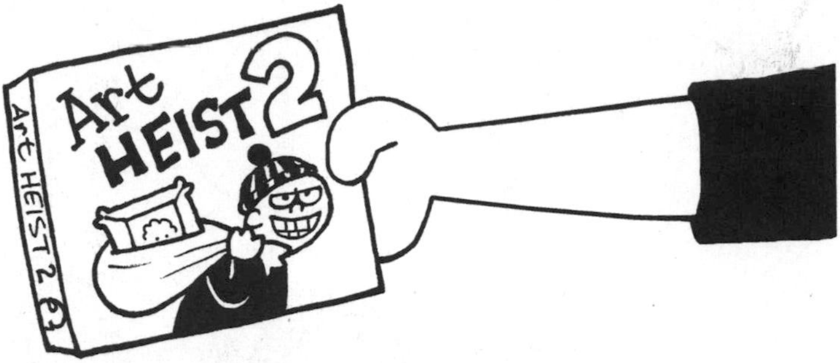
Art HEIST 2
Art HEIST 2

I'll be sure to kick his butt when we play.

My sister gave me these:

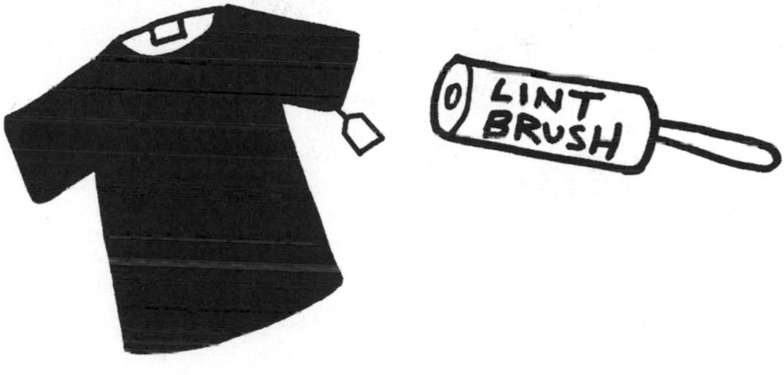
LINT BRUSH

Parker got me a new backpack!

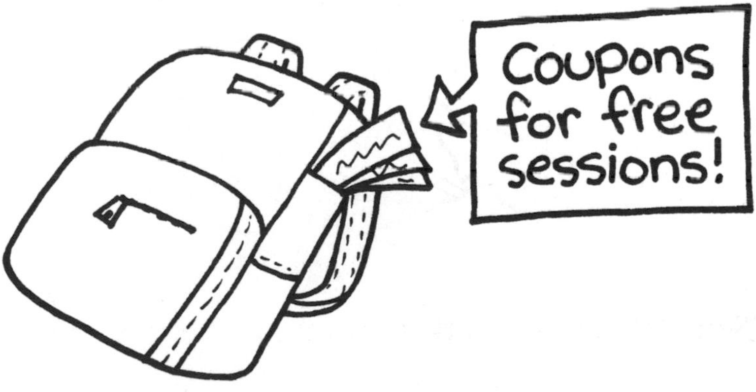
Coupons for free sessions!

My parents got me some books.

TIMMY FAILURE
BIG NATE
DIARY of a Wimpy Kid
LIFE of ZARF
INVISIBLE emmie
LIL RIP HAYWIRE
MY TEACH
IS AN ALIEN

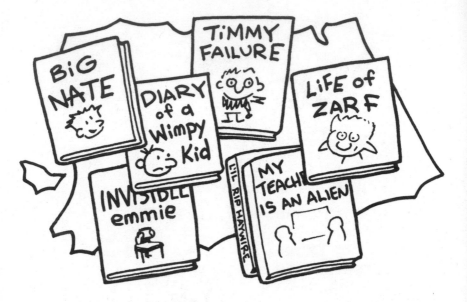

And a new bike!

And a new pogo stick!

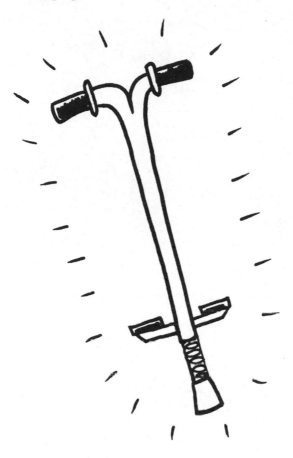

Yes, I know that's confusing.

I also got some cards with money inside, and I have a few ideas on how to spend it.*

One by one, the parents pick up their kids until Parker is the only one left. Her dad hangs out and chats with my parents while Parker helps me clean up.

* On candy.

She tells me she's glad everything worked out.

"Me, too," I say. "But I still don't know who wrote that note."

"You're fun to talk to, Marty."

"Thanks. You are, too, Parker."

"And do you still see that mystery girl? Analie?"

"Nope, she's gone now."

"That's encouraging," she says. "You know you can lie down on my couch any time, Marty."

"It's a love seat," I say.

Parker's dad suddenly comes over and says, "You know, Marty, I could make you a drawing table."

I can't tell if it's an offer or a threat.

As I wave good-bye to Parker, I find a big envelope by the door.

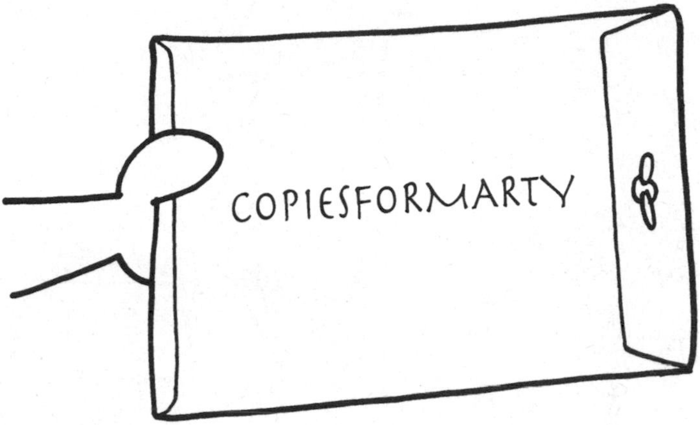
COPIESFORMARTY

It's from Analie! I wonder if I'll ever see her again. I bring the envelope inside and empty it on the floor.

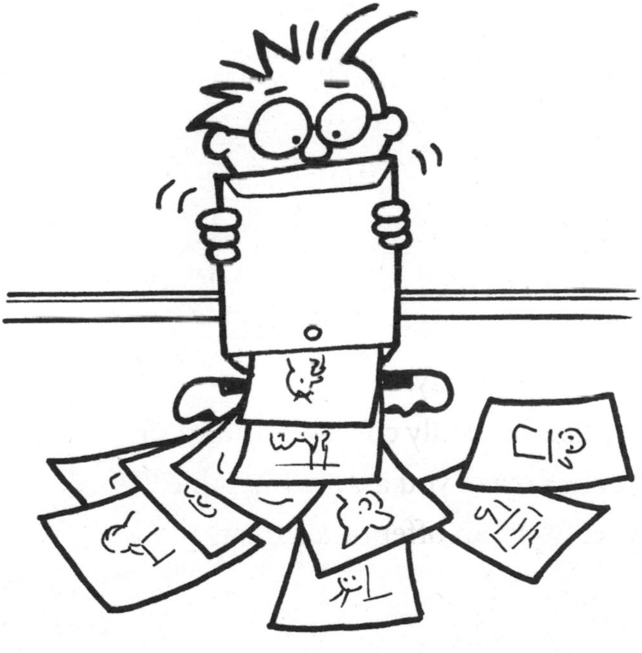

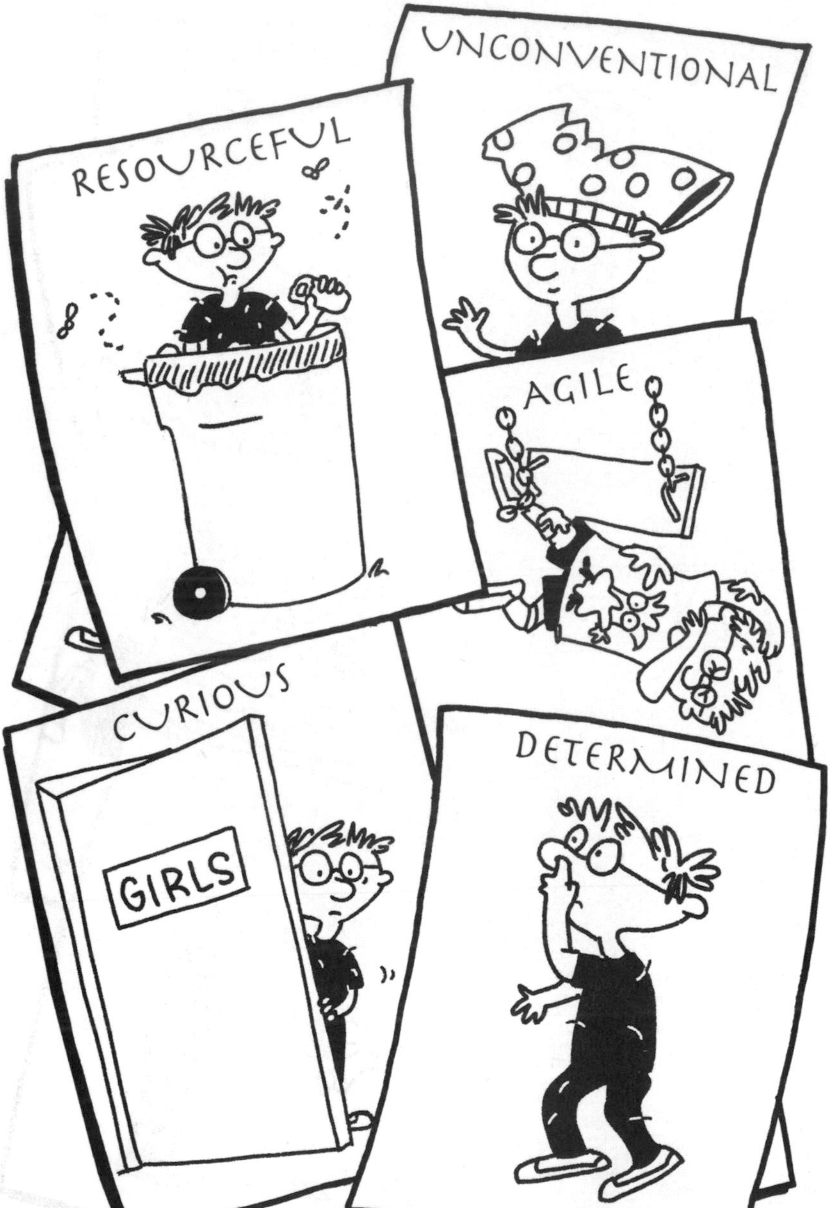
RESOURCEFUL
UNCONVENTIONAL
AGILE
CURIOUS
GIRLS
DETERMINED

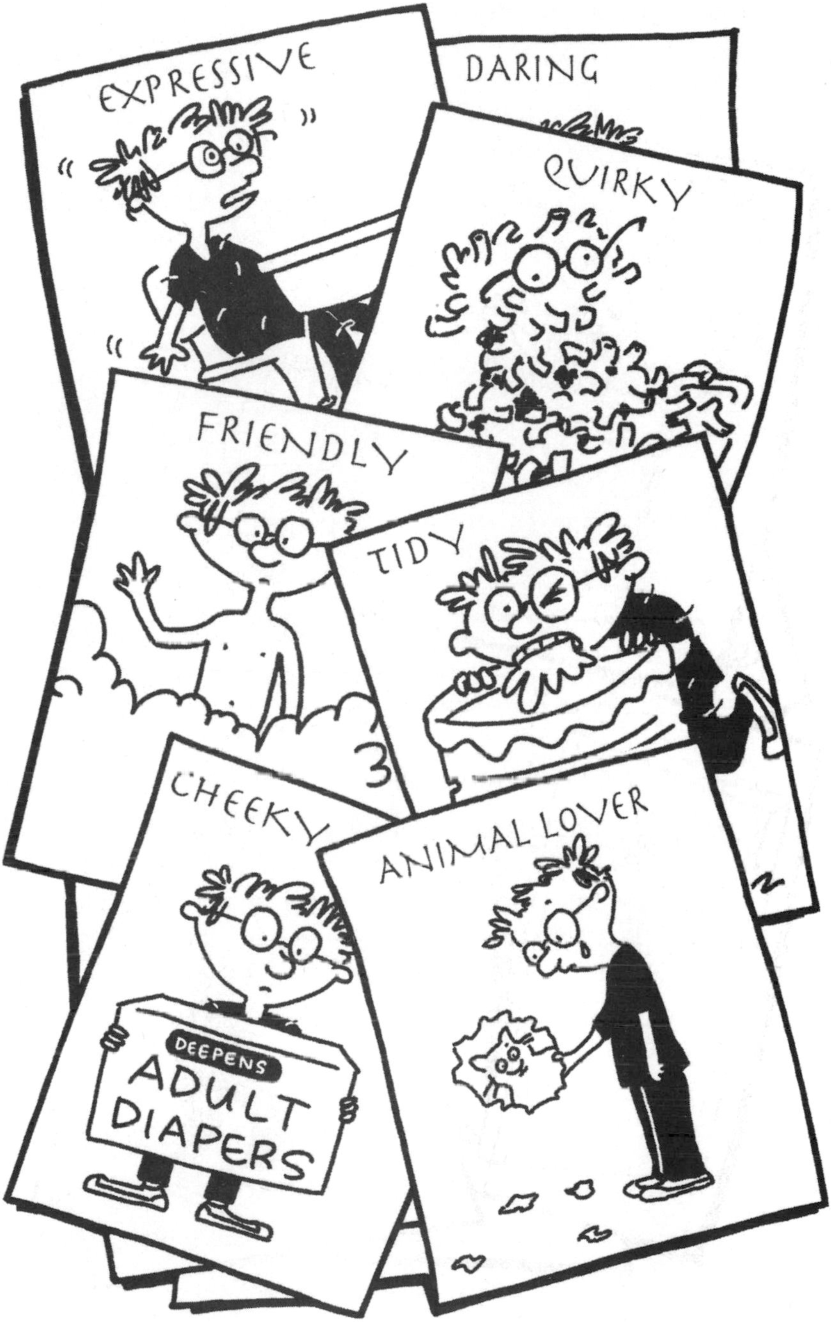
EXPRESSIVE
DARING
QUIRKY
FRIENDLY
TIDY
CHEEKY
DEEPENS
ADULT DIAPERS
ANIMAL LOVER

Analie's an artist, too? I think this is my favorite gift! This and the bike.

Seems she's also a poet. She included this poem.

THERANDOMEARTHLINGIWAS
ASSIGNEDTOOBSERVESHOWSMANY
POSITIVETRAITSANDBASEDONTHIS
INDIVIDUALIRECOMMENDCALLING
OFFTHEEARTHINVASION.

I can't tell what it says, but I bet there's some deep, hidden meaning in there somewhere. Poems are like that. I'm no expert, but I'll guess it's about something delicate, like flowers. Maybe I'll try to decipher it another time, but I'm not really big on poetry.

Hey! I recognize that handwriting! It matches that note I found in my backpack.

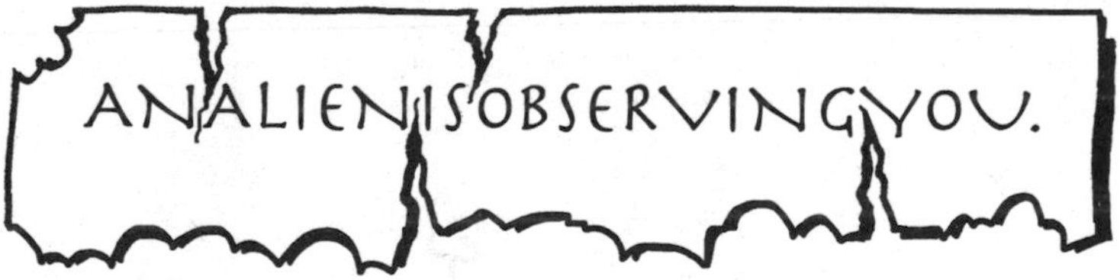
ANALIENISOBSERVINGYOU.

So, Analie N. wrote that note! She knew about McPhee's evil plans and somehow realized I was the one who could neutralize the threat. She knew I could save the planet.

It all makes sense now. At least to me.

CHAPTER 52

that's all, folks

Life is pretty crazy when you think about it. I just confronted an alien intent on destroying the world and changed its mind.

I looked that alien square in the face.

The alien had bad intentions, but thanks to me, the danger is over.

I was the only one who even noticed there was an alien!

I'm sorry. I'm talking about my teacher being an alien, but can't stop thinking of Analie for some reason. I guess I'm distracted.

I take out my list of goals and look at it one final time. I crossed off every single one!

What's this? There's something on here that hasn't been crossed off!

Clean your room!

That's not my handwriting—it's my mom's! Fine. I'll do it first thing tomorrow.

Unless something more important comes along.

THE END

Acknowledgments

I am endlessly grateful to my mom and dad, and my brothers, Nick and Carl, for their encouragement and support. And particularly to Lynn, without whose belief and dedication I may not have become a cartoonist. Thanks to Jen for being incredibly inspiring, and easily the best thing I ever had a hand in creating.

Many thanks to the fantastic team at HarperCollins for their hard work, and making me feel welcome. I cannot thank my editor, Dave Linker, enough for his patient and brilliant guidance, and for sending me that email in the first place. And bonus appreciation goes to Emily Brenner, my HC in-house champion.

I want to thank everyone who read the drafts and gave me valuable feedback: Lincoln, Jen, Lynn, Carl, Cindy, Dan, John, Norm, Ben, Sage, Hilary, and Terri.

Thanks to Andrews McMeel Syndication, my readers, and anyone who's ever encouraged me along the way. Is it weird I want to thank all the pets I've had? Probably.

Thanks to all the artists and musicians I may have referenced or parodied.

Special thanks to the talented Hilary (*Rhymes with Orange*) Price for supplying the art for Analie's drawings.

If I've forgotten anybody, feel free to let me hear about it.

Find out what Marty is up to
in his next adventure:

KEEP YOUR PAWS OFF!

CHAPTER

every picture tells a story

I need to find a baby photo for the class yearbook. Even though I was a totally adorable baby, there don't seem to be many pictures of me.

My sister, Erica, was born first. Here are her baby pictures.

ERICA VOLUME 11
ERICA VOLUME 1
ERICA VOLUME 2
ERICA VOLUME 3
ERICA VOLUME 4
ERICA VOLUME 5
ERICA VOLUME 6
ERICA VOLUME 7
ERICA VOLUME 8
ERICA VOLUME 9
ERICA VOLUME 10

Here are mine.

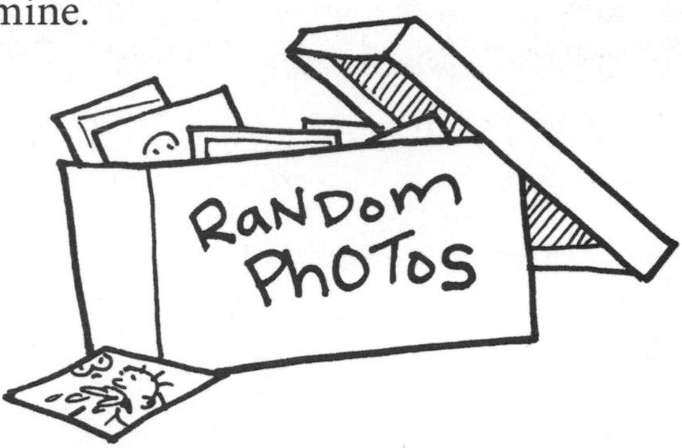
RANDOM PHOTOS

I guess that's how it goes when you're the second child. But once I'm a famous artist, my baby pictures will be like gold, and my parents will regret not having more.

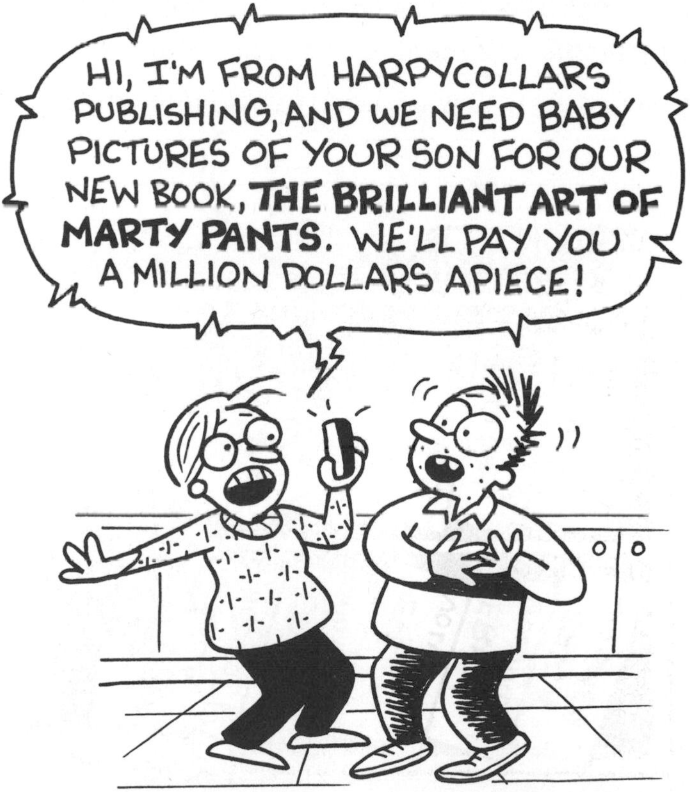
HI, I'M FROM HARPYCOLLARS PUBLISHING, AND WE NEED BABY PICTURES OF YOUR SON FOR OUR NEW BOOK, THE BRILLIANT ART OF MARTY PANTS. WE'LL PAY YOU A MILLION DOLLARS APIECE!

Flipping through the box, I come across an old photo of me with my sister. Look how well we used to get along.

These days it's a little different.
As if to make my point, Erica bursts into my room.

MARTY!

MY KIND, LOVING SISTER →